PRAISE FOR THE INSPECTOR DAVID
GRAHAM MYSTERY SERIES

"Another fabulous installment of the Inspector Graham
series."

"Had me guessing to the end."

"It was so fun to catch up with all the characters."

"Captivating and spectacular."

"Bravo! Engrossing!"

"This is her best book, so far. I literally could not put this
book down."

"I'm in love with him and his colleagues."

"Phenomenal!"

"Alison Golden has done it again."

"Powerful stuff!"

"A terrific mystery."

"These books certainly have the potential to become a PBS
series with the likeable character of Inspector Graham and
his fellow officers."

"Delightful writing that keeps moving, never a dull
moment."

"I know I have a winner of a book when I toss and turn at
night worrying about how the characters are doing."

"Totally great read!!!"

"Refreshingly unique and so well written."

"Alison outdid herself in this wonderfully engaging mystery, with no graphic violence or sex."

"This series just gets better and better."

"DI Graham is wonderful and his old school way of doing things, charming."

"Great character development."

"Kept me entertained all day."

"Wow! The newest Inspector Graham book is outstanding."

"Great characters and fast paced."

"Fabulous main character, D.I. Graham."

"The scenery description, characterisation, and fabulous portrayal of the hotel on the hill are all layered into a great English trifle."

"Inspector Graham is right up there with some of the icons of British mysteries."

"This is her best book, so far. I literally could not put this book down."

"Character development was superb."

"Come on, girlfriend, I need more David Graham. LOL."

"Please never end the series."

THE CASE OF THE BODY IN THE BLOCK

BOOKS IN THE INSPECTOR DAVID GRAHAM SERIES

The Case of the Pretty Lady
The Case of the Forsaken Child

THE CASE OF THE BODY IN THE BLOCK

ALISON GOLDEN

GRACE DAGNALL

Cover Illustration: Richard Eijkenbroek

Published by Mesa Verde Publishing
P.O. Box 1002
San Carlos, CA 94070

ISBN: 979-8340203168

"Books break the shackles of time - proof that humans can work magic."

$\sim$ *Carl Sagan* $\sim$

"Your emails seem to come on days when I need to read them because they are so upbeat."
- Linda W -

For a limited time, you can get the first books in each of my series - *Chaos in Cambridge, Hunted* (exclusively for subscribers - not available anywhere else), *The Case of the Screaming Beauty, and Mardi Gras Madness* - plus updates about new releases, promotions, and other Insider exclusives, by signing up for my mailing list at:

https://www.alisongolden.com/graham

CHAPTER ONE

MELANIE HOWES CAREFULLY positioned a ladder against the outside wall of the White House Inn and, without pausing, climbed it. The back stairs would have been easier, but overnight storm damage made the ladder the only safe approach to what hotel proprietor Mrs. Taylor called the grand attic. At the top, Melanie levered herself through a skylight into the darkness beyond, and when she stood upright, wooden floorboards creaked beneath the soles of her heavy, fireproof work boots. A strong draft and the mustiness of damp wood wafted around her.

The Gorey fire crew manager stood in a corridor that ran from the front of the hotel to the back. The walls, once painted white, were now a murky grey, dust and dirt gathering on the rough surface of the interior stucco. "Uh-oh," Melanie muttered. The upper hallway was a muddied ruin, its roof partially caved in.

Leaning through the skylight, she waved at the ground. Her two companions waved back. "All clear!" she shouted. When firefighter Phil Bevis and Constable Barry Barnwell joined her on the landing two minutes later, their eyes tracked the surroundings, constantly alert to falling debris that might at any moment decide to rain down upon them from the damaged roof above.

Running the entire length of the White House Inn, the giant attic was now cordoned off. And while the Jersey Fire Service inspected, Mrs. Taylor fretted. Having to close the hotel at the insistence of three different local authorities had been a terrible blow. Melanie raised her hand and called out to the two men following her. "I've got smashed tiles and splintered wood. Mind your feet!"

Using Mrs. Taylor's skeleton key, Melanie swiftly unlocked the door midway down the passage. Although invited to witness the inspection firsthand, Mrs. Taylor had thought better of it. How she would navigate the ladder had been one thing. Her distress at what she might find was quite another. "Constable Barnwell has kindly offered to go in my place," she had told Melanie. "But you'll let me know what you find, won't you?"

Once in the attic, Melanie turned to find her firefighting colleague. "Where's Bazza?" she asked him. "Phil, you dozy sod, you didn't forget about him, did you?"

"Right here, matey," called a voice from the landing. "Just taking some photos."

"This isn't a crime scene, you know," Melanie called out to her guest. Taking Barnwell with them on this exploratory mission wasn't in the fire service manual, but she'd accepted the constable's presence as a favour for Mrs. Taylor. "There's no criminal evidence to gather up here. It was the fury of the gods that did this, plain and simple."

Barnwell appeared in the doorway, ducking slightly and dusting off his hands. "Blimey, I've never seen Gorey from this perspective before. Thought I'd take some snaps while I'm up here. Amazing view over the water."

The constable's eyes widened as he took in the state of the attic. An enormous hole blown between the old beams and clay tiles, the gnarly sky starkly visible through it, projected light into the gloomy space. Through it, thunderous clouds shone brighter than the surrounding sky. Elsewhere, tunnels of light protruded through smaller points of damage, like satellite planets around the moon. "Oh, wow."

Barnwell switched his phone's camera to black-and-white mode. Without hesitating, he quickly snapped a shot of Melanie standing beneath the wind-torn roof with its odd-shaped holes, looking up at the desecration of a much-loved Gorey landmark rendered so by a constant foe, the unpredictable British weather. It was a picture that couldn't go wrong—the contrast of dark and light, the moody, debris-strewn foreground, and the single, curious firefighter trying to make sense of it all.

Barnwell was there to catalogue the scene for Mrs. Taylor, but he couldn't pass up the opportunity for some photojournalism. He looked again at his image, pleased with the shot. "You might even call it art," he murmured to no one in particular.

"You'd think we were surveying bomb damage in the Blitz, wouldn't you?" Barnwell showed his picture to the young fireman next to him. "If it weren't for the modern uniforms."

"May as well have been a bomb," Melanie said ruefully.

"Poor old place. It's just not fair what's happened to it." Phil, a born and bred Jerseyman, sounded almost personally offended by the attic's condition, aggrieved on behalf of Mrs. Taylor and her hotel.

What had begun as a sudden squall out in the Bay of Biscay had soon gathered terrifying strength and muscled its way eastwards, causing damage and despair in some of Normandy's traditional coastal villages. But it appeared to the Jersey locals that the storm's actual target had been the island, which it approached from the southwest, preparing to deliver a right-fisted haymaker.

Similar to a storm a few years ago, the island had been in virtual lockdown by midafternoon the previous day. At sunset, Gorey's public was dealing with numerous power outages, no water, and several injuries, all while pummelled by winds that could knock a man flat. The White House Inn, standing alone and proud on a clifftop, had borne the brunt of it.

The following morning should, by rights, have brought a healing spell of bright sunshine, but the weather remained stonily overcast. "At least it's stopped raining," Melanie said. "We can get a sense of what's going on up here without getting drenched in the process."

"Bleedin' chaos," Phil moaned. "May as well tell Mrs. T. right now she'll need a new roof, minimum."

"Only once we're done," Melanie cautioned, taking her own photos. "It's a real mess though. The fabric has taken an almighty whack. You don't need any training to see that. Alright, let's get to it. They've lost about . . . what, forty percent of the roof tiles?"

"Something like that," Phil agreed, peering out through one of the holes. On the tarmac in the car park at the front of the inn, and on the roof of the sunroom, countless angry, star-shaped spatters of terracotta punctuated the surfaces, each the remains of an ancient roof tile swept earthward by relentless winds. It was as though leprechauns had spent the night smashing plates in some kind of gratuitous frenzy.

"And there's structural damage." Melanie pointed to a thick, century-old beam cracked in two as if it had been a length of old, dry firewood. "That'll need to be replaced." She tapped a bevy of words into her tablet, beginning her report of the reconstruction that would be necessary.

Melanie worked carefully, applying nearly twenty years of experience to her review, followed by the ever-curious Constable Barnwell with his camera. "Having fun?" she asked him between phases of the assessment. Melanie and Barnwell knew each other well. They often walked their dogs together—his beagle, her pit bull—at the weekends. Theirs was a friendly, platonic relationship, full of banter and gentle ribbing. "Didn't think you lot would be interested in this. Just the result of wind, rain, and age, really," she said. "Too much of it over too long a period of time."

"I'm here to keep Mrs. Taylor calm. She asked me to accompany you, be her 'man about the house,' if you know what I mean." Melanie frowned. Barnwell, for once alert to the fact that this preference of Mrs. Taylor's might suggest a lack of confidence in the fire service, or in Melanie in particular, patted his buttons and added quickly, "It's the uniform. Comforting." Melanie stared at him, her expression vaguely reminding Barnwell of her dog, Vixen, before nodding curtly and resuming her inspection.

The grand attic was now something to behold. Locally, it was believed that during the war, it had housed young Nazi soldiers, a rumour Mrs. Taylor had been at pains to play down. Later, when the inn returned to its original purpose, it had acted as a dormitory for young men needing cheap accommodation. Now, though, it was full of the flotsam and jetsam of a long-running enterprise that dealt in the business of travelling humans. All kinds of detritus were strewn about, much of it from long ago.

"Flotsam" perfectly described the items scattered mostly against one wall. They literally appeared as though debris from a shipwreck. Wooden chairs tumbled over each other. Overflowing cardboard boxes, wet and ripped, spilled their contents across the floorboards. Furniture had fallen, their heavy weight proving no defence against the forces hurled at them overnight, and some had travelled significant distances before coming to rest in a higgledy-piggledy pile of dark, varnished oak.

"Blimey, it must have been some wind to do that," Barnwell said. "I'm impressed. Everything's been blown over. Even this . . ." He slapped a large dresser that pinned an upholstered winged armchair to the wall. The dresser had flattened the chair, leaving the wings flapping, broken at the joints.

The effect of the wind's force had been to mostly clear the main thoroughfare, pushing everything to one side of the attic. The two firefighters and one police officer walked around the space freely, assessing, cataloguing, and photographing the damage.

As he strolled, Barnwell picked a faded red velvet cushion from the floor. Bedraggled, stringy, frayed tassels hung from each corner. He tossed it on a similarly upholstered banquette that lay in the corner on its own, far from the piles of bric-a-brac and paraphernalia.

Barnwell regarded the banquette curiously, then sat down on it with a hard bump. "Flippin' heck, this is the most uncomfortable sofa I've ever sat on. No wonder Mrs. T. put it up here."

"Probably why it's still in the corner and didn't make its way over there with all the rest," Phil said, lightly testing a beam with his hand. "Solid as a rock."

"You're right. It's as hard as concrete." Barnwell

knocked on the velvet covering. Beneath the fabric, his knuckles met a hard, unrelenting surface. "You know what . . ." Barnwell worried at a tear in the cover's seam and poked his finger through. His fingertip came away dusted with white powder. "I think this *is* concrete. What's a block of concrete doing up here covered in red velvet?"

"Well, that's why it didn't move. Surprised it didn't go through the floor," Melanie said. "C'mon, it's nothing. We're done here. Let's see if we can get down the stairs this time."

But Barnwell didn't hear her. Intrigued by what he was sitting on, he ripped the velvet along the seam. The concrete sat in a mould of red brick. As he opened it to the air, a section crumbled along an edge. He froze.

"C'mon, Bazza. Let's go and get a coffee." Barnwell dragged his eyes upwards to look at Melanie, his mouth open. He remained silent. The fire crew manager smiled. "Alright, see you down there, then."

Barnwell watched her and Phil disappear through the door and waited until he could no longer hear their footsteps as they descended the stairs. He pulled out his phone. Scrolling his contacts list, he tapped a number.

"Sir?" His voice came out croaky. He tried again, stronger this time. "Boss, it's Barnwell. I'm at the White House Inn. Listen, I think you'd better get down here."

A minute later, after describing what he'd found, Barnwell ended the call. His eyes widened again as he regarded the reason he had made it. He blinked several times, his heart beating as fast as it did on one of his runs through the streets of Gorey with Carmen. He squinted, focused, and blinked again.

It was the most extraordinary thing. But there it was, as plain as the Rich Tea biscuit he had dunked in his tea earlier that morning. His mind ran wild as he processed what he was seeing. For if Barnwell's eyes weren't deceiving him, and he fervently hoped they were not now that he had called in his superior, there appeared to be in the corner of Mrs. Taylor's attic, poking an inch out of a concrete banquette, a human fingernail on the end of a decidedly human finger.

CHAPTER TWO

DETECTIVE INSPECTOR DAVID Graham trotted up the steps to the front entrance of the White House Inn. Barnwell was waiting for him. "You know, it's funny. I spent a few months here when I first came to Jersey. I wandered around the hotel a fair amount, but I never made it to the grand attic," Graham said.

"And if you had, you'd hardly have suspected you were sharing the space with a, well, whatever it is, would you, sir?"

"Hardly, Constable."

Half an hour earlier, Barnwell had quietly followed the firefighters down to the ground floor and found a corner in which to discreetly kill time until the inspector arrived. He hadn't breathed a word of what he'd discovered to anyone, not even Melanie. Now he huddled with Graham in a corner of the White House Inn lobby as they discussed the situation.

"Good job on keeping things quiet, Constable. The force that is Mrs. Taylor might be a lot to bear if this is what you think it is."

"We can't keep it from her forever, sir."

"No, but we can keep it from her for *now*. Just until we know more. Who knows, it might not be what it looks like."

"No, possibly not. But it did look like a human finger, sir. I wouldn't have called you if it didn't."

"And you were absolutely right to. Why don't you lead the way, and we'll take a look together? Where is the redoubtable Mrs. Taylor at this precise moment?"

"Talking to that oik, Solomon, about the damage to the hotel." Graham rolled his eyes. A few feet away at the reception desk, Mrs. Taylor was speaking to Freddie Solomon, "citizen journalist," about the previous night's horrors. The blogger's expression alternated between "compassionate concern" and "unexpected Christmas."

"You know, I had a vision!" Mrs. Taylor wrung her hands. Freddie's thumbs flew in a flurry of typing. "A vision of being swept up by the storm, like Dorothy in *The Wizard of Oz*! I thought the whole inn"—Mrs. Taylor gestured to the elegant crown moulding—"would be picked up and thrown into the sea! I'd have believed it, Mr. Solomon!" Marjorie Taylor was desperate for someone to understand. "*Never* been so scared, not in *all* my life."

Mrs. Taylor was, quite plainly, at sixes and sevens. She would take three steps in one direction and stop to glance worriedly at the reception ceiling as though it might decide to collapse out of malicious caprice. Distracted, she would turn and walk six steps in the opposite direction, closing her eyes and gripping her hands together as if in fervent, desperate prayer. Freddie swung between comforting a distressed woman and eliciting from her the most dramatic version of her story.

"Did it feel," he asked her, leaning in close like the

trusted confidant he wished to be, "like the hotel was doing *battle* with the wind?"

Graham grimaced. "She doesn't need that tiresome idiot pestering her today. Perhaps you should escort Freddie out so I don't do it myself and risk losing my temper with the little weevil." Dozens of interfering, speculative articles in Freddie's local crime blog had already put him on Graham's radar, and the blogger was building a history of narrowly avoiding arrest on charges of obstruction, even perverting the course of justice. "And maybe get Janice down here. She could have a word with Mrs. Taylor."

"What kind of a 'word,' sir?"

"A kind one. Janice is good at that."

"I think that would be good coming from you, sir. I mean, a good part of Mrs. T.'s roof just got scattered all over Gorey, the council has designated her business a hazard, and she might be about to learn there's a body encased in concrete in her attic. Lord knows how long it'll take her to recover from all that. I think she'd appreciate a kind word from you as the senior person. And expecting Janice to do it, isn't that a bit . . . what does she call it? Patronising. Expecting her to do 'women's work.'" It was a big, risky speech from Barnwell, but he was correct. Chastened, Graham coughed and stood a little taller.

Among them, only he had the ability to truly imagine the ferocity with which Mrs. Taylor was likely to respond to such news. The fabric, history, and ownership of the building were all part of the same indivisible whole. To injure the White House Inn was to injure Mrs. Taylor. Body and soul of both were inextricably linked.

"Yes, yes. Of course, you're right." Graham opened his mouth to say more, but Barnwell wasn't finished. "And do we really want to put that on Janice? I mean, like, *now*?"

Graham's expression transformed from stern to stricken. "Oh, hell, I hadn't thought of *that*," he said, angry at himself. "The wedding . . ."

"Jan had a block booking here for her out-of-town guests. Mrs. T. gave her a good deal. What's Janice gonna do now? Reckon she won't want their twenty-odd guests staying in a hotel where the wind's whistling 'Here Comes the Bride' at all times of the day and night." Barnwell sighed as he prepared to shoulder the responsibility Graham had delegated to him. "But it's alright. I'll tell Janice. See if she wants to come on down. She's off today."

"On second thoughts, let's leave Mrs. Taylor to Freddie. He'll keep her busy while we slip past."

"What are we going to tell the fire service?"

"The who?"

"The firefighters. I went up with them. They only let me join them because Mrs. Taylor asked specially. They'll want to know why we want to go up there again." Graham huffed.

"Just tell them there's something you want to show me. Keep it vague. But hurry. I don't want anyone to suspect anything." Barnwell lumbered off in the direction of Melanie Howes, who was sitting outside in her vehicle writing a report. Five minutes later, she led Graham and Barnwell into the attic.

They went up the back stairs, now cleared and declared safe, so avoiding Mrs. Taylor and Freddie and the climb up the outside of the building that had proved necessary earlier. "Mind the step," Melanie said. She had insisted on accompanying them. As he entered the attic, Graham, like Barnwell before him, stared at the sky through the huge "porthole" in the roof. "Not so 'grand' now, is it?" Melanie said. "I hope the insurance company is feeling generous because the restoration is going to need a *serious* budget. What is it you want to look at again?"

"Just something that Constable Barnwell was a bit concerned about. It's probably nothing, and we don't want to worry Mrs. Taylor unnecessarily." This seemed to satisfy Melanie, who shrugged and turned down the corners of her mouth but said nothing.

"It's over here, sir," Barnwell said as he walked to the far corner. Graham gazed at the banquette covered in faded red velvet, now ripped and sagging, the grey concrete block and surrounding red brick partially exposed. He followed Barnwell and squatted next to him. "There, sir." Barnwell pointed to a crumbled section of the cement. The grey tip of what was unmistakably a human finger protruded from it.

With his phone in hand, Graham switched on the magnifier. He placed it over the digit and stared for some seconds. Barnwell held his breath, glancing at his boss's face, waiting for a signal that calling Graham had been the right thing to do. At the other end of the room, Melanie stood with her arms folded, oblivious to the men's concern. She stared through a hole in the roof, gazing out at the still-tumultuous sky.

Finally, Barnwell could contain himself no longer. His voice was low. "What do you think, sir? Is it . . . you know?"

Graham turned his phone to examine the fingertip from a different angle. He didn't answer Barnwell but stood and ripped the velvet to reveal the entire block, sweeping his eyes along its length. He might have been examining a work of art or a precious antique.

He knocked on the block's surface and rubbed it, examining the dust left on his palm. With the ball of one foot, he pressed the floorboards next to it. Only then did he suggest that he'd heard Barnwell. He took a few steps to his right and leant into his constable. He murmured, "Seal the room, Barnwell. And call Bob the Builder. We'll be needing tools. I'll call Tomlinson."

CHAPTER THREE

G RAHAM TOOK PHOTOS and, leaving Barnwell to secure the area, headed downstairs to wait for Dr. Marcus Tomlinson. He expected to find Mrs. Taylor in the lobby, and in a terrible state. Both hunches were correct.

"Like the wrath of God!" Marjorie was still exclaiming to Freddie Solomon in an otherwise deserted lobby. "The whole place was shaking, rattling. It was *awful*. You could hear the tiles coming down in twos and threes, hitting the ground like bombs going off. One-half of the hotel had to be evacuated at three a.m., guests in their pyjamas huddling under umbrellas in the car park!" Mrs. Taylor trembled at the memory. They hadn't noticed him, and Graham, shaking his head, quietly made his way to the tearoom.

The tearoom was offering a skeleton service, not least to provide refreshments to the workers who were coming and going, although Graham doubted the finer points of tea-making would be exercised on their behalf. "Builder's tea" would be offered—strong, black, a dash of milk, and two sugars, take it or leave it. No one would leave it, not even

Graham. But after the discovery in the attic, he fancied something fresh, uplifting—a dragon pearl jasmine, or a fruity citrus, perhaps even a green tea. Laura would be impressed.

"What can I get you, Inspector?" Polly, a favourite of his, asked him. She knew just how he liked his tea.

"Let's go for the champagne of teas this morning please, Polly."

"A Silver Needle White it is then, sir. No milk and sugar, correct?"

"The milk is unnecessary, the sugar redundant, so no thank you."

Five minutes later, Polly returned carrying a tray. As she placed the tea set on the table in front of him, Graham sat in his chair, his elbows resting on the arms, his hands clasped in front of him.

"Would you like me to pour? The timer is about to go off," she said.

"I'll do it, thanks." Polly left him to it, and when the final grain of sand had dropped into the bottom sectional of the classic egg timer, Graham leaned over to pour himself a cup of the pale-yellow tea. He sniffed it and closed his eyes as the fragrance of freshly cut hay warmed his cheeks, then took a sip of the hot, slightly acidic yet smoky blend, its warmth bathing him in a seductive, heady, musky blanket. He shut his eyes, exhaled, and relaxed his shoulders.

Just as Graham was draining his second cup, Marcus Tomlinson surged into reception like a caped avenger. He resembled a thunderstorm of his own. He shook rain from his hat and brushed the shoulders of his jacket. "Goodness, Mrs. Taylor, this is a carry-on!"

Mrs. Taylor turned to him without blinking and replied, "Miss Howes from the fire service told me the rainwater has only just stopped coming down the upstairs walls! It's a calamity!" She paused, then squinted. "But what are you doing here, Dr. Tomlinson?"

Inspector Graham swarmed in, intercepting Tomlinson before he could say anything that Mrs. Taylor or Freddie, who was still hanging around, might latch onto. "He's here to meet me for a chat, that's all." Suppressing a wince at his misrepresentation, Graham quickly guided Tomlinson by the elbow up the back stairs. Freddie watched them go, the heavy lids of his green eyes lowering slightly, although Mrs. Taylor seemed too wrapped up in the prospect of her failing hotel to disbelieve the inspector or consider that anything questionable was occurring within it.

"How are things?" Dr. Tomlinson whispered as they passed through the door to the back stairs. "I hear the storm has delivered the hotel a hammer blow. That guests are cancelling to stay elsewhere or fleeing the island altogether. Are things as bad as they sound?"

"Hard to say. The staff are dealing with simultaneous storms on different fronts." What Graham didn't give voice to, not yet anyway, was that the discovery of a body on the premises would likely cause an earthquake capable of upending the other meteorological challenges, thereby ending life as Mrs. Taylor knew it.

He led the pathologist up the three flights to the attic, briefing him as they went. When they reached the top, Tomlinson paused.

"Hold on a second, man. Let me get my breath back." He blew out his cheeks. "It's times like these that I realise I'm not as young as I was." Graham waited patiently, silently berating himself for his eagerness to begin the next part of the investigation into what he was now calling "the body in the block."

Above them, they heard shouts as roofers wrestled with a tarpaulin. Barnwell had followed Graham's instructions explicitly. Crime scene tape crisscrossed the doorway to the attic, and the massive hole in the roof had been covered. Inside, Barnwell stood on a stepladder sealing the smaller holes.

When Dr. Tomlinson had regained his breath, Graham led him to the corner where the banquette sat. The velvet cover had been put back in place, the concrete block now resembling his grandmother's couch. Graham pulled the fabric aside to reveal the concrete-filled brick mould, the incongruity of a finger poking out at one corner stark and obvious.

"Do your worst, Marcus. Is this a prank or some unfortunate person's resting place? Tell me, I need to know."

Tomlinson carefully kneeled while Graham peered over his shoulder. Like the inspector earlier, the pathologist lightly touched the fingertip before reaching into his bag for a tiny brush. With a couple of quick flicks, he wicked away particles of dust before inserting a round, black magnifying eyepiece into his eye socket. Peering intensely at the finger's almost black, wrinkled pad, he sighed.

"If this is a shop dummy, it's a very good one. That is most definitely a fingerprint."

"We have Bob the Builder on standby."

"Bob, eh? He's a good lad. He'll keep his mouth shut too. But before we do anything, I'd like to consult with a friend of mine, Professor Alexander Papadopoulos. He's an archaeologist based on the mainland, but he's on Jersey right now on holiday. He popped in to see me just yesterday. Perhaps he wouldn't mind interrupting his relaxing break to help us with this rather unusual situation." Marcus looked at Graham hopefully. The inspector hesitated.

"We can't just crack on?"

"Honestly, I feel a little out of my depth here, David, but between me, Alex, and Bob, we'll have the best chance of extracting whoever is in here without too much damage. It'll make things a lot easier down the road."

Graham rocked back on his heels. He couldn't risk losing evidence in the name of speed, especially after what was obviously some time. "Of course, whatever you say. It's been here a while, so a few more minutes won't matter. If he's happy to help us, that would be fantastic."

"Jolly good. And David?"

"Yes?"

"We need to proceed on the basis that this *is* a body. We're essentially exhuming it. Respect must be conferred. Just me, you, Alex, and Bob. No . . ." Tomlinson pointed a finger to the ceiling where the stomping of the roofers' boots was punctuated by shouts and laughter.

"Understood. I'll have them down tools. How long will it take, do you think?"

Tomlinson pursed his lips. His eyes lingered over the block. "Who knows? Might be as slow as an archaeological dig, or the concrete might crumble at the first sign of pressure."

"Sir?" Barnwell interrupted.

"Hmm?"

"Sir!"

"What is it, Barnwell?" Graham sounded irritated.

"You, um, might want to come here to see this, boss."

"Excuse me, Marcus. It seems I'm needed elsewhere. You'll call your friend?"

"Will do."

"What is it?" Graham asked Barnwell again, reluctantly turning to walk the length of the attic. As he got close, his eyes landed on what Barnwell was bringing to his attention. It was a very familiar shape, but important parts of Graham's brain were yelling that it absolutely did not belong. "What on earth is that doing up here?"

"That's what I was wondering. And does it have some-thing to do with . . ." Barnwell nodded in Tomlinson's direc-tion. "You know . . ."

"Indeed, Constable, indeed. What make is it, can you tell?"

"Smith and Wesson, sir. It says so right here on the barrel."

CHAPTER FOUR

"**H**ELL'S TEETH." GRAHAM inspected the gun. It lay on the floor next to a chest of drawers.

"Am I calling the firearms guys, sir?"

"Hang on. Let's see what we've got." Graham stepped forward. He retrieved some forensic gloves, a fresh pair of which lived permanently in his inside jacket pocket, and handed them to Barnwell. "Off you go. Pick it up and place it on the top there." He pointed to a table, still upright and undamaged. Barnwell wriggled his meaty hands into the gloves. "And when you pick it up, tell me if it feels *regular* heavy or *extra* heavy."

"Why do you ask?"

"I need to know if it's loaded." Barnwell blinked but lifted the gun delicately by the butt and barrel with his thumbs and forefingers. He gingerly placed it on top of the table. "Doesn't seem particularly heavy, sir."

"Excellent. How did you come to find it?" Graham fixated on the weapon. He donned his own gloves and bent down so that he was at eye level with the gun. He twisted and turned to view it from every angle.

"I was just clambering around fixing holes. These drawers must've been hit by some debris. It looks as though there was a small, red suitcase in one of them. The case must've fell out and burst open. I noticed the gun laying on the floor next to it. My guess is it was forced out of the suitcase when it was damaged."

On the floor was a tomato-red, hard-shell suitcase. Alongside the chrome handle was a label: Tourister. The interior was lined with cream satin. Two elasticised pockets were sewn onto the inside. Graham poked his fingertips inside first one, then the other.

"Aha, here we are." He pulled his hand away and opened it for Barnwell to see. Three bullets lay in his hand.

"These look like thirty-eight wadcutters," Graham said. "What else was in the suitcase?"

"Just some fella's belongings," reported Barnwell. "Stuff from a while back, I reckon. They look a bit dated. Seventies, eighties, d'you think? There's some clothes, books, bits and pieces . . . Look." Barnwell picked up a small item from the floor. "I had one of these. A Walkman. That's definitely eighties. And this." Barnwell picked up the book in his gloved hands. *The Hitchhiker's Guide to the Galaxy.* That was the eighties too, wasn't it?"

"Douglas Adams wrote the first book in 1979," Graham said from memory. Barnwell glanced at him as the inspector took the book from him and flicked through it, his eyebrows raised. "I was something of an Adams aficionado in my day, devouring the books, radio shows, TV shows, films, anything he wrote," Graham added. He scanned the other items. "All this and a large-calibre handgun stuffed in the bottom drawer of an old chest of drawers, eh?"

Putting the book aside, Graham, still fixed on the weapon, turned it over carefully, keeping its barrel pointed at the wall. "Stay this side of me, please," he said. "I don't think it's dangerous, but . . ." He tested its weight. "Alright, it's either unloaded or there's only one round, maybe two, in the cylinder. Revolvers don't expend their bullet casings like rifles and pistols. If someone fired it, the spent round might still be in there."

Graham clicked the release switch to disengage the lock, and the cylinder swung out easily. He gave it a quick sniff. "Hasn't been used recently. And no rounds in the chambers, spent or otherwise." He laid it down again and peered at it. "Do you know what this is?"

Barnwell coughed. "Thought we'd decided it was a gun, sir."

"Indeed, a Smith and Wesson," Graham said before patiently adding from his considerable storehouse of knowledge. "The model twenty-eight, late fifties. Unpolished steel, pretty simple. It was a low-cost revolver called the 'Highway Patrolman.' Very popular with cops in the US back in its day." Even with gloves on, Graham handled the weapon as little as possible. "But no experienced criminal would be caught dead with a relic like this these days. Lord knows what'd happen if we tried to fire it."

Barnwell regarded the gun quizzically. "Big old thing, isn't it?"

"Bit risky to bring this on a job, even back in the eighties, if that's when this is from. I mean, when the model twenty-eight was first manufactured, our grandparents were still spending shillings and sixpences."

"It's a bit rough, I'll give you that, but I bet it gets the job done. Maybe it was all whoever owned it could manage to protect themselves with."

"Possibly, Constable, but the good people of Gorey aren't generally fans of guns." It was pleasingly rare for a firearm to be connected to a crime on Jersey. Graham hadn't come across one yet.

"Well, someone was, as you say, back in the day," Barnwell concluded with a shrug. "They didn't have this big old thing for nuthin'. Do you think this has something to do with . . . ?" He nodded over to the corner where Marcus was talking quietly into his phone. "You know. . ."

"I don't know. Possibly. It'll be our job to find out."

CHAPTER FIVE

I N THE BACK office, Mrs. Taylor hung up. She had just finished pleading with someone about something, successfully it would appear, and like an apparition, when Graham and Barnwell reached the lobby, she suddenly materialised behind the reception desk. She erupted in an explosion of noise when she saw them. "What *now*? What on *earth* is it *now*?" she demanded, seemingly not of the police officers who stood in front of her but of the Almighty as she waved her hands and raised her eyes to the ceiling before noticing that Barnwell held an evidence bag with a gun inside.

"A gun? You found . . . a gun? In *my hotel*?" It was too much. Her eyes welled with tears. "Oh, Inspector Graham, what must you think of us?"

"Please, take it easy, Mrs. Taylor," Graham began.

But Mrs. Taylor was distraught, assailed from too many sides at once on a single, awful day. She began pacing again. "What *will* I tell people? Another big carry-on with the police. Imagine the rumours . . . Oh, the *rumours*, Inspector," she said, clutching her chest. "They'll be the death of me."

Graham attempted to calm her. "It's just an antique gun, Mrs. Taylor. I mean, look, it's virtually a museum piece. Quite harmless." *Unless someone loads and fires it, of course.*

Mrs. Taylor's mutterings continued. "There's that big, new hotel in St. Helier, the LeisureLodge, or whatever they're calling it. Half my prices! I don't know what I'm going to do, I really don't . . ." She wandered back into her office.

Graham turned to Barnwell and leant in. "I've changed my mind. I'm completely serious about getting Janice down here. And as soon as possible. We need reinforcements. All hell's going to break loose when Mrs. Taylor finds out about"—he jabbed a thumb upwards—"*upstairs*. More than anything, she'll need an injection of kindness and calm."

Barnwell conjured up a more extreme solution. "Maybe Dr. Tomlinson injecting her with a sedative would be more helpful."

"No, we need Janice," Graham pressed again. "Tell her things are probably not as bad as they seem if she appears reluctant."

"But what if they are?" Barnwell asked darkly as he dialled Janice's number and waited for her to pick up. "So, we're all up with the patriarchy, then?"

"Wha— Er, yes for now. I'll make it up to her."

"Ah, hey, Janice? What are you up to, love? Fancy an extra half shift?" Barnwell turned away from Graham to focus on his conversation, pressing one finger to his unoccupied ear to drown out the noise of the workmen clearing debris from Mrs. Taylor's tearoom.

Inwardly, Graham cringed. He knew Mrs. Taylor was

right to be worried. People no longer stayed in old grand hotels just for the fun of it. Spiffy, modern places were threatening to take over, but the White House Inn remained special, a genuine landmark, much loved in Gorey, with an unbeatable view. It needed some work—nobody would argue that—but as Mrs. Taylor liked to remind her guests, its imperfections were its charms.

Still, charm didn't come cheap. And reputation was everything. But as he stared at the firearm recently discovered in her ruined attic, Graham realised that now was undoubtedly not the time to remind Mrs. Taylor of the fact.

He focused on the bright side. Maybe insurance-funded renovations would be the boost (and the potential amnesiac) necessary to counter the horror he was about to unleash. Mrs. Taylor would surely need them if the White House Inn were to reopen and compete for tourist's travel budgets.

A continuous stream of people arrived, called on to respond to the storm and its aftermath. These included grey-suited chartered surveyors tasked with drawing up estimates for the repair work. Their presence—and the bowel-roiling expense the repairs would entail—elevated Mrs. Taylor's blood pressure further. It was hard to decide which was worse: the costly and unsightly damage to the inn's century-old roof or the tremulous prospect of closing down the hotel until repairs could be finished. "This'll be the *death* of me," she promised them again, coming out of her office and pacing anxiously, uncertain which crisis to worry about next.

"Do you really think Mrs. T. doesn't know anything?" Barnwell quietly asked Graham once he finished his call. He nodded at the gun. "Jan promises to come down. She seemed quite keen, to be fair. She's showing her mother around St. Andrew's at the moment."

"Judging by her performance, I doubt it, but we'll ask her directly. Once she's scraped herself off the ceiling."

For a minute, they watched a perpetually moving Mrs. Taylor direct her staff, shoo away gawkers, and dispatch a pair of hard-hatted engineers to the basement. Graham hesitated to add more complexity to her day, but the gun was an unusual find.

"I know absolutely *nothing*," answered Mrs. Taylor with total confidence. "Never seen it before, and neither have my staff, I'm quite certain. I'd not have allowed it in the hotel if I'd known. I've no idea how it got there. It's a terrible liberty for a guest to take," she said, disappointed with whoever had been thoughtless enough to leave a *gun* lying around. "Quite against the White House Inn's policies. I mean, it looks old, and if I think about it, it must have been left there well before my time. Yes, yes, that must be it. I haven't been up in the attic in years."

CHAPTER SIX

AN HOUR AFTER Barnwell called her, Sergeant Janice Harding strode into the White House Inn lobby. From the stairs, Barnwell spotted her and trotted down. "Did you manage to agree on the hymns?"

"Not exactly," she answered glumly. "This would all be a lot simpler if we could just have a small beach wedding and be done with it. Is it too late to elope to Tahiti?" She looked around. "Oh, hell. What's all this bloomin' palaver?"

Barnwell looked skyward, aware he was about to deliver bad news. "It's the roof."

"I know about the roof, Bazz. It's all over the car park. It looks like a bomb site out there. I had to park in the public car park." Janice tutted as if the five-hundred-yard walk to the hotel had been a personal insult. "Half the place is closed according to Freddie's blog. My wedding guests are going to be bedding down on yoga mats in our back room at this rate."

"*Temporarily* closed," Barnwell said, doing his best to instil optimism into his voice.

"Right, well, here I am. In uniform, as you asked. What

do you need me for? I don't know the first thing about roofs."

"Yeah, so, some other things have happened."

"Oh?"

Barnwell, faced with Janice in an obviously pugnacious mood, hesitated. "I was poking around upstairs, see . . ."

"Yeah, and?"

"I found a gun." Barnwell castigated himself. He'd bottled it; gone for the lesser bombshell first. But at least Janice's reaction wasn't too bad.

"Oooooooh," Janice said, her eyes gleaming. "Was it big and shiny?"

"Six-shot revolver. A classic, actually. The DI gave me a lecture on the different variants of the model twenty-eight, just in case I ever come across one again. Which I almost certainly won't."

"Was it loaded?"

"Empty. But there were bullets. The interesting bit is where it was found."

"Oooooooh." Janice was thrilled again. This was a lot more exciting than reminding her mother that most people can't hit the top (or even the middle) notes of "Morning Has Broken." Or that Rosemary Harding needed to mend the tiff with her brother—Janice's Uncle Timmy, a Welsh choir mainstay and baritone—if the fifty members of her wedding congregation were to pull off "Jerusalem" as Janice's mum wished. "If he doesn't come, it'll be a lot of people mumbling and mouthing the words with no sound coming out. Your choice," Janice had told her pouting mother as she left her at the church half an hour earlier. "Did you find it in the roof? The gun, I mean."

"We certainly did, Sergeant." DI Graham walked up behind them. "Looks like it was in a suitcase stuffed in a drawer. Fell out when the dresser was karate-chopped by a falling beam. I just overheard Mrs. Taylor on the phone calling someone a 'greedy little so-and-so,' so she might be a while. Once she's done though . . ."

"I should calm her down enough so I can ask her about this gun?" Janice guessed.

Barnwell saw a way in. "Er, yeah. And there's something else."

Graham turned to Barnwell. "You haven't told her?"

"Told me what?" Janice's eyebrows shot up. "What?" she said again, her wide eyes flicking between the faces of the two men.

"I found something else up there. Something different but perhaps related to the gun."

"Really?" Again, Barnwell hesitated. Janice frowned. "Well?"

"Mrs. Taylor's not gonna like it."

"Well, she can't run from it. Come on, tell me."

"There's also a concrete block up in the roof."

Janice frowned and tucked her chin in. "Concrete? Up there?" Her eyes narrowed as she sucked on her lower lip.

"And I noticed that where the concrete had worn away . . ."

"Yes?"

"A fingertip was poking out. Tomlinson's up there now waiting for an archaeologist to advise him on how to excavate it without disturbing too much. Keep it, you know . . . *intact*." Barnwell's words came out in a rush.

Janice's head shot forward, her eyes growing even bigger, her jaw slack. "Wha . . ."

"It might have been there for forty years," Barnwell added.

"For. . ."

"Shush, Jan, quiet," Barnwell pleaded, looking around. "We haven't told Mrs. T. yet. She's gonna go ballistic."

Graham chuckled. "Punny, Constable." Barnwell frowned. "Ballistic? Oh, never mind."

"How do you know it's been there for forty years? The body," Janice whispered.

"There are some things with the gun that look like they're that old. Mrs. Taylor says she hasn't been up there in years. If everything's connected, they could have been in the attic all this time."

"And we were wandering about down here, oblivious. Blimey." Janice was dumbstruck as she thought about the possibilities.

In the distance, they heard Mrs. Taylor clucking as she ordered workmen about before she appeared in one of the doorways that led off the lobby. The three police officers who had been huddling in an alcove under the stairs, immediately sprang apart and assumed casual poses, Barnwell even feigning complete and exhaustive interest in an enormous rubber plant.

"Sergeant Harding, how nice of you to come up here to see us! So good of you. Please pardon the mess. You've no need to worry. We'll have everything sorted out in time for your wedding guests." Thankfully, Mrs. Taylor didn't stop but passed through the lobby, walking outside to look skywards at the roof for the fifteenth time that day.

"I get the distinct impression everyone's avoiding the truth," Janice said. "We're hiding the aggro in the attic from her, and she's not being truthful about the state of this place. There's no way she's going to be open in just over a week."

"Do you fancy a quick jaunt up there? They haven't started drilling yet. We need to collect evidence before they do. You'll need a hard hat and some hi-vis," Graham said.

"Can't wait," Janice said. "Jack reckons I look my most alluring in hi-vis gear."

Barnwell squeezed his eyes tight shut. He didn't want to think of the dependable, motherly, more senior Janice as "alluring." "Enough, enough. Let's go," he said.

CHAPTER SEVEN

B Y THE TIME they reached the top of the stairs,
yellow jackets and headgear in place, Janice could
track some classic smells—dust and mould, the
odour of things covered up and forgotten—and once inside
the attic, she saw why. "You know that secret government
storage room?" she said, struck by the comparison. "Right at
the end of *Raiders of the Lost Ark?*"

Barnwell laughed. "Well, this is mostly just old furniture that didn't get thrown away when it should have long
ago. Plus, a possible body encased in concrete, of course. It's
there in the corner." Janice wandered over. Dr. Tomlinson
sat on an old, metal fold-up chair, scrolling on his phone, his
legs crossed.

"Hello, Janice."

"Bit of a turnup for the books, eh?"

"I'll say."

"You look like you're waiting for a bus, sitting there like
that."

Tomlinson smiled. "I'm waiting for some expert input

from an archaeologist friend of mine. He's on his way." Janice regarded the pathologist. The lines on his face appeared deeper than normal, his pallor a little grey.

"Bazza says you think you've got a body in there. Must have been well sealed not to have been noticed."

"Yes, but if the concrete was thick and dense enough, it would do the trick."

"What's the plan?"

"With a bit of luck, I'm hoping the tomb will have dispelled its secrets by the end of the day. With some good advice and the help of Bob the Builder, we should be able to extract as much of the remains as possible and I can take them to the mortuary for examination and testing."

"Rather you than me, Marcus. Fingers crossed?" Janice smiled and, patting Tomlinson on the shoulder, left him to his phone. She suddenly felt in need of a drink. Or at least most of a bar of good chocolate.

She returned to Barnwell, who stood in the attic's opposite corner. "What've you done with Carmen while you've been doing all this?"

"Uh, me 'n' Melanie left her and Vixen with the hotel's groundsmen until we're done here. They were gonna give them a runaround." He looked at his watch. "Right about now, she's probably snoozing on top of a pile of compost in their big, warm shed. Sounds good to me."

Janice laughed. "Yeah, it does. And I'll have to remember that. Perhaps that pile of compost will be a good resting place for my guests if the hotel isn't back up and running by the time they're due to arrive." She clapped her hands. "Right, then. Show me what's what."

"I'll give you the tour." Barnwell spent the next few minutes showing Janice where the roof's support beams had come crashing down, hurling tiles everywhere and permitting a nightlong deluge of rain to flood the attic. "Melanie reckoned there was a weak spot in the roof that had been holding for a while, but the winds worried at it, and the heavy rain was the final straw."

"It was a downpour to be sure." Janice marvelled at the destruction around her. A full quarter of the White House Inn roof had opened to welcome the elements.

"Yep. Melanie said—"

"Did she now? You're quite chatty with this Melanie, aren't you? Melanie this, Melanie that."

Barnwell held Janice's gaze. "Yeah, so?"

Janice smirked. "Nothing, nothing. Where'd you find the gun, then? Did it get a cold dousing like the rest of the attic?" Yards from the tarped hole, windblown rain still collected in puddles on top of storage boxes and soaked old couches.

"Actually, no. We think it was in this suitcase which opened when a chest of drawers got poleaxed. I found the gun next to it but not damaged, along with some other stuff which is mostly fine. There's the suitcase. All the stuff around it fell out. But the boss found bullets in the inside pockets. Everything needs collecting, logging, and bagging."

"Okey doke," Janice said. "I'll handle it. Poor Mrs. T. must be out of her mind." She rubbed her hands. "Brrr, it's cold and damp up here." She sheltered between a large upright beam and an upturned old bed frame that stood under a part of the roof that remained intact. While the storm had died down, the inn's exposure on the cliff meant the wind still whistled around it. They had to raise their voices to be heard. "Going to need major repairs before this place is watertight again. I wonder what the insurers are going to think of that?"

"From the expression on Mrs. Taylor's face, I'd worry

for my life if I was them. I heard her claiming that the insurers were suggesting that there might have been 'pre-existing structural weaknesses' in the roof. That went down about as well as you might imagine."

The sound of footsteps behind them signalled Graham had arrived. "As one of my early sergeants used to say, 'A copper can always recognise a cop-out.' Sounds like Mrs. T. can too. Barnwell, would you go and chat to the staff while Janice does the bagging? See if you can find out anything about what it was like here forty, fifty years ago. You never know, there might have been rumours passed down. Be discreet. *Don't* mention the . . ." He nodded towards the banquette. "Worth a try at least. Janice can join you when she's done here."

"I'll see you downstairs, Bazza."

As Janice watched Barnwell's retreating back, she sighed. She tried to keep her thoughts at bay, but the White House Inn was central to her wedding plans, and from the looks of the place, it would not be able to perform the role she intended for it.

"Bit of a mess, eh?" Graham seemingly read her mind.

"I'll say so, sir. I've got my nan and step-grandad booked in here along with eighteen or so others. And, to make things easier for Nan—she's eighty-two, the trip over will be quite something for her—we also booked the hotel restaurant for the rehearsal dinner. At this rate, we'll be in the youth hostel and down the chippy."

Janice frowned at the sodden conditions and stepped away to text Jack:

> WHI attic looks like a bomb went off. Hotel closed. Go to Plan B for Accommodation Group Charlie. Repeat, Plan B. 😕

She had time to reach for her forensic gloves and an evidence bag, but her fiancé's reply was near instant and reassuring:

On it. Got six hotels I can try. It'll all be fine!

CHAPTER EIGHT

TO BARNWELL'S IMMENSE annoyance, Freddie Solomon quickly read the changed atmosphere in the White House Inn. As word circulated through the staff that something more than the weather was up, he hovered among them, a watching, listening drone, noting exclamations of shock or a curled lip of disgust. Barnwell had made a list of every staff member and was hunting them down as they helped with the cleanup. All of them were too young to have been at the White House Inn forty or so years ago, but had they heard "any old stories or rumours about criminal activity or a gun, perhaps, anything handed down by previous staff members?"

As Barnwell roamed the hotel and Janice bagged evidence upstairs, Graham sat in the tearoom again, mulling over what he knew, reconstructing what might have happened, and tweaking one variable after another. Following two big discoveries, his senses were sharper, his pulse just a little elevated.

From where he was sitting, he could see Mrs. Taylor

behind the desk, dealing now with a crippling one-two punch—the vengeful storm plus this new embarrassment. She had poured herself a large Bristol Cream sherry from the hotel's bar and, for now, sat sipping as she watched the chaos unfold before her in a post-traumatic daze. She noticed Graham watching her and picked up her glass.

Walking over, she said, "You don't partake, do you?" and dabbed the rim of her sherry glass. She sat in the high-backed rattan wicker chair next to him.

"No, thank you," Graham said. "I can hardly blame you, though, under the circumstances." It was barely lunchtime.

"Is there anything I can help you with? Anything to do with this . . . *gun.*" Marjorie Taylor spoke as though the Smith and Wesson Model 28 was a nasty infectious disease they were all in danger of catching.

"Well, the main thing now is to confirm when it might have been left where it was found. I'm having a bit of trouble working out how we might do that. We'll have to take it to the lab. Run some forensics. See if that yields anything." Privately, Graham thought the concrete block would yield far more evidence, but he didn't want to alarm Mrs. Taylor any more than necessary until it was either prudent to tell her about the body or it became unavoidable.

Before she could take another sip of her drink, Mrs. Taylor had to answer the phone and tackle yet another storm-related problem. In her absence, Freddie sidled up, his target clearly the detective inspector. But Graham, spotting Solomon making directly for him, raised his hand as though he were stopping traffic. Freddie took the hint and, choosing not to test Graham's patience further, slunk in the direction of the front door.

Graham's eye then caught Barnwell, who had just

finished his interviews with the staff. "Anything? You've not taken long."

"Was no need. They're mostly kids, really," Barnwell said. "For them, 'a long time ago' was the week before last."

"Not surprising, I suppose. They'd have to be in their late fifties or sixties to have worked here during the period we're looking at."

"And they were all spooked at the idea that there'd been a gun here. Gawd knows what they're going to think about someone dying and lying for decades directly above 'em."

Graham sighed. "Humanity experiences a one-point-five percent turnover every year. Each of those hundred-odd million people has to die *somewhere*."

"Yeah, I s'pose that's true, but this is the second suspicious death here in recent memory, and there was that monkey business after the last big storm. One of the kids called this place the 'Fright House Inn.'" Graham cracked a smile. It had been a long morning.

More workmen were arriving, vying for Mrs. Taylor's attention at the crowded reception desk. "We're here about the windows, love. Lost a few in the storm, did you?" one asked.

Janice appeared, running down the stairs, passing a couple of smirking builders. "It was *horrible* up there!" she said with a frustrated cry. Ruffling her hair and flexing her shoulders as if to shake off a mat of cobwebs and dust, she shuddered. "There's wildlife 'n' all."

"How wild?" Graham asked her.

"Spiders and stuff. Birds. I disturbed a nest!"

"Of what?"

"I have no idea. That was the worst part. If being a hotelier doesn't work out, Mrs. Taylor can always open a petting zoo for really weird teenagers." Janice handed over the battered red suitcase and two big, clear, plastic evidence bags, one containing the suitcase contents, the other a blue tweed jacket. "Not much, is it?"

"Some people travel light," Graham said. "He probably wasn't planning on staying long. Not with that gun." The inspector focused on the bag of clothes. He could see a thin sweater, a T-shirt, a white vest, a pair of underpants, and a pair of socks, as well as a bulky, midpriced electronic watch, the type that could do calculations.

Just out of earshot but doing his best to overhear anyway, Freddie Solomon continued to lurk, ready to ensnare anyone who might know anything. Having ferreted out the discovery of the gun after Mrs. Taylor's histrionics had given the game away, more intel was clearly of paramount interest, and he was making notes on everything he observed.

"Quite a find, eh?" Freddie began cordially as Graham walked past him on the way to his car. The detective inspector was having none of it.

"Just somebody's belongings, Freddie." Graham was keen to be rid of the man with his twitching thumbs. He wanted word from Tomlinson, who was still standing vigil over the body in the block. He wanted to know the status of Tomlinson's friend, the archaeologist. He wanted to unleash someone on the forensic evidence. And he wanted more tea. Probably in that order, unless the need for tea became preeminent. He most certainly did *not* want to deal with Freddie Solomon.

"A revolver though?" Freddie said, trotting alongside Graham as he seemed so often to do. "Loaded, was it?"

"Be off, you foul creature," growled Graham.

"Then it *was*!" Freddie resumed making notes, still trotting, head down.

Graham stopped and spun around so fast that Freddie ran headfirst into his chest.

"Wow, blinkin' heck," Freddie said, staggering back, his hand reflexively reaching for his forehead. "It's like walking into a *wall*."

Graham brushed imaginary crumbs of Freddie from his jacket. "That'll teach you to bother an officer while he's executing his duties. Now, look, *Freddie*," he said as though unconvinced of the blogger's prerogative to possess a name, "I've warned you about this before."

"It's a very unusual weapon, I understand," Freddie said, keen to press his chance. "The calibre of it, I mean, and . . ."

Graham grasped Freddie's arm with more conviction than Freddie expected. Or, it has to be said, was strictly warranted. "If you print a word about that gun or any other evidence, I'll . . ."

Freddie opened his mouth, ready to protest vociferously against whatever DI Graham had in mind for him, when both men were interrupted by Mrs. Taylor's call from the entryway of the White House Inn. "Detective Inspector! Would you like another cup of tea?"

CHAPTER NINE

"I THINK THIS is him," Barnwell said into his phone. He was standing in the White House Inn's temporary car park, some yards from the regular one that was adjacent to the hotel. The new parking area, a section of the inn's formerly manicured lawn but now a roil of mud and grass, had been so consigned both for the protection of guests' cars from the ongoing danger of falling debris and because the permanent car park was full of fire trucks, pickup trucks, all kinds of workers' trucks.

"All clear" was the reply from Graham in the lobby. "Intercept him and we'll bring him up the back stairs. Mrs. Taylor is in the kitchen."

A few moments later, Barnwell, Graham, and Dr. Alexander Papadopoulos entered the attic, the archaeologist unaware of the clandestine nature of his visit.

"Alex!" Dr. Tomlinson strode across the floorboards, his arms outstretched, evidently relieved to see his old friend. "Twice in two days. That's some kind of record."

"Marcus, it's good to see you again, and so soon. But these appear to be strange circumstances, no?" Dr.

Papadopoulos spoke in lightly accented English as quietly and calmly as he might if he were the narrator of a particularly reassuring children's bedtime story. He was a short, stocky man who wore an ill-fitting brown suit and a brown and yellow paisley-patterned tie. It was strange attire for someone on holiday, but later Barnwell speculated that perhaps Papadopoulos travelled "ready for anything—and, in these circumstances, just as well."

Spectacles with thick lenses were propped on Papadopoulos's pudgy nose, and his eyes appeared unnaturally small when viewed through the prism of the glass. They gave him the appearance of a shortsighted mole. "Your message was intriguing. What do you have here?" Dr. Papadopoulos cast his tiny, glass-obscured eyes around until they alighted on the concrete box in the corner.

"Forgive me for interrupting your holiday, but we've got an unusual case on our hands. We believe we may have a body buried in concrete, and I'd like your advice. I'm not quite sure how to proceed with the exhumation, or perhaps that's *excavation*, without damaging the remains."

"Is that it over there?" Papadopoulos said, not taking his eyes off the corner.

"Indeed," Marcus replied.

Dr. Papadopoulos lumbered over and peered at the concrete through his bottle-thick spectacles. He knocked the brick surrounding it and placed the flat of his hand on top as though testing the temperature. "How old do we think the remains might be?" Papadopoulos raised his head and looked at Marcus, blinking as if he'd just breached the earth's surface after many years in darkness.

"From other items found which we think might be associated with the body, we estimate forty, maybe fifty years."

"Do you have any thought as to the condition?"

"Not exactly, but we have this fingertip." Marcus pointed it out. "Given that it's intact, it's possible the remains might be in a decent state, don't you think? But the concrete's thickness and composition present a problem accessing them."

Papadopoulos reached deep into his trouser pocket to pull out a metal tape measure. Briskly, he measured the length, width, and depth of the block and, tapping his lips with his forefinger, murmured to himself as he contemplated the problem faced by Tomlinson and his team.

"Adipocere appears to have formed which will help, but you'll certainly need to be cautious. Have you considered employing any imaging techniques to get a clearer picture before excavation?"

"Ah, yes, that's a good idea." Dr. Tomlinson rolled back on his heels. "But the Gorey forensic budget doesn't stretch to concrete-penetrating radar, I'm afraid. We don't come across this kind of thing too often, you see."

"Alright, let's make some reasonable deductions. Whoever created this tomb, which is effectively what this is, built a brick exterior around the body and then filled it with concrete. They placed it across the joists for support. If we consider the position of this exposed digit, we might reasonably conclude that the end next to the wall is where we will find the feet. I suggest we start there."

"Right, you are. Anything else?"

"Once we've found the feet, we'll have a better understanding of the body's position, and we can proceed with selective excavation. I recommend using hand tools at first, then we can follow up with a pneumatic saw."

Papadopoulos leaned over and knocked the side of the brick mould several times along its length before continuing with his assessment. "I would endeavour to take the concrete from the top, thereby exposing the body while still supporting it via the concrete underneath. Having it lie on a bed as it were. That will protect the integrity of the remains and help further your study in situ. When you've completed your examination here as far as it can proceed, we can attempt to lift the body for transportation to your lab."

"But surely the body will be in good nick, won't it?" Barnwell whispered to Graham.

They stood a few feet away from the two doctors, along with Bob the Builder. Bob was a stocky lad, a local in his late fifties, a bricklayer since before he left school. Everyone knew him as "Bob the Builder," so much so that only his family knew his real name.

Bob's work took him all over the Channel Islands and sometimes to the French mainland. Having spent most of his life on a building site of one kind or another, he took over his father's construction contracts with local authorities when he retired, and this now comprised most of his work.

Bob had built everything from brand-new houses and barn conversions to shoring up historical stately homes. He was the person everyone turned to for building jobs, although now it was the younger men he hired who did most of the backbreaking work. On Graham's orders, Barnwell had called him in to help, giving Bob strict instructions to tell no one about the details of this "urgent, small job at the White House Inn." Chewing his lip, a bag of tools in one hand, an electric saw at his feet, he looked on nervously.

"I mean, won't the concrete have protected the body from turning to mush?" Barnwell added.

"Not necessarily," Graham said, wincing at his constable's choice of words. "Even if the concrete created an airtight space, the bacteria in and on the body at the point of death will have done their worst."

"Also, how well the concrete was made will have had an impact," whispered Bob, overhearing and leaning in. "Can't imagine anyone making their best mix under these circumstances. They were probably in a right panic. They must have lugged bags of cement, sand, and gravel up here without anyone seeing. And that's if there's a water source up here. If not, they'd have had to have lugged that up an' all."

"How's it going?" Janice said softly, sidling up. She'd been in her car strategizing with Jack about the new accommodation arrangements for the bridesmaids and groomsmen. The conversation had been fraught. "I don't think that's a good idea, Jack. Having Suranne and Ava and Toby and Dexter all under the same roof is asking for . . . shenanigans," she'd said. Jack had eventually conceded the point, and they'd agreed to have a rethink.

"I think they're making progress. Just discussing what to do," Barnwell whispered back. "All done downstairs? Thought you'd have gone back to your day off."

"Wasn't going to miss this, was I? The Gorey equivalent of discovering Tutankhamun's tomb, the Mrs. T. factor notwithstanding. And dealing with my mother was the alternative."

Tomlinson looked over at them. "Okay then, let's get started. Alex will supervise and tell you what to do, Bob."

Straightening his shoulders, Bob picked up his electric saw and wandered with his tools to the corner. Despite working on large, sometimes grand building projects, Bob had never refused a job, no matter how unusual or small. He would lay patios and build outdoor kitchens. He would rebuild low pub walls demolished by patrons who shouldn't be driving. He had even built pigsties around pigs. But uncovering a body in a block of concrete was the smallest, most delicate, unusual job ever asked of him.

"Target this corner here, by hand, bit by bit, please, sir. When you find something, stop, okay?" Dr. Papadopoulos said.

Bob grunted and moved in. With his bolster and sledge-hammer, he broke the brick at one end, then chipped away at the concrete half inch by half inch, watched intently by the four other men and Janice.

Barnwell had silenced the roofers on top. The only thing the three police officers, two doctors, and one builder could hear was the *tap-tap-tap* of metal on metal and occasional gusts of wind as the last vestiges of the storm receded. Clumps of concrete fell to the floor as they waited for a sight or a change in sound that would signal Bob had found what they were looking for.

"Stop!" Papadopoulos cried. Barnwell jumped, startled.

Bob straightened and stood back, wiping his upper lip with the back of his hand, his face puce from effort.

Papadopoulos beckoned Graham and Tomlinson over. At the end of the block, surrounded by near-white concrete, they could see the tip of a leather sole.

"A shoe. Keep going," Graham said. Bob chipped away a little more of the concrete. The tip widened and length-ened to expose a hand-stitched sole of a low-heeled shoe.

"Well, we now know their shoe size. Nine and a half," Tomlinson said, reading the number clearly visible on the leather sole.

Papadopoulos turned to Bob. "Do you have a small rotating saw?"

"I certainly do."

"Then let's move on to the next stage. We'll now

attempt to reveal the body as cleanly as possible. We must shield the area from view and work in silence behind the screen. It is important for the integrity of the burial site and to offer dignity to the deceased," Papadopoulos said solemnly.

"We'll see to it," Graham said. "And leave you to your work."

CHAPTER TEN

"ALL THAT I was told," Mrs. Taylor explained, more composed now that Graham had accepted her offer of tea and was sharing a pot with her, "was that the grand attic was once a dormitory room. I think for unmarried lads back when this place was private apartments, before it was a hotel. In the twenties, thirties."

"Imagine having a whole stretch of this place to yourself," Graham said, admiring the slightly faded grandeur.

"Then the Germans turned it into a military outpost during the occupation," she continued. "You know, Hitler and his lot. Once we kicked them out, nobody paid much attention to the old place. It sat up here on the clifftop empty for a decade or so, then was bought by someone with plans for a retirement home. But they went bankrupt before the idea got off the ground and it was turned into a cheap hotel. Run by a Miss Lovell." Marjorie sniffed and took a sip of her tea. "She was as old as I am now when she took the building over and ran the hotel for twenty years before she eventually died. God rest her soul."

Mrs. Taylor crossed herself and paused respectfully for

a second before enthusiastically returning to her subject. "As a girl, I'd watched this place for years, you see, wondering about it, dreaming. I could see the possibilities, the potential. When it eventually came up for auction, I had just enough money to snatch it up." She sat, her back stiff and straight, puffing out her chest.

"September 1982. I was very young, in my early twenties. Newly married I was. Back then, with a hotel to my name, I suppose I got a bit full of myself. Had some grand ideas, maybe *too* grand. Went around telling everyone I'd be converting the grand attic into a restaurant with an ocean view or some such, I seem to remember. The surveyors and assessors and bean counter people, well, they said not to take the risk, and I didn't. But perhaps I should've. In those days, they doubted a woman could run a place like this and made their views known as plain as day. I was happy to prove them wrong," she said primly, the hotel's decades of success more than enough proof that she was right. "But I did forgo the idea of that restaurant. It would have been difficult with the kitchen on the ground floor.

"Of course, Mr. Taylor helped. In those days, it was different. A woman was often not taken seriously. I could be very stern. I had a confidence beyond my years, but sometimes a man's touch was required. Mr. Taylor was very good. He was usually merely a presence in the background, but there was one time when a guest, a Mr. Madingley I seem to remember, would not accept that he hadn't made a reservation and that we didn't have a room for him. Was causing quite a ruckus in reception, he was. I was about to call you lot, but my Timothy got it sorted. A few quiet words were all that it needed. He was good like that—a help, but he never took over." She gazed into the distance. "I miss him."

After a brief experiment with twenty-first-century tools, Graham had returned to the policeman's traditional notebook and pencil as the means by which he recorded his conversations. As he listened to Mrs. Taylor recite the history of the White House Inn, he created page after page of odd, interconnected symbols. Silent next to him, Barnwell lost track of what Mrs. Taylor was saying as he watched his boss doodle.

Despite their appearance, the scribbles were not meaningless. Graham's pencil made familiar motions, but some strokes were forced into a tight compression, while others were truncated into a complex little graphical suffix. Some marks resembled mini pictograms, as though Graham were borrowing from the Chinese language. Only through context could one even be certain it was English. It was a form of shorthand Graham had devised for himself and appeared to serve as a form of meditation as the detective inspector focused solely on transposing the words to which he was listening. Watching the pencil move up and down and from side to side creating this indecipherable code mesmerised Barnwell.

"In the end, I ran out of money, and I never got around to it," Mrs. Taylor lamented, returning to the subject of the seafront restaurant. "Too much competition, and then the package holidays started. My margins were crunched. We survived all that, several recessions, changes in government. But now? Now I'll be lucky to drum up any business at all." Her voice rose almost to a wail. She began to tear up and dabbed at her eyes with the scrunched-up tissue she held in her hand. "I mean, who wants to stay in an old wreck with only half a roof!"

Graham second-guessed himself half a dozen times but finally put his pencil down and placed a comforting arm around Mrs. Taylor's shoulders. "It's been a rotten day, Mrs. Taylor, but remember something: the White House Inn is a Gorey institution. We can't imagine the place without you." Seeking reasons for optimism was a trick Laura had shown him. "Besides, the surveyors and assessors are working up plans to fix the roof right now. The insurance will prioritise it, and in a couple of weeks, they'll give you the green light. You'll be back in action in no time, you'll see."

"They know your back's against the wall and they'll nip it in the bud," Barnwell added, "if that's not mixing metaphysics or whatever."

"Metaphors, Constable."

"Yeah, them."

Their chivvying seemed to help Mrs. Taylor a little. Sighing, hands clasped, fingertips endlessly clutching at her opposing knuckles while her thumbs tucked the shredded tissue into her palms, Mrs. Taylor thanked the officers, and after draining her teacup, she stoically headed to her office. "That's the body language of someone who has passed through the early stages of grief," Graham told Barnwell, "and is inexorably approaching some kind of acceptance."

"But won't she get thrown right back into the thick of it when we tell her . . . what we've got to tell her?"

"Yes. And that's why we need Janice." Graham looked around. "Where is she?"

"Last I saw, she was talking to Melanie. Having a good chinwag, they were. Had a lot to talk about it seemed. Women in a man's world, I suppose."

"Mrs. Taylor will be alright. At least, I think she will. The carpet still looks good, if a little trodden on by the firefighters, and the old place could never lose its sense of grandeur. People'll soon forget, I'm sure. Don't you think?"

"Yeah, 'course they will. It's a Gorey icon. The place

wouldn't be the same without it. Soon it'll be as good as new 'n' life will carry on as before." The two men looked at each other, unsure as to whether they were being genuine. Secretly, they were jollying themselves along, intent on convincing each other that once word got out that a body had been buried in the White House Inn attic for *decades*, nothing would change for Mrs. Taylor, and she would go on exactly as before. They both knew that was highly unlikely.

"You know, Barnwell, when I first arrived, I wasn't too sure about staying here, but the quality of the tea service persuaded me. I thought I'd stay for a week at most, but then the atmosphere dug into my soul. Did you know I met Laura here?" Graham nodded over to the reception desk, a large, Victorian, oak-panelled affair. "In the lobby, and I like to think especially in this sunlit tearoom, one can hear a faint call from an era when a hotel could be restrained, a true cathedral to travel. A mini palace that one could mirac- ulously call one's own, if just for a week, in the quest for rest, relaxation, and an escape from the trials of everyday life. A place where anything might happen, anything at all —conversations, characters, circumstances, all novel to the traveller. I found it set my Spidey senses alive."

"Blimey, sir, you'll be invoking that annoying little Belgian fella any minute. The one off the telly."

"Hercule Poirot? He would have loved this place, Constable. His essence embodies it. One might imagine seeing him patrol the corridors at night if one believed in that kind of thing."

Barnwell regarded his boss quizzically, then drained his tea with a slurp. "Er, right, sir. Shall we be getting on, then?"

CHAPTER ELEVEN

F OR THE NEXT four hours, under Dr. Papadopoulos's careful guidance, and behind sheets provided by the White House Inn's housekeeping department and hastily erected by Barnwell and Janice, Bob the Builder painstakingly sawed chunks from the block of cement. Dust flew and settled in a field of microscopic particles around him.

Marcus Tomlinson sat quietly on the far side of the attic, away from the dust. Occasionally, Dr. Papadopoulos would request his assistance, and he would disappear behind the curtain, resurfacing a few minutes later. As time dragged on, Graham joined the pathologist, bringing over a chair. They sat in silence as the constant, shrill whirring of the saw filled the air.

Eventually, the saw stopped, the silence ringing in their ears, and the tiny particles of cement that had hung in the air for hours slowly sank to the floor. They settled on the dusty wooden boards already marked with footprints. Papadopoulos swept aside the sheet and peered around it. He was covered from head to toe. A paper suit, booties, gloves, a face shield, a mask over his mouth and nose, and, of course, his glasses, shielded him completely. It might have been impossible to identify him but for his distinctive bottle-glass thick lenses.

"Gentlemen, it is time to show you what we have uncovered. Please come this way."

Eager after so much waiting, Graham and Tomlinson did not hesitate. Similarly suited and booted, they slipped behind the curtain, their eyes widening instinctively as they absorbed the scene.

On a concrete bed lay the body of a man, almost perfectly preserved. He had thin, translucent hair; a short, wide nose; and a pointed chin. Skin around his mouth stretched across his jaws, revealing a set of large teeth perfectly aligned except for a gap between the front two. His eyes were closed, weighed down by large metal washers, and one arm lay across his chest, under which was pinned a bloomless, twisted, thorny stem. The other arm was propped in the air by a crude wire construction as it crossed his body, one finger pointed like he was hailing a taxi. The extended forefinger was clearly the one that had alerted Barnwell to the body's presence.

The man wore a green polo shirt, muddy and faded now, which lay unnaturally over his bony rib cage. An embroidered crocodile motif adorned the left breast. A gold crucifix had settled into the crease of his neck, and jeans, the stain of which was still a pale blue, ended in a pair of black, laced shoes.

"What can you tell us, Alex?" Tomlinson asked.

Dr. Papadopoulos adjusted his glasses before speaking. "Marcus, Inspector, it is quite a rare scene we have here. As you mentioned, we think the body we've unearthed has been encased in this concrete possibly for over forty years.

The concrete has acted as a preservative, albeit a grim one. The body is in excellent condition. However, there are tell-tale signs of decomposition. The concrete slowed the process but couldn't stop it entirely. You'll see that the torso structure has collapsed due to the decay of internal organs, and the legs are wizened to almost nothing. The spongy ball and socket joints have deteriorated. But I believe we have a man who was in his prime when he was struck down. You'll be able to estimate his age from dental records and carbon dating his bones, but a quick assessment tells me that he is a fully developed adult male."

"What about the wire?" Graham asked.

"A rough support we made to preserve the position the body was found in. I suspect rigor mortis had set in when they buried him, which would explain the unnatural pose. When we removed the concrete, the arm was precariously suspended in midair and liable to collapse." Papadopoulos turned to Tomlinson. "I thought it might give clues as to the cause of death."

"Do you have any thoughts about what killed him?" Graham wondered. "I was expecting bullet wounds, but I don't see any."

"That's where things get tricky. The concrete and decomposition have made it difficult to identify his injuries. But I agree, I see no sign of bullet wounds. Hopefully, forensic analysis and perhaps even historical records will help you piece together what happened."

"When we get him back to the mortuary, we'll be able to say more," Tomlinson reassured Graham. "There's a lot I can do."

"I'm assuming his death was intentional. Someone went to great lengths to hide the body. They had to have had a good reason," Graham said.

"It's certainly a possibility," Dr. Papadopoulos replied. "But I wouldn't say it's a certainty."

"No, it's not, but it is curious. Encasing a body in concrete isn't something done on a whim. It suggests at a minimum a deliberate effort to conceal evidence."

"What are you thinking, David?" Dr. Tomlinson asked him.

"My working theory is that he was killed deliberately, and the murderer chose to move the body here for some unknown reason or, more likely, killed him in the attic."

"Or there's another possibility: the man died of natural causes, and someone chose to conceal his body for another reason entirely. But that's more your field than mine," Papadopoulos said, pushing his glasses higher up his nose. He smiled.

"Exactly so." Graham exhaled. "Right, well, thank you for the insight, Dr. Papadopoulos. You've been a great help. Looks like we've got our work cut out for us." Graham turned to Tomlinson and smiled ruefully. "Over to you, Marcus."

CHAPTER TWELVE

JANICE TRIED HER best, but in the end, it wasn't enough. It was likely that nothing would have been sufficient to prevent Mrs. Taylor's bloodcurdling scream when she learned there was a body in her attic. The sergeant bravely tried to talk her down, but it was Dr. Tomlinson with a sedative who saved the day. "I'll sit with her for a bit in case she wakes up," Janice promised Graham.

"Good of you, Sergeant." Graham pocketed his notebook and checked his watch. "Right, if no one here has any ideas about who this guy is, I'm off." He glanced at his car, finding in the early evening light an unwelcome presence hovering next to it like a feverish poltergeist. "Oh, for the love . . ."

"You want me to see to him?" Barnwell offered.

"I've got it. I'll see you tomorrow." Graham strode towards the car and turned his attention to the shivering apparition beside it. "Now, Freddie, where were we?"

"Erm, as I remember, you were threatening me."

"Oh, yes, now I remember. If any of what went on today

goes into print"—Graham opened his car door—"I'll make you write a retraction along with an apology from your jail cell."

"Impinging on the freedom of the media!" Freddie immediately announced to the parking lot like a crier in a market square. "Detective Inspector Graham's oppressing me!" he continued, full-throated. "And denying my reader-ship the—"

"Will you *cool it* this instant?" Graham growled, keeping his voice low.

"Police cover-up!" Freddie shouted. Hearing this, Barnwell came rushing over, Carmen, newly awoken from her peaty potting soil bed, bounding alongside him.

"Trouble, sir?" Graham nodded ever so slightly.

"Free—" Freddie continued to yell.

"Shut," Barnwell said, grabbing Freddie's wrists, "your bleedin' cake-'ole." Somewhere at the edges of the febrile firmament that was Freddie's brain, he felt a cold, metallic handcuff against his wrist, then heard a click as Barnwell locked it.

"Hey, wait just a minute!" Freddie cried. Graham moved to stand squarely in front of him.

"We're in the middle of a serious police inquiry, Solomon. My officers *rely* on evidence, you thoughtless little weasel, and if the guilty party or someone close to them knows what we've found, they can disrupt, pervert, or other-wise counter our investigation. We do not need you helping them do that."

"But there's a *pattern*!" Freddie insisted. Horrified, he glanced down as Barnwell cuffed his other wrist.

"The only pattern around here"—Barnwell gave the chain between the handcuffs a quick tug—"is one of you

jeopardising police investigations when you were specifically told not to."

"But . . ."

"Get in the car, Freddie," said Graham, "or I'll clip you
to the door handle and make you run all the way." It was
just over a mile and a half to the police station, and the
thought pleased Graham immensely, even if he had no
intention of fulfilling his threat. "Then I'll roast you over an
open fire until you understand that investigations require
integrity."

Freddie continued to protest as Barnwell placed a hand
over his head and guided him into the back seat of the car,
the door silencing Freddie's protestations as Barnwell
slammed it shut.

"I never intended to interfere in any . . ."

By now, a crowd of perhaps eight passers-by were
watching the unedifying scene, so Graham climbed in to
continue his telling off. "I don't give a monkey's about your
intentions. You're constantly messing up the juror pool,
directing public opinion, and muddying goodness knows
what else with your brainless ramblings."

"But, the gun, Inspector. It's part of a pattern I'm
researching for my book." News of the remains in the concrete
hadn't appeared to have reached Freddie. Yet. He was still on
about the gun. "It's what I've been waiting for!" Freddie
wailed. "I was just at HMP Holbrooke interviewing two old
guys. Hard lads from the East End who had connections to
Jersey . . ." The rear door of the car slammed as Barnwell shut
Carmen in. She leaned over the back seats, excited to greet the
stranger sitting there. Freddie closed his eyes and cringed as
her moist breath warmed his neck. He wasn't a dog lover.

"It's a nice spot for a relaxing break, Jersey. Loads of

people do it, haven't you noticed?" Barnwell climbed in next to Freddie.

"Hard lads from the East End who had connections to Jersey *before the law caught up with them*," Freddie finished.

"We usually do."

"I think they came to settle old scores and transfer money. I think in addition to Jersey being a tax shelter, it was a bastion for money laundering and a gangster hideout back in the day. Before Spain became the favourite spot for expats wanting to lay low."

"You're taking a couple of random data points, a fanciful imagination, and an ability to write fiction and combining them to create a cockeyed theory that you'll never be able to prove," Graham said from the driver's seat.

"I'm working on it," Freddie said. "Good journalism takes time."

"How would you know?" Barnwell added, earning a silent acknowledgement from Graham for some sharp wit. Graham texted Laura before starting the motor.

"You know, this is typical of you, Freddie. You've never met a conclusion you didn't want to jump to," the inspector added after pressing "send."

"But you've seen it yourself," Freddie pleaded. "You looked back through those old case files I mentioned to Laura. I know you did. You wouldn't have been able to resist. It's all going in my book, you know."

"What are you talking about?" Barnwell said.

Graham eyed Freddie in his rearview mirror. "Mr. Solomon here is researching historical unsolved Jersey cases for a book he's writing."

"Working title: *Murder Island*," Freddie said proudly.

Barnwell rolled his eyes. "That's gonna go down well with the tourist board."

"Listen, there were isolated incidents that don't add up to much, but you've gone and raced ahead yet again, coming to conclusions without *any* proof." Graham shook his head. "Have you learned nothing from wasting my time these past few years?"

Glum and defeated, though never entirely hopeless—it wasn't part of his makeup—Freddie sat in the back seat quietly while Graham drove to the police station. "Um, can I ask a question?" Freddie said when they pulled up outside.

"Hmm?" Graham's eyes flicked to the rearview mirror and caught Freddie looking at him in it.

"I haven't been arrested, have I?"

"Thus far," Graham told him, "you're merely helping us with our enquiries."

"Into what?"

"Into just how much of a bleedin' pillock you are," Barnwell grunted next to him. He had been looking forward to a run with Carmen after a long day. He had hoped to follow that with a nice piece of mackerel gifted to him by one of the local fishermen as he'd patrolled the storm-beaten island before being called to inspect the White House Inn's roof. That seemed a long time ago now.

Resigned to an evening of unpleasantness, Freddie remained determined to defend himself. "Well, according to you, that'd take weeks."

"It's alright," Graham said, bringing the car to a halt. "I've called in reinforcements."

CHAPTER THIRTEEN

"**F**REDDIE! WHAT DID you do?" Laura stood in reception, her arms folded, with a frown so fierce it threatened to crack a pane of glass in the station's window. Barnwell removed a cuff from Freddie's wrist and guided him onto a chair, clicking the empty hand-cuff around the back support. Carmen ran past them and settled herself in her favourite spot under Barnwell's desk. Graham headed to his office, leaving Barnwell and Laura to keep an eye on the meddlesome blogger for a few minutes.

The constable moved quickly to the reception counter to enter Freddie's details should Graham decide to charge him with anything. Privately, Barnwell hoped to avoid the paperwork that accompanied an arrest but looked forward to a lengthy excoriation of Freddie courtesy of Graham or Laura. He didn't mind which.

"This is all just ridiculous. I haven't done anything . . ." Despite her furious expression, the sight of Laura buoyed Freddie. Although not technically a member of the Gorey Constabulary, Laura's proximity to Graham meant that within their ranks she was the closest thing to a supporter that Freddie had. It was kind of her to come out for him, especially considering that running interference on his behalf put her in an awkward position. This time, though, she seemed angrier than usual. "You know what he's like," Freddie said to her, hopeful for an intervention, or at least a soothing word.

"As a matter of fact, I do," Laura said. "And he generally has his reasons."

"It's preemptive censorship," Freddie said haughtily. He turned to Barnwell. "We live in a democracy, you know. You should be ashamed of yourselves."

"Steady on," Graham called from his office.

"Only totalitarian monsters imprison their journalists!" Freddie cried out.

"You've not been banged up yet," Barnwell told him. "But it can easily be arranged." He jostled the keys on his belt to illustrate his point.

"I haven't corrupted any investigation," Freddie insisted.

"No, but it's your habit to do things that make my life complicated, and for that reason, I'm here telling you now: cease and desist before you do." Graham came out of his office and walked towards him.

Freddie answered as though his was the only possible response. "Absolutely not. It's the public's right to know what's going on."

"If you publish details of the evidence found at that hotel," Graham said, "you'll be in trouble. This is an active inquiry, and to ensure its success, *we*"—Graham pointed his thumb at his chest—"decide when to release information, not"—he pointed his forefinger at Freddie—"*you*."

At this, Freddie's indignant, righteous fury evaporated

like water in the desert. His shoulders slumped. "Okay, I understand," he mumbled.

"Alright, then." Graham headed back to his office.

"This is important," Freddie said in a low voice to Laura. "It's about press freedoms. One of these days, he's going to arrest me properly, and there'll be no justification at all."

"Knowing that, as you do," Laura said, "you shouldn't upset him. It's your own fault."

"I didn't *do* anything!" Freddie insisted again. "He's just overzealous."

"He's a professional."

"So am I!" A splutter of amusement from behind the desk told Freddie what Barnwell thought of *that*.

"Oh, yeah, Bazza? Got something to say?" Freddie said, suddenly confrontational again.

"Constable Barnwell to you, Sonny Jim."

"I wouldn't get on the wrong side of the constable either, you know," Laura said. "Look at him, built like a brick house with a mood to match after a long day." Barnwell cackled like an evil super-genius and stroked an imaginary cat lying on his shoulder.

Freddie gulped. "I thought you were my friend, Laura." Freddie's eyes darted around. He was still cuffed to the chair.

"Can I leave now?" he asked Barnwell plaintively.

"No," came Graham's voice from his office. "Sit there and think about what you've done and still might do if you're not careful."

"But I didn't even . . ."

"Constable?" Graham bellowed. "Isn't it about time we recertified the taser equipment?"

"That date's coming up here quick, sir. Yes." Barnwell

regarded Freddie with the *schadenfreude* of happy expectation. "What say we make it a live test, sir?"

"Stop it," Laura said, surprised by their immaturity and cruelty but unaware of the stress of the police officers' day. Though even if she had known, she wouldn't have approved.

Silent while Graham wrapped up his day and Barnwell closed down the station's computers for the night, Freddie's glum, put-upon demeanour returned as he slumped in his chair. But within moments, his affect changed again. He leaned down and, with his free hand, brought out his slender laptop from his satchel. Industriously, his blues forgotten, he balanced the computer on his lap, opened it, and started tapping with one hand.

Laura was worried. "Wait, you're not . . ."

"I'm writing my next piece for the *Gossip,* as you'd expect."

"If there's anything Inspector Graham doesn't like in there . . ."

"I don't write it for him!" Freddie retorted. "I have responsibilities to my readers." He paused. "Do you think I should describe Mrs. Taylor as 'freaked out' or 'losing her mind'?"

"Won't matter," replied Laura. "She'll beat you to death with a rolling pin either way."

"And the inspector's off his rocker," Freddie added, continuing to type, "if he thinks I'm asking permission from the *police* before publishing."

"On this occasion, you can ask first," Barnwell said, "or be told later. And that wouldn't actually be your biggest problem. Let me introduce you to the Criminal Law Act of 1967, particularly section five, subsection two," he said invitingly.

"Eh?"

"'Where,'" Barnwell quoted from his computer screen, "'if a person causes any wasteful employment of the police by knowingly making a false report . . .'"

"I'm doing no such thing!" Freddie protested.

"'. . . tending to give rise to apprehension for the safety of persons or property . . .'"

"Nobody's feeling apprehensive!" Freddie insisted. "I haven't even . . ."

"'. . . he shall be liable on summary conviction to imprisonment for not more than six months, or to a fine of not more than . . .'" Barnwell had to think for a second. "Boss, is it two thousand five hundred for wasting police time?"

"Yep," Graham called back. "Also," he added, "don't forget embracery."

"Last thing I want is a hug, sir," Barnwell quipped. "Especially from him. Or did you mean something else?"

Graham appeared in his office doorway and folded his arms, a sure sign that he had knowledge to dispense. "The offence of 'embracery' involves tampering with a jury to achieve a favourable result. Freddie's obsession with dispensing information in the name of the public's 'right to know' arguably causes him to interfere with potential jurors. Which is," he reminded them, "almost every adult on Jersey."

"It's not like that," Freddie complained.

"Come to think of it," Graham added, mulling over what he knew of this particular law, "I could probably nab you for embracery right now, Freddie."

"I've never heard of it," Laura said.

Graham coughed. "Well, it is a fourteenth-century statute."

"Bang up-to-date, then," Freddie muttered.

"Also," Graham admitted, "the offence was abolished a few years ago."

"So now I'm being arrested for ancient, obsolete crimes?" Freddie sat up straight in his chair, still cuffed to it, and assumed as much authority and dignity as someone could in his position. "DI Graham, you're either going to lock me up for the night on a public order offence or lecture me. But I don't think you'll waste time doing both."

"Rule nothing out," Graham said. "I can be remarkably thorough."

Freddie stood awkwardly, his cuffed hand forcing him to stoop. He was proud of his defiance. Especially in front of Laura, who sat, her arms folded and legs crossed, watching this unseemly drama unfold. Freddie wondered if she found him courageous. Or amusing, at least.

"Are we arresting him, boss?" Barnwell said. "Or should I turf him out so that Miss Beecham and you can get some dinner?"

Graham regarded their prisoner. "Well, Freddie, what do you think? Should we lock you up for the night, bed and breakfast courtesy of His Majesty, or shall we let you go and risk you spilling Crown secrets?"

"I'm not . . ." Freddie caught Laura's eye as she glanced sideways at him. He coughed and sat up straight. "As I have been neither arrested nor charged, I believe I am free to go." Laura raised her eyebrows. Freddie shifted in his seat and lowered his voice. "I think you should let me go . . . sir."

Graham glanced at Laura. She winked at him. He silently counted to five. "Okay, Constable Barnwell, let him go." He glanced at his watch. "I'm hungry. It's been a long day." Barnwell walked around the desk and freed Freddie from his chair. "But Freddie? Listen. This is a warning, and I want you to take it seriously."

Laura leaned in. "Freddie, look, this obsession you've got with 'mobsters' and 'criminal elements' from London—"

"It's not an obsession! You, of all people, know *exactly* what I'm talking about!" Freddie erupted again. "One of them followed you down here and tried to kill you!"

"That wasn't the same thing as organised crime on Jersey's shores, and you know it."

"Alright, that's enough," Graham said, intervening. "I've had enough for one day."

"My research will prove everything!" Freddie cried. "You'll see. And then you'll owe me an apology." With that, he turned and stalked out of the station, his chin high, his eyes shining. Once outside and out of view of the police station, he blew out his cheeks and began the long trudge to collect his car. It was still parked outside the White House Inn, where he had left it earlier before . . . everything.

CHAPTER FOURTEEN

L
AURA FOLLOWED GRAHAM to his office as he finished packing up. "Freddie's not genuinely a danger to anyone, is he?"

"Yes, he is," Graham said pointedly. "And he's the kind of danger one underestimates at one's peril."

"What on earth do you mean? It's a harmless . . . well, *mostly* harmless blog."

Graham was more than ready to think about literally anything else. "Freddie's a complication," he summed up, guiding Laura out and closing his office door behind him. They headed through the reception area. "What are you doing tonight, Barnwell?"

"I planned to go for a run with Carmen." Barnwell looked outside at the now dark evening. "It's not raining, so I'll probably still do that. I have fresh mackerel in the fridge, but I might pick up a Chinese on the way home instead." He rubbed his hands together. "Choices, choices."

"Have you heard from Jim at all?"

"He's busy, I know that, sir. And enjoying it up there in London. He's coming back for Janice's wedding though."

Graham's eyes brightened at this news. "Is he? Top lad."

"We'll have a right old chinwag then."

The inspector smiled. "We will that. Righto, 'night."

Graham had the patrol car for the evening. He was on call, but he and Laura hadn't yet agreed what to do. "I thought we'd hit the Bangkok Palace. It's been a while," he said. "Khun Thongsong said that if I can manage his spicy shrimp *gaeng som*, he'll induct me into the Order of the Perfumed Jewel."

"What's that?" Laura laughed. "Like joining the Freemasons, but for chilli fiends?"

"It's for people who survive food challenges. The ones that are normally fatal. You know, poisonous fish . . ."

"Deadly mushrooms . . ." Laura guessed.

"Psychoactive fruit, that kind of thing."

Laura frowned. "You weren't really going to lock Freddie up, were you?"

Pausing as he was about to start the engine, Graham said. "Maybe, maybe not. Whether it happens in the future, well, that's up to him. I've given him plenty of warning."

"Promise me," Laura said as he got the car going, "you'll talk to me before you do that?"

"If the situation allows it," Graham said, "but I've got to protect our investigations."

"I understand, love," she said. "But there are different methods of getting through to people, and bullying Freddie at the station might not—"

"Bullying?"

"It didn't look that way to you? It did to me."

Uncomfortable at Laura's admonishment, Graham was quiet on the way to the restaurant. As he pulled into the car park, determined not to spoil a night out, he conceded. "I'll find a way forward with Freddie. No one will get charged as long as we can agree on some simple rules."

Laura wasn't sure Graham was seeing the main point. "He's not going to let you censor his writing. And if you insist, then Freddie won't be the only one who's upset about it."

"Come on," said Graham, exasperated. "You know I wouldn't do anything overly vindictive. I've said I'll work it out with him. And I'll only take redress if he steps over the legal line which, to be honest, he's already stepped over multiple times. I'm well within my—"

Laura remained in her seat, expectant but still. "I need you to promise."

"Promise what?"

"That you won't kick off some great big stink and get Gorey Constabulary on the evening news . . ."

"Me?"

" . . . because one of the coppers lost his mind and arrested a journalist who'd written unfavourably about him. Because that's how it will look whether it's strictly true or not. You're in danger of becoming your own worst enemy."

"Look, I'm not going to get a hammer and smash his laptop. Back in the day, illegal publishers had their presses broken by the—"

"Promise you won't stop him publishing."

"Other responsibilities notwithstanding, I so promise."

"And you won't lock him up."

Now Graham was laughing. "Laura, I couldn't even promise not to lock *you* up. That decision depends on what people *do*."

"Not true!" she argued, flipping off her seat belt and opening the door.

Apparently, they were finished with the in-car part of the discussion, which suited Graham perfectly; since breakfast, he'd only eaten a bag of crisps he had snatched from behind the bar at the White House Inn. The *gaeng som* offered itself invitingly. "Really?" he said, climbing out of the car.

"You were all set to arrest Freddie just for talking to others about the case. He could have scared up some useful witnesses . . ."

"Highly unlikely," Graham said. "Oh, good evening." He handed his jacket, and then Laura's coat, to Nan, one of the Bangkok Palace's traditionally attired servers.

"Sir, if I may ask, is it true you intend to order the special *gaeng som?*" Nan asked.

"It is," Graham announced. He licked his lips.

Nan's expression darkened with concern for the condemned man. "And you'd like table seventeen, as usual?"

"If it's free," Graham said. He could already see it was set for two.

The server nodded to a male colleague, who then nodded to another, and together they headed into the kitchen. When they barged back through the swing door, each carried a full-sized fire extinguisher. They set them next to table seventeen on either side of the chair Graham normally sat in. One of the canisters, Graham noticed, had a yellow label.

"Wait, is that a wet chemical extinguisher?" he asked, frowning.

"Khun Thongsong ordered us to be prepared for all eventualities," the server said politely.

Graham couldn't help laughing for a moment, then

explained to Laura. "It contains water and various types of potassium powder used for high-temperature fires."

"Sounds like a sensible precaution," she said, taking a photo of this improvised safety setup. Two other couples, waiting for their starters, glanced over, amused. Graham ordered a pot of restorative jasmine tea, while Laura had a Thai beer poured for her. "Put it this way," she said, jumping back into their discussion about Freddie without preamble, "if you arrest him, he'll become your archnemesis." Graham's mouth twisted, and he raised his hands to wave away her idea. But Laura was having none of it. "No, I'm serious. When he's onto something, Freddie's the veritable 'dog with a bone.'"

"More like a gerbil with an especially annoying face."

"David . . ." Laura warned.

"And no writing talent."

"He's *helped* you in the past." Graham raised an eyebrow. "Well, sort of, and probably will again if you two can work things out. I thought after the successful review of the Sampson's Leap case, things would get better. He's not all bad, not really. He's annoying and inappropriate, but he could become an ally."

"Look, it's really up to him," Graham said. "I won't make things any worse. How about that?"

At least partly mollified, Laura nodded. The double kitchen doors opened to reveal a waiter in a beekeeper's outfit, carefully carrying a tray.

"You alright in there?" Graham asked, grinning.

"No money for hazmat suit," the waiter said as he set the tray down gingerly. "Nearest thing."

"Any advice before I start?"

The waiter reached into his jacket for a slip of paper. "Owner Khun Thongsong says, 'The explosion will be bad, but the resulting black hole will be much worse. Farewell and enjoy.'" The server stared at the note, then looked at Graham through a layer of mesh. "What's it meaning?"

"I suppose we'll see." Graham reached for his fork, the cue for the waiter to scuttle away. "By the way, we found a body today."

"Oh?"

"In the attic of the White House Inn. Freddie doesn't know. But Mrs. Taylor does. I'm surprised he didn't hear her scream. It's been lying there for years."

Laura banged down her beer. "And you didn't think to tell me this earlier?"

"Strictly speaking, I shouldn't be telling you *now*. We think it's been there for about forty years. Marcus called in an archaeologist. It was buried in a block of concrete." Aromatic beyond belief, the curry was a rich yellow broth swimming with large shrimp and chunks of Thai eggplant.

"Well, who is it?"

"No idea. Some guy. Probably related to the gun we found in a drawer."

"A gun?"

"Uh-huh. That's what all the fuss was about with Freddie. He heard about the gun and was fishing for more. Marcus is doing some urgent prelims. He'll try to get the remains to the lab tonight. They'll start decomposing rapidly now that they're exposed to the air." As Graham leaned down to inhale, the chilli fumes hovering above the plate seared his nostrils. By the time he'd swallowed his first forkful, tears had begun; five minutes later, pounding water but undefeated, Graham hoarsely offered Laura a bite.

"I think I'd rather sit on the grass at Chornobyl and have a sandwich."

"It's very tasty," he croaked.

"It's wildly unsafe. They should keep only a tiny sample and lock it away in a lab somewhere. Perhaps Marcus could oblige."

"Where's your sense of adv . . ." Graham started, but the need to draw cool air over his tongue took precedence.

"Adventure? I'm with *you*, aren't I?" Laura laughed. "That's adventure aplenty, thank you very much." She returned to a subject more pressing. "But this body, what are you going to do?"

"We have to wait for Marcus to complete his investigations. I'm a bit worried about him, to be honest. He's looking tired. I think he's feeling the loss of Roach a bit. He says he wants to keep going for a while yet. To give his favourite pinot vines a year or two more to mature in the Napa Valley before he visits, he says, but I think he's feeling his age a little."

The waiter returned with more water, asking anxiously for the fourth time, "Ambulance?"

"I told you, it's delicious," Graham insisted, pushing away his empty plate.

Blinking in disbelief, the waiter withdrew and returned with the bill. Next to the mints lay a small, clear crystal alongside an improvised "Get Well Soon" card. The crystal sat atop a small, red-velvet drawstring pouch, the fabric reminding Graham of that used to disguise the concrete block in Mrs. Taylor's attic. "From Khun Thongsong," the waiter explained. "To welcome you to the Order of the Perfumed Jewel." He bowed courteously, a foot removed from the table, apparently afraid to stand any closer. "He is on holiday in Ireland, but he texted every five minutes to see if you were still alive."

"A very thoughtful host." Graham paid the bill and rose with Laura. "Would you thank him for me?"

"I wish you good fortune in the black hole!" the waiter said as the couple left arm in arm, unaware that the entire cooking crew of the Bangkok Palace had left the sanctuary of their kitchen. Shaking their heads in disbelief, the crew congregated at the restaurant window to peek through the bamboo blinds and watch the mad Englishman and his pretty girlfriend saunter to their car.

CHAPTER FIFTEEN

S TRIDING DOWN THE rain-soaked path from the church to the meeting hall, flanked on one side by ivy and old stone, Reverend Bright reviewed his must-do list. Once this upcoming meeting concluded and the details of the Harding-Wentworth wedding were finalised, he had two calls to make. One to a parishioner, recently widowed, and the other to his tax accountant, ceaselessly scrupulous. After completing both tasks, he had some free time until he had to drive the choir to their concert in St. Helier at six.

"Free" didn't really mean free. It just meant he had time to attend to the myriad of items on his "not-necessarily-today" to-do list that included sermon prep, fundraising, and choosing the dates for next year's church events. Never a dull day, Vicar.

Wait, had he brought the wedding insurance and legal paperwork with him? He stopped by a headstone—lichen-spattered and green-wreathed—to find the papers in his folio. "Okay, good," he told himself. "I'm still with it after all."

"Good morning! You must be Reverend Bright!" called out a middle-aged woman in a striped, cotton dress and straw hat as he approached the church hall.

"Yes, that's right. Joshua Bright," he replied, holding out his hand. "And you are . . .?"

"Rosemary Harding, mother of the bride and mother-in-law-to-be," the woman said.

"Ah." It wasn't the first time Reverend Bright had discussed wedding arrangements with the parents of the happy couple in attendance, especially if they were paying for it, but he did find it set a tone, one that required a certain deftness on his part.

"Now, I know I'm not late, which means you're mad keen to get them married, aren't you?" he said with a smile, bringing out a big iron key.

"Can't *wait*!" Rosemary blurted out, beaming. "Been looking forward to this for a very long time. Ah, here they are."

Janice and Jack swung open the church lychgate and slowly walked up the path to the church entrance. They glanced around them, confused, until they saw Rosemary and the reverend, who waited while they caught up with them.

"And the young couple too, I hope?" Reverend Bright chuckled, his eyes searching them both. "Excited?"

If anything, the couple seemed slightly worn out. "Definitely," Janice said, more with determination than dewy-eyed anticipation.

"Super stoked. Just hoping things go nice and smoothly," said Jack, putting his arm around Janice.

"Of course they will!" Rosemary pronounced. "I'm sure Reverend Bright has done a million of these, haven't you?"

"Maybe only *half* a million," the reverend allowed. "I've

been doing this for over thirty years, and that's sufficiently long for plenty of Jersey folk to fall in love. Let's go to my office."

Reverend Bright walked them to a side door, and soon they found themselves in a sunny, comfortable room. Floral soft furnishings and dark oak dominated the décor, making the room warm and inviting. Bright caught sight of himself in the mirror he used to check his garments before a service. He suppressed a wince. The sun shone unrelentingly, cruelly casting shadows across his face, deepening his lines and making him craggy. The vicar gestured to a deeply cushioned, comfortable armchair. "Please, Mrs. Harding."

"Thank you, Vicar." Rosemary swept her skirt behind her legs and sat down, her handbag upright in her lap, her bottom crushed into the crease between the seat of the chair and its back.

Reverend Bright gestured to a sofa from the same set as the chair. "The happy couple . . ." Janice and Jack sat also, bobbing a little as the springs accommodated their joint weight.

"I simply *love* weddings," Rosemary said. "I've seen our old VHS tape of the Royal Weddings compilation I don't know how many times—"

"Nobody can count that high, Mum," said Janice.

"—so I know *exactly* what to do."

Bright raised a finger. "And so do I. Let's run through my list."

"Yeah, and Mum, remember?" Janice said. "All the ways the royal couples are *different* from Jack and me?"

Jack piped up. "Like, our preference for keeping things . . ."

"Small," Janice said, "with maybe . . ."

"Just us and some friends . . ."

"A few dozen people . . ."

"And not a lot of fuss."

"Oh, it's no fuss, dear!" Rosemary said, proud of her self-declared confidence in matters matrimonial.

Before Reverend Bright could even speak a word, Rosemary was listing the bold, even ambitious elements which comprised, in her view, "the perfect wedding." Janice and her husband-to-be looked on with silent, practiced patience; nothing of Rosemary's performance was unexpected, but all of it was unwelcome, a festival of second-guessing and interference that couldn't end quickly enough.

Rosemary Harding had insisted on coming early to Jersey to supervise the wedding plans personally. "I'll even get on a plane to visit you. And you know how I hate planes!" she had cried. Janice and Jack had simply been unable to shake her off.

"I mean, at the last royal wedding, there were six *hundred* guests!" she exclaimed, turning to Reverend Bright. "As befit such a grand occasion."

"Exactly," Janice said, hoping to press home the point. "Let the extent of the arrangements match the proportions of the event. In our case . . ."

"Small is beautiful," Jack said, returning to one of their themes.

"Not everyone can manage six hundred invitations, of course," said Rosemary, speaking as though she hadn't heard them. "Or even a couple of dozen," she added glumly. Janice's mum had been as disappointed at her eldest daughter's lack of ambition concerning the scope of her wedding and the number of guests as she might have been if Janice had told her she'd opted to study cosmetology instead of neuroscience. It had quite taken the imperiousness out of her for a few days.

"Forty-five," Janice corrected. "Small enough to get married on the beach even."

"The *beach?*" Rosemary shrieked, appalled. "Surrounded by . . . litter? Rotting fish? Seagulls pecking at the ladies' hats? I think not," she said, leaning into the vicar in hope of support. He sensibly kept out of it, happy to have a solid booking, the requisite fee, and of course, the chance to marry a delightful couple.

"Mum," Janice said, a tiny growl creeping into her tone, "these details are decided. They cannot be changed. The invitations were sent out weeks ago. Can we move on?"

"Yes, but to what?" Rosemary said next. Reverend Bright suppressed an eye roll. "Happy-clappy music and guitars? Some folk nonsense about overcoming oppression and smoking whacky-backy?"

"There are no guitars. And they're singing classical, Mum, for heaven's sake."

"Bach," Jack underlined. "Traditional, remember? You know how you like that."

"Very beautiful," Janice said.

"And nearly inaudible," Rosemary shot back. "*Four* choristers? Ridiculous." She suddenly clutched her handbag to her chest as though she suspected that Jack, or the vicar, maybe even Janice herself, might steal it.

Reverend Bright felt it prudent to interject before relations deteriorated further. "I sense that you're a big fan of the royal family, Mrs. Harding?"

"Of their *weddings*," Rosemary specified. "I'll admit I was *captivated* by Charles and Diana in eighty-one. Sad how it all worked out, but the ceremony was unforgettable! I thought Kate's dress rather plain though." She turned down the corners of her mouth. "And as for—"

"Right, Vicar, let's move on, shall we?" Even Jack was getting testy.

"Well, I hope you'll forgive our particular venue its modesty," Reverend Bright joked. "We can't compete with Westminster Abbey, but St. Andrew's can seat around a hundred and twenty in the church, so the planned forty-five guests will be no problem at all."

"Forty-five," Rosemary muttered again, still disappointed.

"Good. Plenty of room to spread out," said Janice, determined to rise above her mother's negativity. Having conceded to Rosemary's wishes for a church wedding, Janice was insistent that it would henceforth follow *her* plan, long considered and carefully tailored to her and Jack's wishes. "So, we've decided on music and readings. Here's a list of . . ."

"The 'Widor Toccata'!" Rosemary exclaimed. She raised her hands and wiggled her fingers, comically emulating the skills necessary to play the famously busy, celebratory piece. "You *have* to!"

Sensibly soothing her temper, Janice proceeded to remind her mother about the wedding details for what felt like the twentieth time. "We haven't hired an organist, Mum. Remember? We said it would feel too formal."

"But the *spectacle!*" insisted Rosemary. "The tingle down the spine!"

Jack jumped in with a smile. "Well, we're getting married, finally. I'm already pretty tingly about that."

"Me too," agreed Janice. "Plenty of tingles to go around."

Reverend Bright was always ready to throw some work his organist's way, but he saw in the eyes and set jaws of this family group that his main role was to ease the tension and lower everyone's stress levels. He would, in the final analysis, most certainly side with the young couple, but he would attempt to do so while not alienating this overly invested mother of the bride.

"No one could hope to make up a bride's mind for her," the vicar said, somehow avoiding criticism of Rosemary's graceless insisting, "but I was at a performance in Chichester Cathedral just the other week, and all the music was *a capella*. You know, without instruments. Just natural human voices in that remarkable space. It was exceptionally beautiful. Talk about tingles,'" he said encouragingly. The story was only partly true—a rapper had been involved—but as a veteran of such things, Bright knew that bridging a widening gulf between mother and daughter was worth a white lie.

"But the 'choir' only has four singers!" Rosemary complained. "And please don't tell me you've forgotten the trumpeter for the processional?"

Janice went through the setup again as patiently as she could. "Look, Mum, no organist, no trumpeter. Just a straightforward choral piece arranged and sung by our friend, supported by four choristers.

"But what about music? You're not going to have recorded music, are you? That awkward pause while the congregation waits for someone to press the right button then gets the wrong one, and instead of Bach's 'Jesu, Joy of Man's Desiring,' we get Kylie Minogue singing 'I should be so lucky, lucky, lucky.'" Rosemary shuddered. "Sherenice had that at her wedding, and you know how that turned out."

CHAPTER SIXTEEN

"NO, MUM, NOTHING like that. We have a string quartet. They're reuniting for us specially as a sort of thank you to Gorey police for rescuing them. Well, Roachie and Bazza found them. They were trapped under the castle a few years ago."

Janice's words seemed to have no effect. Rosemary's arguments continued unabated. "But you only get married once!" she said. "And the church is huge. Have you seen that vaulted ceiling? It's the most special day of your life! And that deserves pomp! Circumstance! A volley of rifles! Isn't that right, Reverend?"

"Er, well, a volley salute is usually performed at funerals, but I take your point. However—"

Jack interrupted. He sensed that if Janice had had three older sisters, her mother would by now have purged herself of the Royal Wedding bug. As it was, all Rosemary's unrealistic, intrusive expectations fell on his fiancée as the first daughter to be wed, and whose plans and protestations at her mother's objections had over the past months fallen on deaf ears. Jack's sympathies lay firmly with his future wife, and he would support her as he should. "For us, Rosemary," he said, "'special' means 'the way we'd like it to be.'"

"But . . ."

"A wedding is a family event," Jack stated firmly, "and it's a simple fact, a power law, that families will argue in inverse proportion to the number of weddings, funerals, and divorces they experience. This is our first," he reminded Rosemary. "And for Janice and me, it will be our last. We will have our wedding the way we wish it." Rosemary, unused to being confronted by anyone, not least her beloved future son-in-law, was momentarily stunned.

"Very nice choices of readings," Reverend Bright said, quickly exploiting Rosemary's breathlessness and shock. "Especially the reading you've chosen, 'Song of Solomon.'" He cleared his throat and quoted with relish. "'Thy cheeks are comely with rows of jewels, thy neck with chains of gold.' Just beautiful, isn't it?"

"At least it's traditional," Rosemary offered, recovering her voice, albeit sulkily. "There's people quoting science fiction, the Teletubbies, and all sorts at weddings these days."

"No one's quoting the Teletubbies at our wedding, Mum. Don't exaggerate," Janice said gently, kindlier than she felt, and, in Reverend Bright's opinion, more patiently than her mother deserved. Janice placed a hand on Rosemary's arm and smiled at her. Her mother sniffed. A hint of a smile fluttered on her lips.

By now, Jack looked mostly poleaxed by the whole exchange, so the vicar blurted out, "I had someone quote a stretch of Michael Jackson the other week. Someone else performed Tina Turner. 'Simply the Best' it was, I seem to remember. And a couple of years ago, we had a funeral at the crematorium, an older fella," he continued, turning to black humour to ease the tension further. "And when they were sliding him in, do you know what music they requested?"

Snapping his fingers, Jack was frustrated that it wouldn't come. "Janice?"

"Nothing yet."

Grinning, the vicar sang softly, "Smoke gets in your eyes . . ."

It was a bad joke, a dad joke at best, but they all laughed. Even Rosemary. The tension dispelled, and with the mother of the bride subdued, if only temporarily, Reverend Bright signed his paperwork, and within moments, the formal part was done.

"I suppose you'll be off to sample cakes or some such?" Bright said, rising. The Harding-Wentworths were pleasant enough people, but the calls to the widower and the accountant were pressing. Taking his cue, his visitors rose also and allowed themselves to be escorted out to the church path.

"There's an idea!" Rosemary exclaimed, appealing to the sky. "A traditional three-tiered wedding cake! With dried fruit! Not the strangest of expectations, now, is it?"

"I told you, Rosemary, my father is allergic to raisins," Jack teased her. "And my mother's gluten-free." He and Janice had decided on the cake ages ago but had chosen to keep its nontraditional details to themselves. They suspected, rightly, that Rosemary wouldn't approve of the layers of chocolate sponge, homemade fudge, and strawberry compôte that would be liberally covered in Swiss chocolate French buttercream pâte à bombe icing.

"There'll be a healthy vibe to the dessert," Janice added.

"It's a selection of fruit," Jack said. Both of them kept a straight face.

"Fruit!" Rosemary cried. Reverend Bright backed away,

disappearing into the church as this new potential for disagreement raised itself. Jack and Janice exchanged looks, wry smiles on their faces. "Slices of orange!" Rosemary exclaimed. "Like it's a hundred years ago or halftime at the football!"

Jack pulled Janice to him and whispered in her ear, "When are we going to tell her?"

"Let's give it a little longer, eh?" Janice kissed Jack on the cheek, and holding hands, they walked down the church path, her mother following them as she continued to exclaim about the aberration of a lack of wedding cake.

"As we've said several times, Mum," Janice called out, "fruit at a wedding is considered auspicious in many parts of the world."

"Like where?"

"India, for one."

"*India*?! But people will be expecting . . ."

"There's a reason for it," Jack said.

"For fruit? What exactly would that be then?"

"It's good for blood flow."

"What?"

"For blood flow, Mum. You know . . ." Janice raised her eyebrows and pursed her lips, a sly smile dancing across them. There was a pause before Rosemary gathered her daughter's meaning. She gasped and clutched her handbag to her.

"Well, really!" Rosemary huffed. "Fruit!" She opened her mouth to say more, but a firm, female hand grasped her wrist.

"People will be expecting me to bring you down the station on a charge of interfering in a wedding if you don't hold your noise soon, Mum. I *promise!*"

Rosemary merely shrugged. "You've been promising to take me there ever since they made you a sergeant."

"The other day, I watched Jan arrest three people for affray," Jack said. "Super impressive."

"Of course she is! This is my Janice!" The wedding was forgotten for a second. Janice relinquished her mother's wrist, and Rosemary put an arm around her daughter's shoulder. "Who did she arrest, anyway?" Janice's mother sensed a story that might just bear repeating to her gardening circle. "And why didn't you help her?" she added, glaring at Jack, suddenly protective. Rosemary believed in the traditional roles of men and women. She didn't hold with "women's lib." It was yet another point of contention between her and her eldest daughter.

"I would have if there was any requirement for it, but Jan is perfectly capable. She didn't need my help. Three lads were fighting outside the pub," explained Jack. "Barnwell hadn't even left the station yet, but Jan's there, wading in to break things up on her evening off. I tell you, she's got a commanding vocal presence."

"They started free, they ended up arrested, that's all. Anyone with powers of detention can do that," Janice said.

"Yeah, but they were punching each other when you arrived," Jack reminded her.

"Leaping into the middle of . . . a *punch-up*? On Jersey? You could have been hurt, you silly girl! Very unladylike." Rosemary had always regarded Janice's choice of career with some distaste, but living on the mainland, she had mostly been able to ignore it. That hadn't stopped her, though, from regaling her friends about her sergeant daughter who was a whizz on the computers, searching out criminal masterminds and bringing them down with her forensic policing skills and a Bluetooth mouse.

Every word from her mother raised Janice's temperature —*silly* was bad, but *girl* was worse. "I wasn't about to fight anyone, Mum. Just shouted a lot and then hauled the three of them away."

"*And* gave first aid to the unlucky one who got the brunt of it all," said Jack.

Rosemary shuddered again, the frames of her glasses shaking slightly. "Drunkards and fighting and dressing wounds . . . You know, I never understood . . ." she said, beginning what Janice knew would be act one, scene one of her mother's ongoing, one-woman play, *My Daughter and Other Needless Tragedies*.

"Jack, I'm off back to work."

"Yep, me too. You alright, Rosemary, or would you like me to accompany you to your B&B?"

"I can find it, dear, thank you," Rosemary said, unusually perceptive for once. "See you for dinner like we said?" She kissed them both, stretching on tiptoes to reach Jack's cheek. She waved goodbye, leaving Janice and Jack watching her toddling down the sleepy, tree-lined lane towards the beach, holding her handbag in the crook of her arm.

"How does she do it?" Janice said.

"Do what?"

"How does she suck the energy out of me and seemingly plug it into her veins? Look at her go! Full of vim and vigour while I feel in need of a long nap."

"Perhaps it's a mother-daughter wedding thing."

"Perhaps."

After leaving the Harding-Wentworths, Reverend Bright found a moment of peace in the church's sanctuary. Meeting the mother of the bride was always an experience, although not all were as overbearing and needy as Mrs. Rosemary Harding. The sunlit late morning and the tall, centuries-old stained glass casting hazy spectra on the pews reminded him to slow down, to take a moment. Sometimes he mused for a while, but today, there just wasn't time to tarry.

For his brief moment of peace, Reverend Bright allowed himself just to be present there in the familiar, glowing space, watching dust motes suspended in the sun's rays. But then he let himself imagine the silliest thing he'd heard in a long time and managed a little chuckle as he headed through to the office. "People quoting the Teletubbies in their marriage vows . . . Whatever next?"

CHAPTER SEVENTEEN

DR. TOMLINSON GLANCED at his watch and then at the arrivals board. Good. The flight from Gatwick was on time. Since Jim Roach had left for the Met, Tomlinson had worked alone in the forensic lab while also fulfilling his regular pathologist duties. He quickly realised that it was too much. "Age catches up with one eventually," he had told Francine.

Francine was his girlfriend. He wasn't too old to call her that. And he made sure they enjoyed life. "At our age, we need to make the most of our time, and I don't have any at the moment."

Acknowledging he was feeling his age was a big admission. Marcus prided himself on his athletic abilities and being more active than men half his age. But he had a professional respect for the inevitable effects of aging, even if he was reluctant to accept them for himself.

Realising he needed help, Tomlinson made a few calls and now found himself awaiting the person he hoped would give him more opportunities to enjoy life—life with Francine, with wine. Heck, even a nap in the afternoon would be nice. Yesterday was long, with more work ahead, and he eagerly looked forward to sharing his responsibilities.

Jersey Airport wasn't large. The flow of crowds came in waves as planes landed and the passengers disembarked. The pathologist had arrived amidst a lull, and after checking the state of play concerning flight EJ203, Marcus ordered himself a coffee and sat down to wait. As he sipped his drink, he scrolled through his phone, looking at the photographs of the remains they had unearthed the day before.

He had spent the previous evening taking samples and measurements, then overseen the extraction of the body from its bed of concrete prior to its transport to his mortuary. There, the remains could be protected from further degradation by the sterile, climate-controlled environment and with the liberal use of chemicals. With Dr. Papadopoulos's help, the extraction had gone well, and the body had been moved almost entirely intact.

Marcus had never had such a case in his nearly fifty-year career. Despite examining countless bodies in that time, he had never encountered one squirrelled away in concrete. For the person he was meeting, he was certain the same was true. For them, the case they were about to embark upon might prove career-defining.

Exhumations of any kind were extremely rare. Marcus had only been involved in two. In one instance, a family accused a care home of the misidentification of a deceased relative, suspecting that the burial of the wrong person had taken place. Marcus was able to prove the accusers wrong, and no further action was taken. In the second instance, where a family sought to repatriate remains to the deceased's home country, he attended the exhumation and confirmed the identification of the remains before release. In each case, there had been coffins and the exhumations performed within months of death. The extent of Tomlinson's work had been to take DNA samples and report the findings.

It was more common for bodies to be referred to him following some period of decomposition. It was not unusual for someone to die alone and remain undiscovered for a while. Marcus would be required to determine the cause of death in those cases. The identity of the person was almost always known or suspected.

Drowning victims weren't rare during his long career either. On occasion, he was tasked with identifying bodies of fishermen or swimmers washed ashore. He would use either dental records or other DNA evidence in these cases.

The remains found in the concrete at the White House Inn were a different proposition altogether. He needed to perform tests and procedures to determine the cause of death, extract DNA for help in identifying the man, perform ballistics on the gun, and examine the body and belongings for any other evidence that might help Inspector Graham and his team solve this very cold case.

Alexander Papadopoulos, accustomed to centuries-old remains, had been ecstatic to find the body in such good condition, especially how it had held up after being moved. Marcus, his experience confined to working with recently expired corpses, was more challenged. But it was a case he was pleased to pursue with the help of the young person whose plane, according to the announcement to which he was now listening, had just landed.

Marcus looked out of the window at the aircraft cruising into view. He watched it park, waved into place by a marshal, their gender extinguished by an excess of hi-vis gear. The door behind the cockpit opened. Steps were wheeled and secured into place.

Passengers hauling children, backpacks, and carry-on luggage, much of which seemed to be in excess of the cabin's weight restriction, exited the plane as Marcus attempted to identify his new helpmate. He had interviewed her via video and checked out her social media, so he knew what she looked like. But his eyes weren't so good at this distance, and there were a lot of potentials. He watched as the first passengers reached the terminal, then headed to the gate.

As they walked through the terminal door, it was obvious from their attire that the vast majority of passengers were tourists. Marcus could see no one he recognised, his heart beating faster with every person who passed him, citing no recognition. After the last straggler drifted away, Marcus glanced at his watch and the arrivals board. Maybe she hadn't made it. Sighing, he pulled out his phone.

"Dr. Tomlinson!" Walking towards him, a tall woman—slim, brunette—rolled a large suitcase behind her. She was wearing a T-shirt and jeans. On her feet were deep blue ballerina flats. At this distance, she looked like Laura's younger, darker sister. The woman strode up the tunnel as Tomlinson waited. Three feet from him, she stuck out her hand.

"Good morning, Dr. Tomlinson. I'm so happy to be here."

"And I'm very happy to see *you*, Fiona."

CHAPTER EIGHTEEN

"SO SORRY IF I worried you. My luggage was too big for the overhead. It was stored in the back of the cabin so I had to wait for everyone to get off before I could retrieve it."

Marcus laughed. "You did worry me a bit. But you're here now, and that's the main thing." He took the handle of her rolling case. "Here, let's go to the car and I'll take you to your digs. I hope you've come ready to work because I've got something special for you. Just popped up yesterday. Literally."

The automatic glass doors opened with a shush in front of them, and they stepped out into the bright, warm sunshine. Fiona gazed at the cloudless sky. "As we flew in, the island looked beautiful, but I can't wait to get to work."

They found Tomlinson's old silver Mercedes at the furthestmost point of the car park. "It's good for me to stretch my legs," Marcus said as he lifted Fiona's bag into the boot of his car. "Jump in, and I'll take you to your flat." He checked his watch again. "We've got plenty of time before the tide goes out."

Fiona looked at him askew. "What's that?"

Marcus chuckled. "You'll see."

A few minutes later, he smoothly spun the car's steering wheel as he expertly navigated Jersey's winding, narrow roads. Fiona sat beside him looking out of the window, drinking in the view. He had purposefully taken her the coastal route, doing everything he could as a good host and a hopeful mentor to imprint the delights of the island in Fiona's mind.

"When you're settled in, you'll have to come for dinner. Francine, my girlfriend, is a wonderful cook."

"Sounds fab," Fiona said. "I'm delighted to be working with you, you know. When I heard from Bert you were looking for someone, I jumped at the chance. Did you know I worked with him and Inspector Graham on the "screaming beauty" case?"

"Of course I did, Fiona." Marcus took his eyes off the road for a second and winked at her. "I did my homework. Bert Hatfield is an old, trusted colleague, and because he'd worked with David in the past, I gave him a call to see if he knew of anyone. He mentioned you immediately. He told me you'd kept in touch throughout university and medical school, said you were interested in becoming a pathologist, and here we are."

"And here we are," Fiona repeated, turning her face to the warm sun. "Where are we going, anyway?"

"Ah-ha! I heard from Bert you were up for an adventure, so I thought I might give you one of the best." When they reached St. Helier, Marcus pulled into a parking space on the cobblestone seafront. "We'll leave the car here." He placed his "doctor on call" card on the dashboard.

Fiona giggled. "Should you be doing that?"

"Not really, but it's technically true. Plus, I know an

inspector who'll help us out if I get dragged across the carpet." He led Fiona a few yards down a concrete ramp to a bus stop. Fiona frowned. Marcus smiled at her confusion. "It'll be a bit of a squeeze with your luggage, but there's no better way to travel. Ah, here she is."

Fiona turned to look out to sea. A brightly coloured blue ferry was coming in, but as soon as it left the water, she saw it had wheels. It covered the ground like a bus.

"This is the amphibious ferry. It'll take us over the water to your digs."

"What? Over there?" Fiona pointed to the ruins in the distance.

"Elizabeth Castle, yes. There's an apartment there. I thought you might like to stay in it for a while. You can walk along the causeway when the tide's out or take the ferry at any time. Francine was a bit worried it might be too remote. You're welcome to say no, and we'll find something else, but I snagged the flat while I could because it's very popular."

Fiona's eyes gleamed with excitement. "I'm going to stay there? On an island? In my very own castle? Looking out to sea?"

"That's right. It's rather cool, isn't it?"

"I'll say!"

"I can drop you off, let you get settled in, and come back when you're ready if you like."

"Oh no, I can explore later. I'd like to see the lab if I may and be briefed on this very interesting case you mentioned."

Marcus exhaled. Relief flooded his body. He hadn't realised how much he had enjoyed having a young, curious, hardworking mentee until Roach left. Fortunately, Fiona's enthusiasm appeared to match her predecessor's. Which was just as well. They had their work cut out for them.

"Alright, if you're sure, we can go straight to the lab, and I'll introduce you to Mr. X."

Fiona raised her eyebrows. "Mr. X, eh? Sounds intriguing."

"Oh, he's intriguing alright."

CHAPTER NINETEEN

G RAHAM HUMMED SOMETHING operatic and triumphal as he pushed open the doors to the Gorey police station. "A palace," he said to no one in particular as he breezed in, "dedicated to the pursuit of truth and justice." He hung up his coat and greeted Janice and Barnwell, who were already at work. He glanced at his watch. It had just gone eleven. "Morning, all." Carmen trotted up to him, her lead in her mouth. Her big, brown eyes looked up at Graham hopefully.

"Not just yet, Carmen." Graham bent down to give her a series of pats and scrubs. "I'll take you later." Carmen must have understood because she good-naturedly wandered off and curled up under Barnwell's desk for a snooze.

Barnwell manned reception while Janice, already exhausted by the meeting at the church, attempted to ignore texts from her mother by attending to the following month's shift roster. She would be on honeymoon for part of it, and the Gorey team would need backup from headquarters.

"Morning, sir," they chorused in unison.

"You're in a very chirpy mood this morning, sir," Barnwell said.

"And so I should be. I have a great team, and we've got this knotty cold case to get our teeth into. My office, five minutes." It wasn't a question.

But then the inspector's phone rang. His hands full with his briefcase, jacket, and keys, Graham could either open his office door or answer the phone. He decided on the former, so the call had to wait. "Hang on, hang on," he said, dropping his stuff on his desk. *Click.* "DI Graham here."

"David!" came a familiar voice.

"Ah, Marcus." Graham flipped on the kettle and flopped into his seat. "How're things going?"

"With Mr. X?"

"Is that what we're calling him?"

"That's what I'm calling him for now. I need the go-ahead for some lab work," Tomlinson said. "We'll have to forward some of this stuff to Dr. Weiss in Southampton, and you know how the bean counters make us justify every *minute* on the UV spectroscope."

"Go ahead," said Graham. "I'll keep things straight with Finance. How are you doing without Roach?"

"I miss him, of course. He was a fine young man." There was a pause as Tomlinson remembered his former protégé, now living the high life policing the mean streets of London.

"He was," Graham said. "Still is. Thanks for looking after him while he was here. You were a great fount of knowledge and a fine mentor to him. He wouldn't be where he is now if it weren't for you. You know how much I appreciate that."

"Will you get a replacement, do you think?"

Graham pursed his lips. "Hmm, not sure. I'd like to see

how we do, just the three of us, for a while. It'll save a bit of money that I can put towards training or some new equipment. But probably not for long. We need some resilience in the team, and with just us three, it leaves us a bit thin. We'd be underwater in no time if anyone was put out of action or wanted a change of scenery."

"Have there been any rumbles? Anyone wanting a transfer?"

"I don't think Barnwell's thinking of going anywhere, but with Janice's wedding coming up, she might feel like a change, and then we'll have to take action PDQ."

"Hmm, Roach taught me a valuable new skill."

"Really?" Graham asked, surprised.

"*Delegation*, dear chap! *Del-e-gation*! I've recruited a new assistant, someone to replace young Roach. She's just looking around her new flat. Her name's Fiona Henson. She worked with you on the "screaming beauty" case. I tracked her down via Bert Hatfield. Do you remember her?"

It didn't take more than a few nanoseconds for Graham to pluck Fiona's name and her contribution to the case from his memory. "Rather. She was the reason we cracked it. She made the connection to the lottery ticket."

"That's the lass."

"Fabulous. I'll meet her when I come down for the postmortem. What time will you start?"

"Four p.m. on the dot. Come earlier if you want a cup of tea beforehand. It'll be a curious one. Not sure how the body will react, but we'll do our best."

"See you then."

CHAPTER TWENTY

JANICE AND BARNWELL waited for Graham's call with Tomlinson to end and then assembled in Graham's office as instructed. Steam rose from Graham's teacup.

"Right, team, so what do we think happened at the White House Inn? We have a body concealed in cement and abandoned in the attic for some unspecified amount of time. We have a gun and some items that presumably belonged to the body. What can we deduce?"

"Well, sir, we can definitely date the scene to sometime after 1979 because, like you said, that's when *The Hitchhikers Guide to the Galaxy* came out *and* that particular book had a publish date of 12 October 1979 on the copyright page. It is a first edition. I took a look before it went off with the forensics guys," Barnwell said, proud of his initiative.

"Good work, Constable. So, we can set an outer boundary at the end of 1979."

"But that still gives us decades to play with," Janice said.

"Right, but we know that Mrs. T. took over the hotel in

September 1982. She denies any knowledge of the body. She told me she hadn't been in the attic for years. I think we can assume that this happened before her time."

"So, we're looking at the period from October 1979 to September 1982," Janice summed up.

"A period when the hotel was owned and run by a Miss Lovell, deceased," Graham added.

Barnwell piped up. "Could it be, sir, that someone killed him, decided to bury him on the spot, shoved the belongings in the drawer, and scarpered?"

"That's one theory, Constable."

"But how would they do that without being seen? I mean, that was a lot of cement they had to mix," Janice said.

"And all the way up those stairs 'n' all. Would need to be strong."

"And determined," Janice added.

"Well, if you've just killed someone, I suppose you would be." Barnwell was thoughtful. He stared at the floor as he imagined the scene.

"They'd need to have time, sir. To do the work I mean. How long would it take?" Janice asked Graham.

"They could bury him during a night, I should imagine. The cement would take a while to dry, but if no one was going up there, it would work out with a bit of luck."

"But why were his belongings, and the gun, shoved in a drawer?" Janice waggled her head from side to side. "Seems a big oversight if you've just spent the night going to the effort of burying the body."

Barnwell had an idea. "Perhaps the murderer forgot them when they scarpered." He paused as he thought some more, and then raised his eyebrows as another idea came to him. "Maybe they thought if they shoved the belongings in the drawer, they'd be long gone before the items were found. I mean, maybe they just wanted to delay the body being discovered until they were far enough away that we couldn't catch them. Maybe the burying was just a delaying tactic, and it was dumb luck the body wasn't found until now."

Graham wasn't so sure. "Hmm, maybe. The effort they went to suggests to me that they didn't want it to be found for a very long time. I mean, burying a body in the attic is a bit like burying a body under the patio . . ."

"While you carry on living there," Janice said.

"Exactly, Sergeant."

"But let's keep an open mind on that. Both theories are valid."

"One thing that's bothering me, sir."

"Yes, Barnwell, out with it."

"It might be nothing, but . . ."

"Yes?"

"Well, that velvet covering. The thing that made it look like a sofa. It was sewn to fit. Someone must have made it special-like."

Graham's eyebrows shot up. "You're right, Barnwell. The person who buried him had to be a man given the physical effort required. But maybe a woman was involved somehow."

"I know! While the murderer was doing the heavy work, she was running up a little number with her Singer sewing machine!" Janice exclaimed.

"Isn't that a bit sexist?" Barnwell was disappointed in Janice. "Could easily have been a man. Even I've been known to do a bit of sewing here and there." Graham and Janice stared at him for a moment, processing this unanticipated piece of Barnwell knowledge.

"Right, Bazz, but we're talking 1982. It was different then. It's unlikely."

"He's right, though, Sergeant. It could have been a man, an enlightened one, perhaps."

"Yeah," Barnwell said. He pursed his lips, pleased to be supported. "Anyhow, we should follow the evidence, sir. That's what you always say, right?"

"Yes, Constable Barnwell. Let's focus on that timeline until Marcus gets back to us with some results. He successfully moved Mr. X to the mortuary last night and will be performing a postmortem this afternoon. He's also hired a new assistant from the mainland to help him." Janice and Barnwell exchanged looks. "She'll be taking over the responsibilities previously fulfilled by Sergeant Roach, so I'm hoping for some quick progress. But we need to do our bit while we're waiting. Any guesses as to what that might be?"

"Something to do with mispers, sir?" Janice ventured.

"Exactly, Sergeant. What can we do to push that along, eh?" Graham looked meaningfully over the rim of his teacup as he brought it to his lips.

Barnwell stiffened. "No," he said, the whites of his eyes showing.

"Yes, lad."

Barnwell shivered. "You're not really sending me down there again, are you?" He remembered past forays into the basement filing room. Remaining to be digitised were twenty-five large boxes of old police records, many of them unopened and unexplored.

Moving to calm the officer's nerves, Graham said, "It's a specific search this time."

"Last time was 'specific,'" Barnwell recalled, "and I was down there for eight hours."

"It's all terribly inefficient, I understand, but I can't

think of another way. You look for files on missing persons registered with Jersey police over the past, oh I don't know, let's start with thirty years, fifteen years before and after the period we're looking at."

"*Thirty?*" Barnwell almost screeched before clearing his throat. "Ahem, thirty years, sir?" Graham stared back at him, unblinking. "I mean, it's a lot. A very lot."

"Yes, it is, Constable, but you're up to the challenge, aren't you? Or would you rather I do the searching, and you go to the postmortem in my place?"

Barnwell most definitely would not prefer that. He took a deep breath, straightened, and pushed his shoulders back. "No, sir. Yes, sir. I understand, sir."

"There can't be that many people who've gone missing on Jersey. It's a small place."

This didn't alleviate Barnwell's desire not to spend his day amid clouds of dust, looming darkness, poorly labelled files, and possibly the odd small rodent, but he considered the alternative. "Have we spoken to Mrs. Taylor some more, sir? Can she help?"

"She might, and we could. But that won't get you out of going down to the basement, Constable. Nice try though." Graham turned to his sergeant. "Sergeant Harding, cross-reference anything Barnwell might find with the PNC database."

"Yes, sir."

"Excellent. Off you go, then."

"Sir, so you're going to the postmortem?" Janice asked.

"I was planning to. Why, are you volunteering?"

"Thought I might, sir." Janice was standing very upright and staring straight ahead. "Not every day you get to observe one on a body so ancient." Graham paused as he considered this. "Okay, why not? Good experience for you. It's at four p.m. Full report on your observations by—"

"I'll get them to you today."

"Alright, Sergeant, if you're sure."

"I am, sir."

When they left Graham's office, the gloomy expression on Barnwell's face gave Janice a dark laugh. "Let's hope you find something, Bazz."

"Bet you a tenner it'll be a wild-goose chase."

"Yeah, maybe, but the boss wants it done. Might as well get it over with."

"Alright." Barnwell groaned, low and long, as though anticipating a twelve-hour patrol in the rain. "'If I die,'" he said dramatically, "'think only this of me . . .'"

"'That there's some corner of a police filing room that is forever England'? I daresay you'll survive. It is a post-war building, after all," Janice reminded him. As she shepherded Barnwell down the hallway to the door, rarely opened, that led to the basement, she awkwardly attempted to put her arm around his burly shoulder before giving up. Her arm simply wasn't long enough. "The electric lights might even be working again down there."

Another groan and Barnwell opened the door. Darkness loomed ahead of him.

"But, Jan, why do you want to go to a poxy postmortem? You don't normally do them."

"Stop yer stallin'. Get on down those stairs." Janice patted him on the shoulder, and Bazza reluctantly pushed off, descending the steps to begin his task.

CHAPTER TWENTY-ONE

"WE'VE MOVED THE REMAINS to the mortuary, but I want you to get a feel for the case." Marcus had driven Fiona to the White House Inn and, deciding not to trouble the front desk, led her up the back stairs to the attic. "This is where Mr. X was found."

Fiona looked around her at the attic, still tarped and draughty. She took in the motley collection of furniture and bric-a-brac that congregated in one corner. "We found a gun amongst all that lot," Tomlinson said. "An old one, along with some items that we think date from the eighties. There was a 1979 copy of *The Hitchhikers Guide to the Galaxy* amongst the things. It'll be part of our job to date the body. We don't know his name or how he died."

"Huh," was all Fiona said.

"Our man was over there." All that was left in the corner where Barnwell had stumbled upon the concrete grave were chunks of cement, broken bricks, and a pile of crumpled, faded velvet. "A chance find. They were examining the storm damage when a police officer got curious.

The cement was well-made and dense. It protected the body from decay. It's in remarkable shape—you'll see when we get to the mortuary."

"How was he not found earlier? Did no one report him missing? Did no one wonder why this immovable object sat here for so long?"

Tomlinson shrugged. "Your guess is as good as mine. Out of sight, out of mind? Mrs. Taylor, the present hotel owner, claims she hasn't been up here in years. I guess no one else came up here much either."

"And due to minimal bacterial activity and the composition of the cement, any odour would be brief and faint."

"That's right."

"You mentioned Mrs. Taylor is the present owner. What about the former?"

"Long dead, so no help there."

"Curiouser and curiouser," Fiona said. She grinned at Tomlinson. "Let's go and see the main man, shall we?"

"Beautiful, isn't it?" Tomlinson said. Fiona stared out the side window as they drove to the mortuary, taking in the sights: the pretty, brightly painted buildings that bordered Gorey harbour, the wide open green fields, and clear, sandy beaches.

Fiona was a naturally pretty woman, with small features and straight, dark hair that she pinned off her face with a sparkly clip. Her plainspoken manner and unadorned appearance transmitted a no-nonsense approach that Marcus suspected would go down well, especially with Janice and Laura. Francine would appreciate her enthusiasm and energy. Graham would enjoy her intelligence.

And he, Marcus Tomlinson, looked forward to benefitting from her willingness to get stuck in, literally and figuratively.

"It certainly is," Fiona replied. "How far is it? The mortuary."

Tomlinson smiled. "A few minutes, that's all.

When they got there, Marcus pushed open the doors for her and introduced Fiona to his mortuary assistant, Aidan, a big, bearded bear of a man with a plethora of tattoos. Aidan nodded a curt welcome and continued with his work cataloguing lab samples.

"A man of few words, Aidan. Great worker though. And a gentle giant. Perfect for what we do here," Tomlinson whispered. Raising his voice to a normal volume, Marcus added, "First, let's get you suited and booted. I'll show you where the gear's kept."

Once they had donned their paper suits, Marcus directed Fiona to the bank of drawers that lined one wall. "We'll have to get you put into the system," he murmured as he used his fingertip to unlock one of the drawers. A sound —a "clunk"—could be heard from deep inside the drawer as the mechanism unlocked and it opened. Fiona's eyes widened as the body slid into view in front of her. "Have a good look and tell me what you think."

"Wow, you were right. He *is* in good condition. Almost mummified." Fiona's eyes scanned the body.

"Already air exposure and movement have caused some deterioration. The rib cage is more concave, his facial features less distinct."

Fiona's eyes raked the body from top to bottom, taking in the arrangement of his limbs, facial features, height, and clothing. "Was he discovered in this position, with one arm raised and the other across his chest?"

"Yes. What does it suggest to you?"

"Hmm, either that he was buried in that position or rigor mortis had set in beforehand and there was no alternative."

"Agreed. Any preference for either theory?"

"I favour the latter."

"Why's that?"

"Because of this. Was it a rose at some point?" Fiona delicately pointed at the thorny stem that had been threaded beneath the man's palm lying across his chest.

"Yes," Tomlinson confirmed. "It certainly looks like it. The petals had disintegrated. But why does that make you believe rigor mortis had already set in?"

"Because unless he died clutching the rose like that, whoever buried him took care to put the rose there. That suggests consideration. If the body was still malleable, given that level of care, I would have expected them to lay this suspended arm across his chest if they could."

"You think the person burying him in concrete in an attic was being thoughtful?"

"Yes, but for what reason? Concern, respect, or . . ."

"Some diabolical purpose?" Tomlinson processed this new theory. It was unsettling.

Fiona moved on. "Hmm, the clothes aren't very helpful. This is a brand-name T-shirt. They've been around for years and still going strong. Quality brand. The jeans are jeans and the shoes are shoes. Can't see that they can tell us anything at the moment. Can we get DNA?"

"Yes, I'm hoping he's on the database. If not, it'll be like looking for a needle in a haystack. If we can't identify him, the police will have to search old missing persons records going back decades, following up on many lines of enquiry."

"What about the cause of death?"

"Well, that's also interesting. As I said, we found a gun among some effects in the attic. Maybe related, maybe not. But there's no sign of a bullet wound. The cause of death isn't immediately obvious to me. So that's our other challenge. I'm hoping the postmortem we're going to spend this afternoon performing might turn something up. The police certainly hope so."

"Well, you were right when you said you have an intriguing case. Shall we get to work?"

Marcus smiled. "I was hoping you'd say that."

"I'll make a start on his belongings."

"I think that would be excellent. We have an appointment with the ballistics centre in a couple of days, but for now, take a look at what the police found in his suitcase. It's over there." Tomlinson pointed to a metal counter on which lay several bags of items collected by Janice the day before. Next to them was a small, bright red suitcase."

"That was his case? Bit feminine for a man."

"It also looks older than the period we're considering. You might want to look it up. I'll leave you to it. Aidan will get you a password so you can access the computer systems."

"Leave it with me." Fiona donned a new pair of forensic gloves as Tomlinson returned to his office. He watched her through the glass as she carefully opened the bags and laid the items in them on the counter. But soon, Marcus's eyelids flickered, and his breathing slowed. Yesterday was catching up with him. In moments, he was quietly snoring.

The lab was almost silent as Fiona carefully catalogued all the items. Tapping their details into her tablet, she handled them as though they were delicate, precious, laying them side by side on the sterile metal counter as she processed them.

They didn't amount to much: a blue jacket, thin sweater, T-shirt, white vest, underpants, and socks. Fiona peered inside a tan leather wallet, but it was empty. Toiletries were limited to a disposable razor and a toothbrush, along with a flannel. She put those to one side. Picking up the large, chrome electronic watch with its digital clock face and calculator buttons, Fiona stared at it for some seconds. She had never seen anything like it.

The Walkman was new to her too. She pressed a button on the side of the black plastic case and a drawer popped open. Inside was a cartridge tape, "Dire Straits" printed on the side.

Next, she flicked through the pages of *The Hitchhikers Guide to the Galaxy*, checking to make sure nothing was tucked inside the pages. She noticed an address written in blue ballpoint at the bottom of the inside back cover: 4 St. Julian's Road.

After noting the address on her log sheet, Fiona turned her attention to the suitcase. It had already been dusted for fingerprints, and the talcum-based white powder coated the red exterior unevenly. It reminded Fiona of the big, fluffy powder puff her grandmother used on her face and neck before going out.

The fine powder had turned up nothing useful. Fingerprints last indefinitely, but temperature, humidity, and exposure to the elements can erase them. Fiona popped the clasp and looked inside. The satin lining was smooth, silky, and cool as she ran her gloved hand over it. She slipped her fingertips inside the elasticated pockets sewn into the sides.

They were empty, the bullets Inspector Graham had found having been removed and bagged with the gun.

But as she examined the lid, Fiona noticed the lining stitches had frayed. The satin had detached from the hard shell of the case. The corner of something flat poked out. Using tweezers she inserted into the gap in the lining, she teased it out, careful not to damage or crease it. It was a card, still in its cellophane wrapper.

Fiona turned it over. On the front, two cartoon bees were surrounded by red hearts. Above them was printed "Bee my valentine!" Fiona studied it for a moment before making a note and placing the card next to the other items on the counter.

Looking through the glass into Tomlinson's office, she saw that he was asleep. They still had an hour before they were due to start the postmortem. A movement in her peripheral vision alerted her to Aidan's presence. He lumbered into view. Fiona exhaled, lifted then relaxed her shoulders, releasing the tension in them. "Fancy a cup of tea, Aidan?

CHAPTER TWENTY-TWO

The Gorey Gossip
Saturday

Let's just be honest, squelch our natural reserve, and say it out loud: Jersey is a seriously attractive island.

We've got beaches to rival much of Europe. We've got history—no visitor could ignore the splendour of Gorey Castle, the War Tunnels, *or* the haunting Elizabeth Castle. We've got a first-rate zoo too. There are idyllic country lanes to potter down, parks for picnics, and walks for walkers. Our restaurants, everything from posh places to unpretentious pubs (see the *Gossip's* new review section, "The Dine Mine") offer *truly* great fresh, locally caught seafood at fantastic prices prepared to top-notch standards.

But just as a school of fish attracts a

variety of predators, occasionally encountering something large and truly dangerous, Jersey can fall prey to undesirable elements. I'm afraid that in the past some of our visitors were *not* here to support the local fine hotels or to catch up with friends in one of our elegant tea rooms.

Sadly, and steadily, alongside its beatific scenery and delightful communities, Jersey of the past accrued a history of violence, and I'm not just talking about the Nazis. Couples fall out, friends come to blows, and idiots throw punches in the pub indeed, but these London-based gangsters came to our island to cause *mayhem and misadventure*.

I'm talking about the Mob, so named due to their enigmatic nature. The mainland police forces tend to see gangs as monolithic, all linked and gathered under a single umbrella. My research is showing that they couldn't be more wrong.

Small gangs, quite separate from any larger organisation, attracted by the remoteness of our beautiful island, its status as a tax haven, and its sunny climes, have used the Channel Islands to make dead drops, deposit money, launder cash, meet with co-conspirators and, yes, to threaten and in some cases inflict violence on one another. In studying Jersey's past, I've uncovered evidence of *at least seven* mob-related murders here

since 1950. These killers are profession-
als. Their crimes are premeditated, not
opportunistic.

In yesterday's post (*A Storm, A Gun, and
a Thousand Questions*) I laid out evidence
relating to the discovery of an ancient gun
at the White House Inn. Today I am learning
about the unearthing, just a few feet from
said gun, of a body encased in concrete,
the unfortunate victim likely having lain
there for decades. It doesn't take a detective to understand that a powerful handgun
and a secreted death do not belong, but it
does need a detective's acumen to make the
connections that reveal the truth.

In these pages, I labour to convey
reality along with integrity and sincerity.
As loyal readers, you know that accuracy is
my priority. That said, I am not bound at
the ankles by evidence or beholden to any
authority.

These freedoms let me speculate that the
man found dead in the White House Inn
yesterday didn't meet a natural end. He
carried a gun, after all.

We don't know who he is yet, but he had
no discernible occupation or business on
the island. If he had, his disappearance
would have been noted and we would have
learned of him earlier. So we ask: Had he
been to Jersey before? Was he here to
commit an act of violence? Did he succeed?
Or did violence arrive at his door first?

The evidence is mounting quickly, and it all points to one thing: mob warfare raging on Jersey in the latter part of the last century. Considering the desirous nature of our wonderful island, it only stands to reason that gangs with their depraved motives duelled and competed and settled scores here. *Maybe they still do.*

CHAPTER TWENTY-THREE

"JUST A PRELIMINARY update. I've got good news . . ." Tomlinson began.

The pathologist had spent twenty minutes taking notes, peering through magnifying instruments, and completing a couple of simple chemical tests.

"Great! Let's have it!"

"If I may finish, David . . ."

"Sorry."

"Good news, bad news, and a question. What would you like first?"

"Start with the bad, move onto the good, and leave the question until last."

"Fair enough. The bad news is that the belongings don't give us much to go on. The wallet is empty, and there isn't much to be said about the rest of his things."

"Capital," Graham moaned. "And what's the good news?"

"I'm sixty percent sure I can recover a usable DNA sample from his effects. His hairbrush is our best bet. We can also try for some from the bones."

"The DNA database wasn't set up until 1995. That won't be much use."

"Ah, but it gives us a base sample in case more evidence appears. Like a match with a family member who *is* on the database. So, it's worth doing. Of course, it's entirely possible these clothes, and the gun, have nothing to do with our Mr. X."

"Yes, it's possible, but I find it hard to believe a gun and a body found within feet of each other are unconnected. What about his clothes?"

"A jacket, sweater, T-shirt, a white undervest, underpants, a pair of socks. That's it. An overnight kit, basically. The suitcase was an older model, popular in the sixties, mass produced, nothing very notable."

"Our guy didn't plan on staying very long, then. A quick in and out."

"Looks like it. Could be a salesman. They move around all the time."

"Sure. Most of them don't carry a model twenty-eight though."

"I was just about to mention that," said Tomlinson as he walked over to Fiona, who was examining the revolver. "We'll do some tests on it, get a ballistics sample for comparison."

There would be a record if the handgun had been involved in a crime. *Provided it's been digitised.* Graham winced. He had heard stories from veteran detectives recalling the terrible delays to investigations while ballistics samples spent weeks crisscrossing the country; nowadays, the process took mere moments if they had been catalogued in the system.

"We did find something else. It was stuffed between the

suitcase shell and the lining. Fiona seems to think it wasn't hidden as such but put there for safekeeping."

"Oh, what was it?"

"A Valentine's card. Just a store-bought one, nothing special."

"Was it written in?"

"No, still in the plastic wrapper. Not sure it means anything but wanted to mention it."

"Huh, perhaps all this happened around Valentine's Day then."

"Yes, remember the rose stem in the man's hands?"

"Hmm. You said you had a question?'"

"Ah, yes."

Graham heard Tomlinson move away from the soft, rhythmic whirring of a laboratory centrifuge and close his office door.

"David, how did Mrs. Taylor come to have this man's belongings?"

"She didn't say much. She was a bit, ah, shocked at the time. But she claims no knowledge of any of it and believes whatever happened must have taken place before she took over the hotel. She says she never went up into the attic, nor did anyone else. I'm leaning towards accepting her explanation. Maybe someone, at some point, innocently or not, cleaned up the room and popped the belongings in a drawer. Then, for some unknown reason, they were forgotten."

"They thought it best to forget about a *firearm* belonging to a man who had *died* and store it away in the attic?"

"When you consider someone encased a body in concrete and stored it for decades, it doesn't seem so strange. In fact, nothing makes sense in this case. The whole thing seems odd."

Marcus composed a thought carefully. It took a moment. "David, perhaps I could throw an idea into the air?"

"Always."

"Maybe whoever stored the things *didn't know* there was a gun in the suitcase. Just stashed it away."

"Indeed, another possibility. One of many."

"Is there anyone *at all* from the time who's still there? Maybe one of the older staff might remember an incident."

"Not many people work in the same hotel for forty-odd years," Graham replied, "but I'm going there this afternoon. If Mrs. Taylor hasn't gone supernova, I'll have the chance to ask."

"I've been a pathologist since I was twenty-six. There's something to be said for institutional knowledge. I'm a big believer in it. So rare these days though. People move through and on so fast."

"They do. Good record-keeping helps, I find. Let me know as soon as you discover anything, even if it's inconclusive."

"Will do."

"By the way, Sergeant Harding is attending the post-mortem in my place."

"Okay, that's unusual."

"Yes, she volunteered. Not sure why. Not her regular beat."

"Well, she can meet Fiona. Oh, and David?"

"Hmm?" The DI was on his feet, already distracted by the next thing on his list.

"It *is* possible this Mr. X is just a regular guy who died of natural causes, you know."

"Of course."

"It's just everyone's heading off in different directions, and someone needs to say the simple, normal thing."

"I'll grant the importance of varied viewpoints," said Graham, "but to me, this case feels neither simple nor normal. Being buried in concrete doesn't suggest either."

CHAPTER TWENTY-FOUR

DISTRACTED BY THE blue tarpaulin still spread across the roof, Graham drove up the drive to the White House Inn. He sighed. It would take weeks for the hotel to recover, and for many visitors—and at least one anxious engaged couple he knew of—the storm had tossed a serious spanner in their works.

At least the car park was cleaned up. Only some faint smudges and the odd nick in the tarmac where roof tiles had succumbed to wind and gravity remained. The car park was, however, almost empty. Not a good sign.

Mrs. Taylor was at the reception desk, holding the old-school phone receiver tight and close. It was clear her stress levels had not dissipated. She tapped a pen against the counter as she listened.

"Right . . . right," she said, then ran her finger down the page of her reservations book, also old-school. Mrs. Taylor wasn't one for using the latest "fandangle thingamabob" when the old methods worked for her just as well and, she was wont to exclaim, added to the hotel's charm. "Three doubles, a single, and then another single with a cot. You're a marvel, Derek. Thanks for taking in some of our displaced guests."

She replaced the receiver and, unaware Graham was steadily approaching, allowed herself a vigorous, unrestrained jiggle, shaking her arms and shoulders until her fingertips tingled. Then, with a deep breath, she looked up. "Oh, Inspector! What a *time* I'm having thanks to this storm! My business and livelihood are under real threat. I'm having to re-home some of our most faithful guests. And then there's your nasty business." Mrs. Taylor closed her eyes and shuddered. "I don't even want to *think* about what you've come for."

Mrs. Taylor's litany of disasters had lengthened: water damage was suspected in several top-floor rooms, the silent, invisible threat of mould not far behind. "They want to come in here," she said, appalled, "and rip down all the old walls on the second floor!"

"Ghastly state of affairs for you."

"They're going to charge me a king's ransom for some fancy sealant. Did you ever meet anyone with such bad luck?"

"Mrs. Taylor, it's a rotten time for me to ask a favour, but I need some help."

"Oh, don't worry, Inspector! You're about the only person around here I'm not furious with!" It was only half a joke; such a series of crises would give anyone a stern test. "I held a staff meeting, you know. Told them what happened. We're determined to carry on as normal. You've taped off the attic and we will not go up there. Not that we ever did, or we might have found that poor man earlier. I blame myself." Mrs. Taylor's hand fluttered at her throat.

"You mustn't do that, Mrs. Taylor. No one could have susp—" Graham stopped. "Anyhow, we'll keep things discreet. Only disturb what we have to, when we have to. Right now, we're narrowing down the period during which our man in the concrete met his demise. You wouldn't happen to have any records for the period 1980 to 1982, would you?"

"You know me, Inspector Graham. Never throw anything away. I have all the reservation books from the day I took over, but not from before my time, no. There was nothing left for me like that at all. I had to start from scratch. But that wasn't necessarily a bad thing." Mrs. Taylor folded her arms and sniffed.

"Okay then, did you hire any of your predecessor's staff?"

Mrs. Taylor sniffed again. "I don't take kindly to her being referred to as my predecessor, young man."

"Oh?"

"The hotel was a *very* different type of establishment back then."

"How so, Mrs. Taylor?"

"It was more . . ." Marjorie looked skywards as she searched for the words. The quest for an appropriate euphemism ultimately required more energy than Mrs. Taylor could muster, and she found herself defeated. Her shoulders slumped. She whispered, "Downmarket. The hotel had a *reputation*."

Unwilling to let her off the hook, Graham raised his eyebrows. "For what?"

"Oh, Detective Inspector, must you make me spell it out? This place was cheap back then, run down. It attracted, you know, the wrong sorts. There were stories about women of the night visiting. Even plying their trade in the bar!" Mrs. Taylor voiced her feelings about such enterprise with a downturn of her mouth and the employment of stringy neck muscles. "It was why I was able to pick up the old place for a song. Nobody wanted to touch it. I even changed the name to the White House Inn to make a clean break of it. It used to be called The Grange."

"I see. So, you didn't keep anyone on when you took over?"

"Now, I didn't say that." Mrs. Taylor snapped her fingers and pointed. Graham took this to be an excellent sign. "Janet Northrop, the lady who comes three times a week to help with afternoon tea." It didn't take any time at all for Graham to locate a memory of the slight, efficient, somewhat taciturn, white-haired woman who ran the tearoom. "She's here today, helping out. A real trooper, she is. Mrs. Northrop would know far more about that time than me. Let me get her. She's in the kitchen putting Polly and Raj to work. Wait there a moment."

The two younger staff members claimed they could manage without Mrs. Northrop's oversight for a few minutes, and a petite woman came through to reception to speak to Mrs. Taylor and the detective inspector. Energetic and slender, Janet, bedecked in a red-and-white checkered apron, had only recently turned sixty. She had a school-teacher's manner, highly organised, and always on the move with sinewy forearms that were marbled with veins so big Graham suspected Barnwell would covet them.

"Has Mrs. Taylor presented you with your Long Service Medal yet?" Graham asked. "Quite a tenure you've had here."

"The people are wonderful. Our staff and the guests both. And at my age, everyone needs *something* to keep them out of trouble," Janet said brightly. She laughed. Graham sucked on his bottom lip. He hadn't heard Mrs.

Northrop laugh before, and he had been in the tearoom during her shifts aplenty.

While Mrs. Taylor fretted behind the desk, shuffling invoices and trying not to overhear, Graham asked Mrs. Northrop about her time at the hotel before Mrs. Taylor arrived. "I know you've heard the news. What we found upstairs in the grand attic . . ."

"Not so grand with a great hole in the roof," Mrs. Taylor muttered.

"Well, it's from a while back," he said, taking Mrs. Northrop's arm and steering her out of Mrs. Taylor's earshot, "and we're trying to figure out how it got there. Do you remember anything that might help us? Would have been between late 1979 and October 1982." Janet Northrop's first instinct was to glance at Mrs. Taylor, now studying the reservation book with the fervour of a student up against a deadline. "Mrs. Taylor didn't take over until in September 1982. This was during Miss Lovell's tenure. Do you remember?"

"Do I remember?" Janet Northrop raised an eyebrow. "Marjorie showed up here with the deeds to the place and not two pennies to rub together. And yet she announces that we're reopening 'the grandest hotel on Jersey' in only three weeks!"

CHAPTER TWENTY-FIVE

"I T WAS *MARVELLOUS*," Mrs. Taylor called over, her hearing newly appreciated by Graham for its acuity. Easily nudged into nostalgia, she added, "We begged and stole and . . . well, not *stole*."

"We were very creative," Janet Northrop said, raising her eyebrows at the inspector.

"More like 'extended borrowing,' eh?" Graham suggested.

"That's right."

"So, before Mrs. Taylor bought this place," Graham said, now guiding Mrs. Northrop into the conservatory, "do you remember a guest passing away in one of the upstairs rooms?"

"Freddie Solomon's been writing about him, hasn't he?" Janet said.

Graham's eyelids dropped a fraction of an inch. "Mrs. Northrop, please put out of your mind anything you might have read and simply answer my questions." Graham's words were clipped, his tone hard.

Janet Northrop frowned and looked down at her hands. "And this was 1980 to 1982, you're saying?"

"Yes, there are reasons to think it might have happened in February. Around Valentine's Day."

Mrs. Northrop gave it her best, rapidly tapping the pad of her forefinger against her thumb as memories built themselves. "It's an awfully long time ago," she said. "And in 1982, I wasn't even here. I went to the Scilly Isles. I remember that because my big sister treated me for my eighteenth. First time on a plane for both of us, it was. We went for the weekend. My birthday isn't until June, but she couldn't afford it then, so we went in the low season. We had a lovely time. Even in February, would you believe? Beautiful sunshine. I loved it."

"And you went around Valentine's Day?"

"Yes. I remember because someone from the local flower farm handed us bunches of white narcissi as they met us off the plane—they're famous for those there. Anyhow, we were told the flower was called Scilly Valentine in honour of it being Valentine's Day that weekend." Mrs. Northrop's eyes glazed over before snapping back to the present. "But I remember nothing about anyone dying. Ever."

"Please think carefully," Graham said.

"No, I'm sure of it," Janet replied, pressing her forefinger into her shoulder. "You'd remember something like that, wouldn't you? And I don't remember anything about Valentine's Day in 1980 or '81. In '82, I wasn't back before later in the month. I didn't hear of anything happening while I was away."

"Ah, well," Graham said. "It was worth a try."

"I feel so awful that he died," Janet said. "That man. And under our roof, of all places. Must be quite a test for you, the case I mean. Being so old and such." Janet Northrop continued to deliver a speech that was very familiar to Graham. It was entitled, *Why I Love Police Mysteries on the Telly*. When she paused midspeech to take a breath, he politely thanked her and stepped away to finish his handwritten notes.

"Not very helpful, was she?" Mrs. Taylor said, appearing moments later at his shoulder. "I wish we could help more, not least because the sooner this mystery is solved, the better it will be for all of us."

"You've got enough on your plate, Mrs. Taylor," Graham said, putting away his notebook. "You leave the mysteries to us," he said kindly. He smiled at her.

"I'll be getting on, then," she said, politely returning his smile. From far away, up many flights of stairs, came the distinctive crunch of an old beam being taken down, followed by a burst of hammering. Mrs. Taylor winced, standing still for a pained moment before finding whatever energy was needed to press on.

Graham called Janice. "Mrs. Northrop's reaction was interesting. Her story was quite elaborate and precise. Almost like it was rehearsed."

"Well, she's worked there forever, sir, and the roof has just caved in. She must be a bit upset. Perhaps she's over-compensating."

"I've watched Mrs. Taylor's staff cope with a missing turkey delivery at eleven p.m. on Christmas Eve before now. I've seen Mrs. Northrop face up to a hundred of the most entitled tea drinkers on Jersey without blinking, all in one afternoon. Her prep guy, Raj, once told me that when things get hectic, she can command a kitchen like she's mobilising an infantry battalion."

"So, Mrs. T. and Mrs. Northrop are both forces of

nature," Janice replied. "Even institutions are allowed to throw a wobbly now and then. Might be worth talking to her again. Want me to bring some charm to the proceedings?"

"I think I've got it for now, Sergeant, thanks." Graham chuckled. "How was the postmortem?"

"Unpleasant, sir. As you know very well."

"Any findings of interest?"

"Male, midtwenties. The cause of death was a heart attack. Dr. Tomlinson said the heart looked healthy, other than the dead bit, of course. That was a bit unusual. They're doing further tests on the shirt he was wearing, tox screen, et cetera. Other than that, nothing stood out. I ran his fingerprints through the system—nothing."

"Hmm, mundane."

"Precisely. What do you think we're looking at, sir? If it's a heart attack, it's natural causes, surely?"

"Possibly. Bit young though."

"Young men do suddenly drop dead occasionally. There was that lad playing football for St. Helier that time, remember? Fell like a stone on the pitch. I remember Roachie talking about it."

"It does happen, of course, but if it was natural causes, why was the body secreted as it was?"

CHAPTER TWENTY-SIX

"**D**ID IT COME through?" Tomlinson asked Fiona. He sat in an office chair, gently pressing the floor with his foot so that he swung from side to side.

"Yep," Fiona said, sitting at her workstation so that Tomlinson could see her screen. "Doesn't look much like the original object though."

"Ah, yes," Tomlinson said. "Wavelengths of light. It's all about the wavelengths." He raised his voice. "Isn't it, Dr. Weiss?" Dr. Miranda Weiss was head of the forensic science lab in Southampton, to which particularly complex Jersey cases were referred. The lab possessed an array of technology not available on the island, which regularly both challenged and excited Marcus.

Over the speaker, Fiona and Tomlinson heard her chuckle. "Let me know if this gets too *Star Trek* for you, Marcus."

When it came to refuting ageism, Tomlinson's pump was already primed. "I understood every word of the briefing you gave me."

"Even the parts you slept through?"

"My elbow," he explained slowly, "merely slipped off the table. You had my full attention."

"And I assume I still do." Dr. Weiss shared her screen with the Jersey pair, quickly adding layers of colour and detail to the image on it. "There, that's better."

In front of them was a roughly symmetrical shape, not unlike an inkblot test but which resembled nothing in particular. "I have no idea what I'm looking at!" Fiona admitted in a tone similar to one she might use when she couldn't wait to open her Christmas presents.

"You created the image yourself not half an hour ago," Dr. Weiss told her.

"Wait . . . This is from Mr. X's shirt?" Fiona said. "Wow! I thought it'd be like looking at a close-up photograph."

"You're thinking of an electron microscope, Fiona. These are results," Tomlinson said, "from an ultraviolet spectroscope. A spectroscope interprets a different kind of light. Different animal. Dr. Weiss has even more sophisti-cated gear up there in the buzzing metropolis of Southamp-ton." He returned to the image on the screen. "And what kind of animal are we looking at right now, Miranda?"

"We're seeing varying levels of reflectivity," said Dr. Weiss. "I know it's your first time with one of these, so I'll go slow." At her end, Dr. Weiss used the mouse to point out a roughly symmetrical pattern at the top of the screen. "If it's a different colour, it's a different chemical. Everything has its unique way of reflecting light. That's where the rainbow comes from," she explained simply. "Ultraviolet light is special because it can show us whole categories of chem-istry. Over here," she added, circling a broad, dull area, "is just normal carbon weave. The black stuff is the polyester.

No surprises there, but these lighter marks near the buttons of his shirt . . ."

"They're a different chemical completely," Fiona said. She leaned in and added, "But they're not part of the shirt."

"Why do you say that?" asked Tomlinson.

"The marks are inconsistent, spread out over his shirt in a random pattern."

"You think they're random?" came Dr. Weiss's voice, leading Fiona onward. The young woman appeared stumped, a tiny furrow forming between her eyebrows.

Tomlinson's experience allowed him to race ahead. "Could we say in this case," he asked, not even looking at the image now as he made quick notes in Mr. X's file, "that the majority of the substance is down the centre, below his shirt buttons? And that the rest is divided, so we see about forty percent on his right side and sixty on his left?"

As Dr. Weiss adjusted the view, it emerged that Tomlinson was right about the dispersal ratio.

"Huh, interesting," Fiona said. "So, what does that mean? And what kind of chemical is this, anyway?"

"Ever eaten a Cornish pasty? A really flaky one?" Tomlinson asked her.

"Wouldn't have them any other way."

"Messy, aren't they? Crumbs everywhere."

"Yes," Fiona admitted, "but it's well worth the mess."

"Really? Personally, I'm not much of a fan."

"Madness!" Fiona exclaimed. "They're delicious."

"I have the sense Mr. X would have said the same," Dr. Weiss said.

"Wait . . ." Fiona gestured to all the machines and screens and accoutrements of modern forensic investigations that lay around them. "Was all of this just to discover he spilled puff pastry on his shirt?"

"Ha-ha, no, but there are two things we can say with reasonable certainty," Miranda Weiss said, her low, rumbly voice reverberating through the screen. Reaching for his phone, Tomlinson said, "He's right-handed. I'd bet my wine cellar on it."

"And these marks," Dr. Weiss said, "are a lot more exciting than whatever your Mr. X had for lunch."

"Cocaine?" Graham sat up straight.

"Probably," Tomlinson said. "I'm judging from experience. It's a white amphetamine powder. I'll show Fiona how to do some more chromatography and some mass spectroscopy, then we'll be sure."

"Well," Graham said, "there's a thing."

"The pattern suggests a right-hander, albeit marginally. Small amounts spilled down either side of his shirt buttons."

"That'd explain it," said Graham. "Our victim enjoyed too much Bolivian marching powder and keeled over."

"Or just enough of it," said Tomlinson. "As far as I could tell, his heart looked in decent condition, but it's possible he was a habitual user, or he mixed the cocaine with alcohol. If any of those were the case, he'd have been at risk."

"Wouldn't have to be an overdose, you mean?"

"Not necessarily."

"Curiouser and curiouser. So, we have a young man visiting Jersey between 1980 and 1982 while in possession of a gun who dies of a heart attack while snorting cocaine during his stay at the White House Inn, aka The Grange. Identity and reason for visit and gun still unknown."

"That's about the sum of it so far. Ballistics soon. We'll

see what that throws up. How are you getting on trying to find out who he is?"

"Nowhere yet. Barnwell's still in the basement. Janice found nothing in the databases. And Mrs. Taylor doesn't have any record. We're drawing a blank at the moment."

"Fiona's sent off hair samples for DNA analysis. That might help."

"Thanks again, Marcus. Anything else comes up . . ."

Tomlinson assured him, "You're always my first call."

CHAPTER TWENTY-SEVEN

F IONA GRACELESSLY PLONKED Marcus's mug in front of him although she didn't seem too put out by his request for yet another cup of tea. "In a rush to go somewhere?" Tomlinson said.

"Yes. My next task is to verify the quality of the cocaine on Mr. X's shirt. I'll be back shortly." Fiona turned to leave before pausing. "You know, there's some AI software that takes skeletal data to generate an impression of how that person might have looked when alive. Maybe I could try that?"

"Sounds expensive."

"I could log in to the software in my previous office and do it remotely, if you like. There's also a free app that enables you to age a person from a photo so you can see what they look like at different points in their life."

"Hmm, interesting. Let me talk to Inspector Graham. See if he thinks that would be useful."

As Fiona got to work, Marcus quietly sipped his tea—he liked it piping hot—as he listened to the tapping, whirring, and whooshing sounds coming from the lab. The sound of a door opening interrupted him. Fiona appeared in the doorway, flushed and frustrated. She waved a piece of paper and wiped her brow with the back of her wrist. "I need some help. The spectroscopy tests spit out some strange results I've not seen before. Either I haven't done it properly, or Mr. X's coke contained a *lot* of adulterants. The chart shows not only multicolour spikes in the right areas of the chemical spectrum for cocaine, but also others I can't identify. Come and see it on my screen. It's nearly a third of the mass."

By the time they got to Fiona's desk, the software had come back with a solid hit for the variances in the chart. Fiona pointed to her screen. "What's that?"

Tomlinson cleaned his glasses and squinted at the results. After a few seconds, he straightened, peeling his glasses off one ear and then the other. "That, my dear, is a reason for Detective Inspector Graham to stop what he's doing right now and give us his attention."

"Poisoning?" Graham exclaimed for the second time that day. Then, in almost the same breath, "*One* cause? There were others?"

"I think whoever did away with Mr. X went a little overboard. If they hadn't, we might not have caught it. You see, the cocaine which drifted down onto his shirt contained traces of two different old-fashioned rat poisons."

Pen already flying, Graham visualised the scene. "Alright, so our killer couldn't make up his mind, or used two poisons just to make sure?"

"Hard to know. The red squill is a cardiotoxin. It works by causing heart attacks, usually in rats. It's a common rodenticide."

"How quickly are we talking?"

"Extremely quick. As far as I can tell in this case, death appears to have been immediate. If he clung on for more than a few moments, there'd be signs of internal bleeding. There were none that I could identify."

"Could they have been hidden by the effects of decomposition?"

"I would have seen some sign even at this late stage. There were simply none. The state of the remains is really rather remarkable."

"What about the second poison?"

"Ah, that's different. If he'd lived longer, we'd have seen the effects of thallium poisoning."

"Flu symptoms," Graham recited from memory, "stomach trouble, tingling in the feet, and hair loss. Kills slowly though. A week or more."

"My opinion is that the heart was stopped by the red squill, and death was instantaneous. The thallium served as backup but became unnecessary. Mr. X was fortunate his ticker gave out as soon as it did."

"One method causes immediate death, the other a lingering agony. Sounds like our murderer was organised or maybe determined enough to give the Grim Reaper some options. Who would choose to poison an enemy in such a way?"

"Indeed," Tomlinson added. "And why."

When Graham put down his phone, he fired up his computer. Pursing his lips, he idly tapped a few words into the search bar and pressed "enter," pausing to read the entries that the internet produced. He typed again, refining his search, and this time, his eyes widened as blood rushed to his cheeks. He sat up straighter in his chair before jotting some notes in his notebook, abandoning his computer, and shrugging on his jacket.

As he walked through the main office, Carmen's head popped up. Hope sprung into her deep brown eyes. Graham paused to scratch her head.

"Sorry, Carmie, not now."

"I'll take her when Jan gets back," Barnwell said. "She just popped out. Something about her mother and flowers, she said."

"Okay, good. I'm going out for a bit."

"See you later, sir."

CHAPTER TWENTY-EIGHT

SINCE THE STORM, the White House Inn had transformed into a building site. People were up on the roof tossing down ragged, smashed pieces of tile and split timbers. Inside the grand attic, the site having been released as a crime scene, a workshop was being set up to install the new beams. All of this generated a near-constant hailstorm of noise.

"It's like having surgery!" Mrs. Taylor said to Graham between the many bouts of drilling. "Like they're replacing my hips without anaesthetic!"

Graham murmured sympathies, but he was there on police business. "I wonder if I could bother Mrs. Northrop again?"

More drilling almost drowned out Mrs. Taylor's reply; it seemed to resonate all the way down, through the walls, to the foundations of the building. "Again? Must be important."

"We're making progress," Graham told her. "So, is Mrs. Northrop here?"

Janet Northrop took a moment's finding, but Mrs.

Taylor found her in the walk-in freezer. She meekly followed Mrs. Taylor into the reception area. Her reluctance was obvious from the set of her shoulders and her expression, which was a mixture of resentment and resignation. "It was so very long ago," was the first thing she said, anticipating Graham's questions. "So very long, and—"

"Tell me again about the Scilly Isles," said Graham companionably. "The week you spent there with your sister."

It was a surprising turn, but Mrs. Northrop recounted again the same memories as before—the unseasonably sunny weekend of sand and sea with her sister. "It was lovely. Once we both got married and her first husband landed that job in Copenhagen, I hardly got to see Judy. But we made the best of the time we had before that."

Animated flipping of the pages in the inspector's notebook brought Mrs. Northrop to a halt, as he'd intended. "Ah, here it is, yes." He read aloud from what sounded like a weather forecast. "Twelfth to the fourteenth of February 1982. Scattered showers on Friday, heavy rain almost continually from Saturday morning to Sunday teatime." He closed his notebook. "Sounds awful. Must've been cold too. The original, authentic 'wet weekend' in all its glory. Isn't that right, Mrs. Northrop?" The woman's gaze faltered, and she broke eye contact with Graham, glancing at the ground, murmuring something he didn't catch.

"Hell's bloomers! That's not for *this* weekend, is it?" Mrs. Taylor asked, wrongly overhearing and horrified that her roof would be open to the elements.

"Second weekend in February, 1982," Graham informed her. "The date of the weekend you say, Mrs. Northrop, you spent with your sister. A happy, *sunny* weekend, you said. 'Thunderous rain' was the weather reported for Cornwall and Devon that weekend, which includes the Scilly Isles, of course. It's amazing what you can find out these days."

Janet Northrop stared at him. Mrs. Taylor stared at her. "Janet?" she asked. "Are you *positive* about those dates?"

Mrs. Northrop immediately crumbled. "I'm not . . . I mean, I didn't . . ."

"Would you like to go into my office for a quiet chat, Inspector?" Mrs. Taylor offered. Unusually for Mrs. Taylor, she sensed the mood. She didn't want yet another public scene.

Inside the office, pulling up the guest chair for her tearoom manager, Mrs. Taylor gestured to her office chair for Graham. As she reached for the door handle to give the pair some privacy, Janet Northrop piped up.

"C-could Marjorie sit with me? We go back a long way. It would help calm my nerves." In a flash, Mrs. Taylor was by Mrs. Northrop's side.

"We do, Inspector. We really do," Mrs. Taylor said. Graham looked up from his notebook and regarded the two women, one eager, the other pleading. "Very well, but please don't intervene, Mrs. Taylor. You're here to support Mrs. Northrop only."

"Yes, of course, Inspector." Mrs. Taylor pulled out another chair and sat next to Mrs. Northrop.

"That means don't say anything, Mrs. Taylor."

Marjorie slowly clasped her hands in her lap and, gazing steadily at the inspector, lowered her head, still holding eye contact with him. "I understand, Inspector. Please, proceed." Feeling he was already at risk of losing control of the situation, Graham continued as smoothly as he could.

"Mrs. Northrop, it would appear that the dates you gave

us for your trip were not, in fact, accurate. Was there a reason for that? Did you get the dates mixed up?" Comfortable answering his own question, he added, "Or perhaps it was because you wanted to convince me that you weren't here during the period we're investigating. When, in fact, you were."

"It was *so very* long ago, Inspector."

"So you keep saying, but we don't normally forget our eighteenth birthday celebrations, Mrs. Northrop. Especially when they involve once-in-a-lifetime activities."

"I'm an old woman, you know," Janet Northrop said, her hands curled in her lap. "Things aren't quite as good up here," she said, tapping her temple.

"Poppycock," muttered Mrs. Taylor, defending her friend but also undermining her claims. "You're as sharp as the chef's knives, Janet."

Graham glared at her. Chastened, Mrs. Taylor bit her bottom lip and settled into her chair some more. The inspector resumed his questioning.

"I'll just ask this: What happened after the body was found?"

Now Mrs. Northrop was shaking her head. "You don't understand. It was Miss Lovell. I was too young. I didn't know what to do. She said not to mention him, the man who died. Not to say anything to anyone."

"Why?" asked Graham.

"Our reputation!" Janet said as though it were obvious.

"But people die in hotels all the time without it resulting in disaster."

"No, it's the weather that does that," Mrs. Taylor muttered quietly.

Graham ignored her. "Mrs. Northrop?"

Fear brightened the woman's blue eyes at the inspector's prompt. "Well, I wasn't the boss, was I?" she protested. "I was eighteen, for heaven's sake. And if Miss Lovell said, 'Not a word to *anyone*,' she got silence from me. What right did I have to question her? It's not like there was a lot of employment on the island for someone like me in those days. I wanted to keep my job."

"So, what happened? Tell me," Graham said.

Mrs. Northrop folded her arms and looked away defiantly. "I'm not saying anything."

Graham leaned forward. "I really think you should, Mrs. Northrop. There's a family out there who lost someone. And they don't know what happened." Mrs. Northrop was unmoved.

"And you're implicated in the concealment of a body. Perverting the course of justice. You clearly lied to deflect from your involvement." Still, Mrs. Northrop didn't return his gaze. Graham glanced at Mrs. Taylor.

"Before my time," Marjorie said, quickly distancing herself from the situation. She, too, looked away and folded her arms, pursing her lips. Then she turned back and appealed to her friend. "But, oh, Janet, what on e*arth* happened back then?"

At her appeal, deeply uncomfortable at being forced to wade through this historical territory, Mrs. Northrop deflated. She reached out to grasp Mrs. Taylor's hand for comfort, perhaps for fortitude. "I wouldn't go back in there, Marjorie. Not into that room. Oh, it was awful. I found him, you see. 'Natural causes.' That's what Miss Lovell told me. But I knew something was wrong. He was staying in the attic, you see. It was a guestroom back then. After I told Miss Lovell about him, she went into the attic alone, and closed the door so, so quietly."

"How long was she in there for?"

"Ten minutes, maybe less."

"What was she doing?" Graham asked carefully.

"I don't know. Didn't see. And like I said, no way was I going back in there."

"What do you *think* she was doing?" Graham was determined to press Mrs. Northrop, his only true lead.

"I'm not a mind reader," Janet Northrop retorted sharply. But then she felt Mrs. Taylor's hand on her shoulder. Marjorie leaned over to whisper. Noting Graham's frown, Mrs. Northrop said, "Marjorie here wants me to tell you everything I know. She's a good egg, isn't she?"

"An excellent egg," the DI agreed.

"Go on, love," Mrs. Taylor said softly. "It might help the inspector. And with your nerves. You know how they affect you."

Janet Northrop closed her eyes and sighed. "I was so scared I stayed as silent as a mouse. I've never told anyone. Even when Miss Lovell died, I didn't want to rake it all up. I saw her go into the attic and that was the end of it. I don't know what happened, and I never wanted to find out. I assumed that the body was taken away in the dead of night and disposed of. But obviously, that isn't quite what happened."

"Do you remember his name or anything about him that might be relevant? We're still tracking down his identity. You could help a lot with that."

"His name was Mr. Smith. I'll never forget." Janet thought back. "He was in his mid to late twenties. A heavy smoker. We didn't have no-smoking rooms in them days. Drinker too. But he was charming, with a nice, big smile."

"You remember his smile?" Graham frowned.

"He was a flirt. I was young, remember? Bit of a looker I was back then. And it was Valentine's Day 1982. He said he didn't have a date but that seeing hearts everywhere was making *his* heart 'go all aflutter.' He was a bit leery, I thought. Trying it on. Well, he didn't get anywhere. Not with me."

"What nationality was he?"

"He was English. London, I'd say."

"Why didn't you say all this when we spoke before?"

Mrs. Northrop made to apologise, her palms open. "I was told not to, wasn't I? And I didn't want to get involved. I wanted . . . I *want* it all to go away. I don't want to remember what I saw. Or that I was told to look away and say nothing. And I . . . well, I committed a crime, didn't I?"

"Why do you think Miss Lovell didn't declare the body?"

"I should imagine it was because of what it might lead to."

"And what might that be?"

"There were rumours . . ."

"Of what?"

"That she had a side business. That the hotel wasn't her only source of income. Perhaps not even her main one." Mrs. Northrop looked down at her hands. Graham glanced at Mrs. Taylor.

"*Drugs,*" she mouthed. Graham's eyebrows shot up.

"You mean Miss Lovell might have supplied him with something that could be traced to her? Something that caused his death?"

Janet Northrop squeezed her eyes tight shut and nodded. "Hmm. Or she simply didn't want the police poking around. She was in her last months, although I didn't know that at the time. Miss Lovell had cancer, you know. She died about six months later."

Graham sat back and paused as he processed this information. He lifted his chin, stretched his neck, and breathed out through his nose.

"Who would have helped her with the concrete? She couldn't possibly have done it by herself."

"I don't know."

"Surely you've some idea. Can you give me a name?"

Mrs. Northrop screwed her eyes up tight again, her lips pinched together. When she relaxed them, she said, "I would try Neville Williams. He was her grandson. He was in the building trade back then. Just a young lad, an apprentice. But I've no idea where he is now. We're talking over forty years ago." Graham flipped his notebook shut with a flick of his wrist. "We'll find him. Thank you, Mrs. Northrop."

"Will I . . .? Will I be charged?"

"Well, technically . . ." Graham caught sight of Mrs. Taylor's expression. It conveyed that her tolerance of his presence in her tearoom was subject to conditions. "Uh, it's unclear at the moment. I do require that you not leave the island, however."

"How did he die, Inspector?" Mrs. Taylor said.

"Heart attack."

"Hardly surprising, I suppose, given his habits."

"Smoking, drinking, even to excess, don't normally lead to heart attacks in otherwise healthy young men, Mrs. Taylor." Graham stood, preparing to leave. "But the two kinds of rat poison he inadvertently snorted up his nose could easily be judged as the *decisive* factor."

CHAPTER TWENTY-NINE

"**M**URDER? In my hotel. Again!" Three of her staff took Mrs. Taylor to the quietest part of the hotel, providing tea and sympathy and shielding her from new stresses. Before she left, Mrs. Taylor clutched the hotel's reservation book to her as though someone had threatened to steal it, taking small comfort in the hotel's future bookings, unseasonably thin as they now were.

"I'm sorry to have to break it like that," Graham said to Mrs. Northrop when Mrs. Taylor had gone.

"The poor man," she said. Then with lip-curling distaste, "Up his nose, did you say?"

"That's the most common way with cocaine. It's also typical," Graham pointed out, "for innocent people to speak the whole truth first time around when interviewed by a detective. Again, I can't help noticing you chose not to do that." Mrs. Northrop was silent. "I'm trained to regard that as suspicious, madam."

Janet Northrop remained calm for a second before erupting into a fireworks display of apologies. Someone brought tea, for which Graham could have awarded them a medal, and it gave Mrs. Northrop a moment to collect herself.

"When the body was found, I wanted to see if the man's death would be ruled an ordinary one, or if something would turn up about drugs," Janet Northrop explained quietly, keeping her voice level. "I was aware of the rumours about Miss Lovell at the time."

"But why the hesitation? Why wait to see if we found anything? Why did you not simply tell us? You have to admit it looks suspicious and forces us to look at you and what you've told us very carefully. If you're innocent, why put yourself in this position?"

"I didn't know about the rat poison," Janet said firmly. She was trembling. "Only the drugs. She was a very forceful personality, Miss Lovell was. A bit of a bully, to be honest. And she made me *swear*."

"As she was your boss and the hotel owner, I appreciate Miss Lovell had a great deal of influence. You were young. But, and I know it's not nice to think about, laws were broken. A man died," Graham reminded her. "And the authorities weren't informed. His family hasn't known what happened to him all this time." Mrs. Northrop shrugged and cast her eyes downwards into her lap. "It was decades ago. Miss Lovell is long dead."

Janet Northrop shook her head, unable to explain.

"How old was Miss Lovell?"

"She was nearly eighty. She seemed ancient to me at the time. Tiny thing, she was. If you sneezed, you worried you'd blow her over. And then you wouldn't hear the last of it. My, she had a temper. Lorded it over everyone, she did. We were all terrified of her."

"Hmm, it seems to have been quite the cover-up Miss

Lovell was hatching. I know why *she* did it, and honestly, I can understand why you kept things quiet at the time. But you're not eighteen any longer, and you haven't been for a long time. You *stayed* silent. Even when Miss Lovell died, even when you learned the body had been found."

"I don't know. I was scared you would put me in prison, I suppose. For not telling the truth at the time or since." Mrs. Northrop was grey with fatigue. Graham sighed.

"Did you see what Miss Lovell did with his belongings? Especially the gun?"

"I don't know anything about a gun. I didn't see one at the time," Janet said.

"And what about a suitcase?"

Janet shook her head. "I remember him arriving with it. It was red. What happened to it after . . . you know, I have no idea."

"And it was definitely red?"

"Yes. It was very noticeable. Unusual." There was a pause. Janet rubbed her top lip with the tip of her tongue. Graham sensed that she was wrestling with something. He waited until what was lighting up her brain's synapses faded as they were vanquished, and her eyes dulled.

"Perhaps she didn't know it was murder," Mrs. Northrop said. "Miss Lovell. I mean, if there was poison in his mixture, could Miss Lovell have not known about it?"

"Well, we can't know for sure. She might not have been the source of the drugs that killed him. And if she was, was she the one cutting it, or was it cut before it got to her? Either way, she committed several crimes—not reporting a death to the authorities, disposing of a body, and the perversion of the course of justice. And that's just in relation to this case. It's enough to be going on with, but I could continue. I suspect Miss Lovell knew that, and once she'd started down the path of obfuscation and denial, getting off it became almost impossible."

Janet rubbed her face with her hand. "So who exactly *was* he, this 'Mr. Smith'?"

"Well, that's a bit up in the air still. But your evidence has given us some leads to chase."

"Well, that's good. Can I go now, or do you have any more questions for me? Things have been *awful* lately, what with the storm and now this. For Mrs. T., the staff, everyone. I'm not sure how much more I can take."

"No, no more questions. Not today anyway. If I think of some more, I know where to find you. If you wake up at three a.m. with a blinding flash of insight or a memory, call the station. If no one picks up, leave a message and a sleepy constable will call you back. And please, Mrs. Northrop . . ."

"Yes?"

"Try to be honest from here on out, okay?"

There was a knock at the door. Graham opened it and found Mrs. Taylor gripping an old reservation book bound in green cloth. "I had another look, and I found something, Inspector."

Before she continued, Janet Northrop slipped between the two of them, muttering about "getting back to the tearoom."

When she and the inspector were alone, Mrs Taylor spoke again. "I called in two of my bar staff to help me. You see," she explained sincerely, "I can't have rumours again. You know, like before. The ghost stories and the gossip . . ."

"I understand," said Graham. "We'll do everything we can to clear this up quickly."

"Exactly." Mrs. Taylor opened the book. "From '82. Before my time." Opening a page marked with a yellow sticky note, she said, "I think this might be him. Mr. John Smith."

Graham snorted. "Of course." The "4" next to his name had been struck out with a red pen.

"What do you think that means?" Graham wondered.

"He was booked in for four nights." Mrs. Taylor added woefully, "I suppose the strike-through means that he didn't complete his stay. On account of him, you know . . . dying." Graham coughed. "As I said, Inspector, this was *before* my tenure."

"Alright, so, as best you can recall, Miss Lovell never mentioned anything to you about this?"

"Not a word, not a word." Mrs. Taylor looked weary, beset by the most debilitating of challenges: those that arrive *all at once*.

"It's just that there was an unregistered firearm and an unidentified body in your attic, Mrs. Taylor, and that's obviously not the best thing to happen."

"But I didn't know they were there!" Mrs. Taylor replied. "Isn't that obvious?" Her face fell.

"You also didn't mention the rumours about drugs."

"Oh, I'm sorry. I've been so upset about the storm and my business and . . . Am I in trouble?" she asked thinly, clasping her hands once more. "Oh, Inspector, if I'd known anything . . . oh, for heaven's sake, I'd have told you in a flash! Back then, I was so busy renovating the hotel and learning the business, getting my first guests . . ." Marjorie shook her head. Her hand-wringing intensified, and she turned away from him, overwhelmed.

"You're not in any trouble, Mrs. Taylor," Graham said. "We don't believe this situation has anything to do with you." Amid this crisis, it was churlish to harangue her, but finding a dead, armed man in her loft *was* a serious situation. "Are you sure you can't tell me anything else about the victim? This Mr. Smith?"

Marjorie saw Graham's frustration in his body language and the angular symbols he made with his pencil in his notebook. "I'm just trying to make sure I don't tell you something that isn't accurate," she said. "I know how important these details are. And, I'm sorry, I can't help you."

"Very well, Mrs. Taylor. I'll take my leave. No need to see me out."

When Graham left the hotel and reached his car, he dialled Marcus Tomlinson's number. "We have a breakthrough, Marcus. A date. February 1982."

CHAPTER THIRTY

"**B**ARNWELL!" GRAHAM HAD barely opened the doors to the police station before he was bellowing for his constable. Barnwell wasn't on reception. No one was.

No one appeared to be in the main office either. But when the door swung closed behind the inspector, Carmen came bounding towards him, her long, floppy ears bouncing around her.

A hand appeared on a desk, and Barnwell appeared red-faced, puffing with effort as he clutched onto the desktop to lever himself upright. Janice appeared a second later, looking awkward and straightening her uniform.

The inspector looked at them curiously, but the urgency of his order superseded his interest in whatever Barnwell and Janice were doing on the floor. "We've got a date and a suspect. My office." Barnwell and Janice clocked his mood immediately and followed him.

"Sounds like you've been busy, sir," Janice said as Graham dumped his keys and notebook on the table before flicking the kettle on.

"Mrs. Northrop spilled the beans. She said she went to the Scilly Isles for her birthday in February 1982. Said the weather had been lovely. Just a hunch, but I looked it up. It's amazing what you can find on the internet these days. Anyhow, her memory and the reality didn't match up, so I went back to question her, and I got quite the story."

"What did she say, sir?" Barnwell had brought a packet of Viennese Whirls with him. He offered it to Graham.

"Oooh, don't mind if I do." With his fingertips, he delicately picked one up, careful not to squeeze it too hard in case the jam and cream filling fell out from between the two soft, sweet, crumbly biscuits they were sandwiched between. Janice declined Barnwell's offer with a shake of her head.

"Mrs. Northrop told me that it was she who found the body. His name was John Smith, but I think we can assume that was fake. Can you check the police database though, Janice? Midtwenties. British, perhaps from London. Smoker, bit of a drinker. Drug user, unless it was forced down him, which I think unlikely."

"Sir." Janice acknowledged his order.

"When Mrs. Northrop found the body and raised the alarm, the owner of the hotel, Miss Lovell, took charge. She forbade Mrs. Northrop from mentioning anything about the death, and that was the last she heard of it. She told me that she had kept schtum all these years. Not told a soul."

"Wow, why would she do that?" Barnwell wondered.

"More recently, Mrs. Northrop thought we might arrest her for not saying anything, rightly as it happens. But back then, it sounds like Miss Lovell ruled the roost with a rod of iron."

"You're mixing metaphysics, sir."

"Wha—oh yes. Anyway, our Miss Lovell, who was a mere eighty years old at the time, had a side hustle. Drugs."

"At the White House Inn? Are you serious?" Barnwell struggled to comprehend the idea.

"Mrs. Taylor said there were rumours at the time. It would have been in Miss Lovell's interest to cover up the death if the rumours were true."

"Blinkin' Nora." Barnwell was still struggling to imagine the graceful, elegant hotel as a drug den.

"But do we think she murdered him, sir? Did she add the rat poison to the drugs?" Janice asked.

"That's for us to find out, Sergeant. We need to follow up on the drug-dealing angle though, and hunt down a lead that Mrs. Northrop offered. Miss Lovell is long gone. She died of cancer about six months after our Mr. X, but she had a grandson who lived on the island. He was in the building trade—an apprentice, and a young lad at the time." Graham consulted his notebook. "A Neville Williams. We need to find him."

"I wonder if Bob the Builder knew him," Barnwell said.

Janice reached for a calculator on Graham's desk and tapped in some numbers. "They'd have been about the same age in 1982. Perhaps even apprentices together, working for Bob's dad."

"Good thoughts. Constable, you follow that up." Graham bounced a pencil in his hand. "Did your exploits in the basement bear fruit?"

Barnwell suppressed a shudder. "Not a sausage. No missing persons from the period we're looking at at all.

"Nothing on the mispers database either, sir. Nothing that I can tie to Jersey, at least, but now we have more intel and a tighter timeframe, I can run some more checks."

"Someone must have missed him. He can't have just

disappeared into a block of concrete without *anyone* noticing."

"What about Dr. Tomlinson, sir?"

"He's still waiting on the DNA results. And there's the ballistics to come. Perhaps if you need a break, Sergeant, you might like to have another cup of tea with Mrs. Taylor. She's still struggling."

"Perhaps I'll send my mum over. They'll get on well."

"Right, off you go, the two of you. Let me know if you turn up anything. I'm going to take Carmen for a walk." Barnwell and Janice turned to leave, but Graham stopped them. "Oh, and . . . what were you two doing on the floor?" Barnwell and Janice glanced at each other. Janice flushed. "Or should I not ask?"

It was Barnwell who spoke. "Just putting Jan through her paces, sir." Graham raised his eyebrows. "A few press-ups, sit-ups, you know." The inspector stared at them, the explanation he so obviously needed hanging unspoken in midair. Janice blinked.

"I've been stress eating, sir. After all these months of dieting and exercise, a few days before the big one, I'm struggling to get in my wedding dress."

Barnwell raised his head as soon as he heard the doors open. Carmen entered the station first, Graham following, the red lead he held in his hand connected to a similarly coloured harness around the beagle's body.

"Found him, sir! Neville Williams. I was right. Bob the Builder did know him. They were apprentices together until Williams disappeared in, wait for it, 1982. He's not been on the electoral roll on Jersey since. He lived with a

Dorothy Williams, presumably his mother, now deceased; she was the daughter of Emily Lovell, owner of The Grange, also deceased; then the trail went cold. No criminal record, but I tracked him down with the help of the DVLA and confirmed with Bob that it's him."

"Where is he?"

"In Bournemouth, sir."

"Excellent work, Constable. Fancy a day trip to the south coast?"

CHAPTER THIRTY-ONE

"YES?" THE DOOR opened only as far as the chain would allow. A man squinted through the opening.

"Neville Williams?" Barnwell raised his police ID so the man could see it. Graham, standing behind him, did the same. The IDs were only partially glanced at. Williams's eyelids flickered. "Can we come in, sir? We'd like to ask you a few questions." The man hesitated, then closed the door. Barnwell braced himself, then heard the chain rattle and the door opened wide.

A skinny man with long limbs, his face ravaged by hard living, stood on the dirty hall carpet. He didn't look at the two police officers but waved them in, his other arm dropping resignedly to his side where it dangled like a forlorn windsock.

Barnwell passed him, followed by Graham. As they walked down the hall, Barnwell peered into the rooms that led off it. "Anyone else here with you?" he called over his shoulder.

"Nope, I live by myself. Always have and always will,"

Williams said. "Go into the living room. I've been waiting for you. Do you want a cup of tea?" Barnwell looked to Graham for guidance, who gave a minute shake of his head.

"No, thanks. You're fine."

The three of them moved into the front room, cluttered with newspapers, pizza boxes, and takeaway wrappers. Graham walked over to the windows and opened them.

"Please sit down, Mr. Williams," Barnwell said.

"Wha—oh, alright." Neville Williams folded his long legs as he sat on a cracked and peeling synthetic leather chair. He was awkward like a giraffe and nervously picked at his cuticles, giving Graham the impression he was on something, or at least jittery, nervous. "Aren't you going to sit down? You're making me nervous standing like that," Williams said.

Barnwell sat on the sofa. Graham peered at a framed poster on the wall. A man with a huge afro, exotic features, and a long, lanky physique riffed on a guitar. Underneath was printed "Thin Lizzy, Fort Regent, Jersey, UK. 1981."

"Mr. Williams, I'm Constable Barnwell. This is Detective Inspector Graham. We're from Gorey. You grew up there, I understand."

Williams's eyes flicked around the room, unsure on what to alight. Eventually, he nodded. "Yeah, but I haven't lived there in decades. Left when I wasn't even twenty. Too small for the likes of me. I lived with my mum." He didn't continue, so Barnwell prompted him with a turn of his head as he raised his eyebrows. Williams sighed like a teenager being asked to lay the table.

"Left school as soon as I could. Hated it, you see. Got an apprenticeship with a local builder—Bob the Builder. Bob Simms, senior. Good man. He's dead now, but his son carries on, or so I heard through the grapevine." Williams looked out of the window at the narrow, quiet street lined with terraced houses and their owners' cars. With another sigh, he turned back. Graham moved on from the poster, peering at a mess of papers and unopened envelopes on a sideboard.

"So why did you leave?" Barnwell asked Williams.

Williams shrugged. "Wanted something more. I was a young guy. Gorey was much too small for me. Needed the bright lights."

"You just hopped it and left?"

"More or less. I had no ties, nothing to stay for. Nothing much, anyway." Williams stopped and seemed to have come to the end of this branch of his life story, so Barnwell shifted tactics.

"What about your grandmother, Emily Lovell? She ran a hotel in Gorey, so we heard."

Williams shifted in his seat. "Yeah, my nan. My mum was her only child. They're all dead now, long gone. What about her?"

"And she ran the hotel until her death in 1982?"

"She died of lung cancer, yeah. She chain-smoked. Hopeless case. Nothing would stop her. Didn't matter what we said."

"See, there's been suggestions that the hotel was a place you could go to get drugs and that Emily Lovell was in the middle of it. What do you know about that?"

Williams shrugged once more but broke eye contact with Barnwell and looked out at the street again. Two teenage girls walked by in their school uniforms, gossiping, their ties—as bright blue as their blazers—askew against their white blouses. Williams didn't answer Barnwell's question.

"Mr. Williams? Neville?"

When Williams continued to ignore Barnwell, Graham leaned forward and tapped him on his knee. Williams looked vaguely at Graham as if seeing him for the first time.

"The thing is, Mr. Williams, we believe that Emily Lovell was selling drugs out of the hotel."

"The drugs had nothing to do with me," Williams answered quickly. The words came easily, eagerly even. "Yeah, she was on the make, at least that was the rumour, but I never saw anything of it. Nannie Em was always telling me to stay away from the stuff. She was pretty hard, my nan." Williams's eyes cleared.

Seeing he had his attention, Graham pressed on. "While the drugs might not have had anything to do with you, something related did happen in which you got caught up, didn't it?" Williams glanced outside at the street again. They could hear the jingle of an ice-cream van pealing repeatedly.

"Mr. Williams, when you opened the door, you said you had been waiting for us. We gave you no advance notice of our visit, so what did you mean by that?"

Williams dragged his bottom teeth against his top lip and dug in so hard that Graham expected him to draw blood. But Williams pressed his lips together, rolling them between his teeth. "Nothing."

"Nothing? Doesn't seem like it would be nothing to me."

"Look, it was nothing to do with *me*, okay?" Williams glared at Graham. "The drugs, none of it. It was all her."

"What was all her, Neville? What wasn't anything to do with you?" Williams twisted in his seat, lengthening his long legs, and began to rock, his hands on his knees.

"I can't tell you."

"What can't you tell us, Neville?" Graham prodded.

Williams continued to rock, his eyes focused on his hands. Slowly and gently, Graham placed his own over Williams's, and gradually the distressed man ceased his rocking.

Suddenly, Williams pulled his hands away. After a series of deep breaths, the words he had been refusing to speak came forth, first in staccato bursts, then in a torrent.

"She asked me for help . . . She was my nan. I was only seventeen. . . What could I do?" Williams sniffed, then began to sob. He grabbed Graham's wrists. Barnwell tensed.

"All my life I've waited for you to find me. I can't believe it's taken you this long. Why did it take you *so* long?" Williams's wild eyes looked into Graham's calm ones. "This could have been over long ago!" He released Graham's wrists and pushed them away, almost in disgust. "You've no idea what my life's been like. Always looking over my shoulder. Never feeling safe. And the nightmares! You can't imagine!"

Williams glanced at Barnwell, his eyes appealing. It occurred to the constable that the distressed man could have confessed at any time. He chose not to.

"What happened, Neville?" Graham asked. "Did your grandmother call you for help?" He leaned against the mantelpiece, seemingly unperturbed by the man's erratic behaviour.

"She said to get down to the hotel. I was due at work, but she said she had a more important job and that I should call in sick."

"When was this, Neville?"

"It was the day after Valentine's in 1982. A Monday. I'll never forget."

CHAPTER THIRTY-TWO

"**E**IGHT O'CLOCK IN the morning. The cleaning person had found a . . . body in his room. It was awful, it was." Williams sobbed and slapped his palms forcefully across his eyes. Barnwell winced. That had to have hurt. "He was lying on the floor next to the bed. Looked like he'd fallen off it."

"What was your grandmother doing?" Graham was as cool as ice. Calm.

"Not much. She just stared at him, like. Then she told me to 'deal with it.' I said, 'What do you mean?' She said, 'Deal with him. I don't want him found.' Her cancer was terminal, you see. She'd only a few months to live. 'I recognise him. I gave him the drugs that killed him, Nev,' she said. 'I'm not having my last months messed with. No one must find out about this until I'm gone.'"

"What did she mean by that?"

"She had it all worked out. She wanted me to bury him in cement. She told me I had to build a brick frame and mix and pour the concrete into it halfway. When I'd done that, we put the body inside and covered him up."

"Sounds like hard work."

"It was. I had to lug the bricks and mixes up the back stairs and do it without anyone seeing. I laid the bricks, then filled it in like she said. Nannie Em helped me with the guy, but by the time we moved him, he was stiff as a board and hard to handle. Regardless, I got the job done. It wasn't the best. The mortar between the bricks wasn't completely dry when I poured in the cement. I was worried it would fall apart, but I propped the brickwork up with lengths of wood in the hopes that it would hold. And it must have."

"Then what did you do?"

"I tell you what I didn't do. I didn't hang around. I got out of there as soon as I could. I moved away immediately. I couldn't stay there, not on Jersey. Not with the memories and living with what I'd done. I've hated myself ever since. What happened ruined my life. I never married, never had kids, always going job to job, looking over my shoulder. I mean, Nannie Em, she was a mean old bird, always was. You did what she told you, no messin', and you didn't argue if you knew what was good for you. I wanted no part of anything to do with her after that. I left the island, and I haven't been back since."

"And nothing was ever said?"

"Nothing. It was like it never happened. No one came knocking. As far as I know, Nannie Em lived out her last few months with that . . . that . . . thing above her, and everyone was none the wiser. Then she died, lucky old bag. I still can't believe that bloke's laid there all this time without anyone finding him."

"Take me back to when your grandmother called you. What did she say?"

"Oh gosh." Williams put his hand to his head and looked up at the ceiling. "It was a long time ago."

"Broadly, then. What did she say?" Graham sat now in an armchair facing Williams.

"She didn't tell me why until I got there. She showed me to the attic. We went up the back stairs, and she pointed to the man on the floor."

"And what did you see?"

"He was fully dressed, lying next to the bed. There was a glass coffee table beside a sofa, and it was obvious that he'd been snorting cocaine, then perhaps stumbled to the bed and didn't make it or did make it and rolled off. His hand was clutching the bedspread across his body like this." Williams crossed one arm to his opposite shoulder and made his hand into a fist.

"We had to prise the bedspread out of his hand. The other lay on his chest. He was on his back. His eyes . . ." Williams wiped the back of his hand across his top lip. "Oh." He exhaled. "They were open, and they *wouldn't* close. They stayed like that the whole time I was working. I had to put the bedspread over him. Terrible, it was. In the end, I found some washers to weigh down his eyelids."

"And your grandmother didn't want to declare the body because . . ."

"I told you. Because she had supplied him with the cocaine. She said so. He must have overdosed. That's what she said, anyway. 'I'm not having my last days on this earth spent on remand for supplying,' she told me. I knew she was ill, but I didn't know she was definitely dying, so that surprised me. I was in shock. I was just a lad. It was . . . horrific. I've regretted it every day since. I asked her, 'What about me? They'll find him eventually and come after me?' But she didn't seem to care nothing. Just shrugged. Said I was young enough to deal with it. Bloody old hag, she was. Before it happened, I didn't mind her, but afterwards . . . "

"Would your grandmother have cut the cocaine? You know, made it go a little farther, more profit for her?"

Williams's eyes grew wide. "No, I don't think so. But then, what would I know? I was just her wet-behind-the-ears grandson. And I wish it had remained that way."

"Did you see a gun in the room when you were there . . . mixing?"

"A gun? No, nothing like that. I'd have remembered."

"What about a red suitcase?"

Williams screwed up his eyes as he cast his mind back. "Er, yeah, maybe. But Nannie Em dealt with all that. I was just the mug who had to bury the body. Nothing more, nothing less. That was enough."

Graham sat back in his chair and leant his elbow on the arm, thumb under his chin and his forefinger laying on his cheekbone as he regarded the man, only seventeen when this crime was committed but now nearly sixty.

"Mr. Williams, I am sure you'll understand that, while perhaps coerced into this action and only a minor at the time, you have kept this knowledge to yourself for over forty years. That's forty years during which the family of this man has had no idea what happened to him, causing trauma to them. And"—Graham's mind drifted to Mrs. Taylor—"to others who have been affected by the discovery of his body and the knowledge that it lay there as they lived their lives." Williams stared at the floor and nodded.

"As such, it is required that we arrest you in connection with charges that relate to preventing the decent burial of a corpse, disposal of a corpse with intent to obstruct or prevent a coroner's inquest, and the perversion of the course of justice. There may be further charges to follow. Do you understand?" Williams continued to stare at the floor. Again, he nodded.

"Constable Barnwell, would you please . . ."

Barnwell stood and, putting a hand around Williams's arm, lifted him to standing. Williams offered him his wrists, and as Barnwell read him his rights, he locked the handcuffs around them.

"The local police will take you to the station and we'll liaise with them in connection with your case. It will be the local court's decision whether to let you out on bail or place you on remand."

Williams fixed his eyes on the floor before raising them. "I want you to know, I gave him a decent burial . . . in the circumstances. Said a little prayer, I did. And I laid a rose across his chest. It wasn't much—the rose had wilted—but it seemed the right thing to do."

As they left the house an hour later, Barnwell closed the front door behind them quietly. "Poor lad. Getting caught up in that when you're only seventeen."

"He had forty-two years to confess," Graham replied. "He didn't, and now he's reaping what he sowed."

Barnwell straightened his uniform jacket. "Yep, you're right, sir. Should've taken his medicine long ago. Wouldn't have been nearly as nasty."

"No, and if he had, this wouldn't have been our case to clear up. It would have been someone else's. As it is, we've still got a long way to go. Miss Lovell didn't adulterate that cocaine with rat poison. A supplier would know it would kill and their business would go poof. Also, there were no other deaths at that time that would suggest a bad batch. No, that rat poison was placed in Mr. X's cocaine deliberately. Someone wanted to kill him, specifically him."

"But who?"

"Who indeed, Barnwell. Who indeed."

CHAPTER THIRTY-THREE

LAURA BUSIED HERSELF making sure the research desk was in good order before the lecture finished. In a few minutes, thirty-five or so enthusiastic and newly informed amateur genealogists would be hungry for resources. Her role would be to guide them to the icon on the library website for the digitised parish records and then answer questions about a hundred different other things. With the lecture wrapping up, she was pressed for time.

Freddie Solomon hovered. He would take the number of questions she had to answer to a hundred and one. Or a hundred and twenty-five. There was no telling with Freddie.

So far that afternoon, he'd asked her all manner of random questions—about the library's *whole* range of programs, planned renovations to the annexe, meeting room bookings—everything *except* about the case of the unfortunate Mr. X, in which she suspected he was mostly interested.

"There's no point dancing around, Freddie."

"Aww," he complained, "that's a shame. You're quite the dancer. I've been watching you."

It was a tactic of Freddie's that Laura knew well: keep her talking until she either inadvertently revealed something or lost her patience and told him to clear off. "Please, Freddie. I'm about to get slammed. What do you want?"

"Any news on the White House Inn mob case?"

"Crikey, if David hears you calling it that, he'll slap the cuffs on you again."

"I'm a member," Freddie proudly reminded her, "of the Fourth Estate."

"Yes, well," Laura replied, stepping away as the lecture crowd streamed through from the annexe. "The way David is with these things, I wouldn't be surprised if he's already burned down the first three. So, you'll be next whether you like it or not." Laura continued forward and headed off the genealogists at the pass. She sent one group to the computers and the other to a suite of desks flanked by shelves and displays: the library's new Local History Resources Section.

Once the chaos was reduced to a simmer, Freddie sidled over again. "I'm going to sound like a broken record . . ."

"My grandmother recommended fixing electrical things by giving them a stout slap," Laura said with relish. "If you get stuck, I can perhaps help you out by following her advice."

"These guys did all kinds of things back then, Laura. You know it and I know it."

"Stop inferring." Her eyes still on her patrons, Laura scowled. "You have no idea what I know. We're past the time when men get to speak for women, Freddie."

"I mean you're from that part of the East End," he said.

"I'm from Kent, not Albert Square. I only worked in the

East End peripherally and only for a very short time. It just happened to be a momentous one. Thanks, probably, to my friendly and reliable manner that causes people to trust me sometimes"—Laura leaned in close to Freddie and opened her eyes wide—"*prematurely.*" Laura had ended up on Jersey having entered a witness protection scheme after overhearing details of a diamond heist while working in a pub.

Characteristically, Freddie didn't respond to her corrections of his assertions. To do so would be to admit that he had been wrong. He simply acted as though he hadn't heard her. "These guys, the ones in HMP Holbrooke that I've interviewed, they *used* people to take down the competition and punish snitches, and yet they've gone down for precisely a single armed robbery apiece despite a career spanning *decades.*"

"So? They're in jail, Freddie. And they're in their seventies, aren't they?"

"Seventy-nine," he said. "If we could get another conviction, that would bring closure for somebody, surely." Laura ignored his use of the word "we."

"And plenty of new readers for you." Laura turned away.

"My blog is both a thriving business and service to the public," Freddie said, apparently unaware of how puffed up and ridiculous he sounded.

"I'm quite sure." Laura coughed. "But consider this. Even if you uncover a hidden truth and deliver some 'just desserts' that'll satisfy your readership, how much would the extra life sentence matter?"

Freddie raised his voice just enough to press home the point. "Justice. I believe in punishing criminals."

Laura sighed. "Look, what is it that you *want*, Freddie?"

194 ALISON GOLDEN & GRACE DAGNALL

"I want to help in the Mr. X case!"

"And what is it that you want from *me*? Because I'm sure you're not here to admire my latest 'New Books' display."

Freddie shifted from one foot to another. "I thought maybe you had some intel you could toss my way. Or . . ."

"Or?"

"Or you know someone who might." Laura had had more than enough of Freddie for one day. She turned away again. "I thought you believed in justice!" Freddie hissed, mindful of the library's rule on silence.

"I believe," Laura said, heading away, "in providing high-quality local library services. Toodle-pip."

Thwarted in his mission, Freddie didn't leave at once. He continued his systematic search of the Channel Islands press, but as usual, there wasn't any mention of the incidents he was chasing up and nothing that pertained to the identity of Mr. X. "Officialdom, pressurising the media," he muttered, "forcing self-censorship to spare an inevitable panic. That's what this is."

There was nothing for it. He had to return to his source —happily, a pair of sources—who had so far helped him outline his book. *Murderer's Island* (working title) would be a gritty and exciting narrative, his first entry in the true-crime genre.

But it would only work if the two men, Arthur and George Parnaby, a pair of former gangsters who Freddie had befriended, would speak freely. They'd both spent twenty-five years in prison and, for one of them, justice had already come knocking. He was terminal. Freddie hoped that death for one and grief for the other might spare the pair for another few weeks. Just until he could apply for another HMP Holbrooke visitor's pass.

CHAPTER THIRTY-FOUR

"WOW," FIONA EXCLAIMED, lifting off her ear protection. "This thing is a *monster.*"

"Even underwater apparently," said Tomlinson. "Let's be grateful it wasn't a high-speed weapon."

"Why's that?"

"The water tank can only slow down a bullet so much. If it starts out too quickly, it'll make it all the way through the glass . . ."

"And ruin the experiment," concluded Fiona.

"And flood the place. And I remember asking for *two* rounds, young lady." Tomlinson peered into the water tank as the waves slowed their sloshing. "But if I can still count, and I believe those capacities are still in place despite my advanced years, that was six."

"Got carried away," Fiona said with a rueful grin, releasing the Smith & Wesson from its mount by the tank and setting it on the table.

"Easily done, I suppose. It's not every day you get to fire one of these." Tomlinson bent over, his hands on his knees.

He regarded the firearm suspiciously. "Now we've got our impressions, what does Detective Inspector Graham want done with this fiendish thing?"

"He said to store it in the new 'Ancient Arms Room,' wherever that is." Fiona bagged up the weapon and the pair stepped into the hallway.

"One level down," the on-duty firearms sergeant said, looking up from his screen. "You, er, you like guns, then?" he asked Fiona.

"Ooh, yes. Not in a weird way though," she added quickly.

Tomlinson followed Fiona from the ballistics room, past several other labs and a small open-plan IT hub until they reached a keypad that opened one door, and then another. They eventually arrived at an electronic, heavy metal slider that was operated by a guard once they showed him their passes. Entering a white-painted room, the walls lined with shelving, they glanced around. It would have been a routine storage space except the shelves were crammed with guns.

"Stone the crows!" Tomlinson exclaimed.

"Or," Fiona replied, looking at the vast arsenal, "we could just shoot them." She grinned. Tomlinson rolled his eyes.

"Clever. Half of this stuff is from the Jerries by the looks of it. That's an old MG forty-two." Tomlinson pointed to a machine gun standing on a bipod. "Bloody *lethal*, they were."

"I didn't know you were into that sort of thing." Fiona was toying with a handgun so ancient it was partly rusted. "Perhaps I should have something like this back at the castle. To defend myself in case anyone tries to storm the battlements."

"How are you getting on out there? Not too eerie, is it?"

"Yes, it is. And I love it!"

"Ah. Bert was right then."

"How so?"

"He said you were a game girl, not easily frightened."

"That sounds about right. I like novel, exciting, strange." Fiona opened a velvet-lined drawer and peered at a short-barrelled pistol laying inside.

"That's a Sauer 38H you're looking at. Favourite of the German police during World War II."

"Looks posh." Fiona stared at the gun's ivory grip and gold inlay. There was an engraving on the side.

"They were sometimes presented to Nazi officials to commemorate things."

"You mean like tankards for long service, or gold watches?"

"Something like that. Ah-ha! I knew there'd be one in here." Tomlinson spied a black, stubby weapon and pulled it from the shelf. "Ever seen one of these?"

"Only in documentaries."

Marcus set the Sterling submachine gun on a table near the door. "Got your phone?" he asked her, clapping his hands and rubbing them together.

"Yeah, why?"

"Set the stopwatch."

"Okay, ready."

"Go!" The elderly physician's hands became a studied whir of motion. Pieces were coming off the gun, large and then smaller, until it was set out like a manufacturer's diagram: muzzle, barrel, magazine, stock, firing pin. "Finished!" he said, stepping back and standing neatly to attention. His hand twitched as he almost saluted.

Staring at the pieces as though Marcus had forged them

from thin air, Fiona finally said, "You know what? I work with the *strangest* bunch of people."

Marcus laughed and used his handkerchief to clean his hands of gun oil. "Army Medical Corps for three years in the seventies. When patients were few, the other doctors and I got competitive about the *silliest* things. Anyway," he said, a little bashful about his field-stripping ability, "let's find Mr. X's revolver a home."

It went into a padded drawer labelled and electronically tagged. "What do you think it means that Mr. X was carrying this gun?" Fiona wondered as they headed out.

"Could be all manner of things," Tomlinson said. "Difficult to speculate."

"I mean, it could punch a bullet through a brick wall. You could stop an elephant with it. How often are charging bull elephants a genuine risk to the average person?"

"Not often, that's for sure. Let's find out where it's been, shall we?"

The ballistics discovery process, courtesy of the National Ballistics Intelligence Service in Birmingham, was almost entirely digital, but on this occasion, the test's findings required another quick phone call to Miranda Weiss. "The striations are a perfect match. The incident was in the late seventies," she informed Tomlinson.

"What kind of incident was it?" Dr. Weiss hadn't referred to a murder or even a crime.

"Best I can tell, some lunatic got trigger-happy outside a pub and shot up his mate's car."

"Heroic."

"I see you sent six images," Miranda said as she finished

downloading the high-definition scans showing microscopic analyses of the bullets. "Did your assistant get trigger-happy too?"

"Something like that. She's new and prone to the odd moment of giddiness."

"Well, tell her never to get giddy around firearms again. And," Miranda added, her tone softening, "that she's welcome to come to Southampton anytime. I've got a pile of stuff waiting to be analysed, and my best technician went into labour two weeks early."

"If Jersey can spare her and we don't find another collection of weird evidence in someone's attic, I dare say she'll accept," Tomlinson said, winking at Fiona next to him. "Will you let her play with the new UV setup, the one with the—"

"View that integrates three wavelengths at once? Maybe, if she's good." When combined, the separate feeds— visible, infrared, and ultraviolet light—revealed *everything*.

"Is it really like having X-ray vision?" Tomlinson said.

"Yes, and half my incoming calls are about borrowing it. I wrote a nineteen-thousand-word proposal to get that thing, Marcus, and it's *mine. All mine.*"

"What kind of evidence would someone need to get some time on it?"

Dr. Weiss thought for a second. "Jack the Ripper's underpants, still with the label on."

Marcus laughed as he brought the call to a close. "I'll see what I can do."

Fiona continued to puzzle over photographs of the gun. "What can we deduce from this?"

"Difficult to speculate. But if he was planning to deprive another human of life, he must have been danger-ous. Dangerous people aren't always the smartest. They do stupid things, like carrying a gun already known to the police."

"A galumphing, great *big* gun already known to the police."

"The heavier it is, the less likely that he was an accomplished hit. Pros like them small, fierce, quiet, and efficient."

"I see what you're saying. If our guy was here to target someone, he was setting himself up for difficulty, if not failure. Not being very bright. Suggests inexperience."

Tomlinson turned to Fiona, her eager face full of intelligence and curiosity, her eyes alight. "Exactly so. But perhaps he was here on a suicide mission, literally. Perhaps the drugs and his heart got to him first. We don't know that he intended the bullets for someone else. Maybe he decided to do away with himself on a beach overlooking the ocean." Tomlinson's phone pinged. The DNA results were in. Marcus handed Fiona a mug. "Would you be a dear and make me another cup of tea?"

When she had gone, he quickly switched to his computer screen to open the email. He scanned the report, his temperature rising. Picking up his phone, he sent a text.

Ballistics and more. Interesting.

Over a hundred miles away, Barnwell was driving to Poole where he and Inspector Graham would catch the ferry back to Jersey. His senior officer focused on his phone. Tired and puzzled after his interview with Neville Williams, Graham tapped the screen as he placed a call.

"Marcus? What have you got? Something good, I hope."

"The bullet striations show that the gun was used in 1978. Man in a car was shot at."

"Got the C/N?"

"Yep, 15635897."

"Great. I'm on my way to catch the ferry back. Could you send the info to Sergeant Harding? She'll look it up. What was the other thing you had to tell me?"

"We got the DNA results from the hairbrush, but our man doesn't appear on any database." Graham scrunched up his nose and pursed his lips. "But there was a strong match with someone who does." Graham sat up a little taller. "Twenty-seven percent—with a certain Angela Dillon."

"Twenty-seven percent? What does that mean?"

"My guess would be a cousin, aunt, maybe a half sister."

"Hmm."

"Fiona told me she could reconstruct our guy's face from the remains and some sorcery using artificial intelligence jiggery-pokery. Would you like her to do that? It wouldn't be perfect, but it could help. It would provide you with a picture of what Mr. X might have looked like when he died."

"Brilliant. That would help a lot. Send everything to the station. I'll take it from there."

"It's simply amazing what they can do these days. If we had a photo of him, she could manipulate it so that we could see what he looked like at any age, she said."

"Well, let's hope we find out who he is soon. Good work, Marcus. Thanks a bunch. And thank Fiona too."

"Angela Margaret Dillon, date of birth March sixth, 1968. Wandsworth. String of arrests for prostitution starting in 1983, last one 2013," Janice told Graham over the phone.

"Long career. Where can we find her?"

"Her last known address was 43 Walking Topham, Leeslake." Graham looked it up.

"Are you sure?" he said, frowning.

"That's what it says. Posh, isn't it?"

"I'll say. What was her last arrest for?"

"Soliciting."

"Nothing about keeping a brothel or anything more lucrative?"

"Nope."

"Okay, see what else you can find out about her. We may need to pay her a visit too. What about the gun?"

"Ah, yes. 1976, Clapham. Tiff between two small-time gangsters. The suspect was Arthur Parnaby. At the time he was known for piddly stuff—laundering, a bit of dealing—but seems to have escalated: protection with menaces, violent assault. Currently well into a twenty-eight-year stretch with his twin brother. They're in HMP Holbrooke for armed robbery."

"Holbrooke?"

"That's right, sir. Security guard killed. No charges were ever brought in connection with the earlier gun incident and no further record of the gun until it turned up in Mrs. Taylor's attic."

Graham squeezed his eyes tight shut as fragments of a memory swooped around his brain, gathering force and substance. Freddie. He mentioned having sources in HMP Holbrooke.

CHAPTER THIRTY-FIVE

The Gorey Gossip
Monday Evening Edition

You already know what some say about me:
I'm an irritant, a fly in the constabulary's ointment, a man the police could
never trust. I get emails calling me a
"crank," a "conspiracy theorist," and a
"dull, unenterprising wordsmith." (Of the
three, only the last stings.) Detective
Inspector Graham and his team dismiss me,
most recently as a "thoughtless little
weasel."

But I know a thing or two about right
and wrong. A man died in his room at the
White House Inn on the evening of Sunday
14th February 1982. His body was not
disclosed and left to lie undiscovered for
over forty years until it was recently

unearthed in a roughly hewn concrete tomb. That is wrong.

But here's what is true: Jersey is neither as safe as we hope, nor as it could be. I'm certain that a sequence of mob entanglements has marked the last several decades of our island's history.

It stands to reason, given his inauspicious burial, that the man at the White House Inn did not die from natural causes. And after speaking with my sources deep inside the dangerous world of London's organised crime, I'm certain I'm right to doubt the Gorey police investigation. Given what I know, DI Graham's work so far has been slow and incomplete. Simply put, they are going in the wrong direction.

Because the past has chosen to present itself and because our law enforcement appears to be going down blind alleys, I am compelled to speak out. I am not party to the intimate findings of the investigation, and my suspicions are speculative, but they are grounded in intel gained from insider sources and combined with a good dose of common sense.

I suspect that the dead man was the target of a diabolical, premeditated murder. I believe it is likely that he was on Jersey for nefarious reasons. And that the gun in his suitcase was either to perform a hit or to protect himself as he completed whatever job he was here to perform. I also suspect his death is maybe the tip of an evidentiary iceberg. Are there, in fact, other shoes still to drop?

I hope I'm wrong, but everything so far—including years of reporting on Jersey's criminal community—is telling me that I'm right.

CHAPTER THIRTY-SIX

"WHEN I SAY *immediately*, Freddie, I don't mean whenever it suits you." Detective Inspector Graham was standing in reception when the blogger finally arrived. Graham's plan had been to close out the day and go home, but Freddie's blog post had compelled an explanation. He had been summoned to the station.

"And I don't recall being a member of the constabulary," Freddie shot back, "so I don't have to follow your orders."

"Doing anything *other* than that," Graham argued, "would be considered impeding my duties. Or is that your intention?"

"*Impeding* your . . .? You work for me, remember?"

"The longer a murder remains unsolved, the more you can write about it in your ridiculous blog. More sensational articles mean more revenue from your advertisers—"

Freddie interrupted the inspector. "They're called commercial partners these days."

"All of whom need their heads examined, if you ask me. I'd sooner partner up with half the cons in Strangeways than with you. So, investigative delays serve your purposes quite well, don't they?"

"What delays?" Freddie demanded.

"I could be working on the case, but I'm here, having to yell at you for imperilling my investigation. *Again.*"

"I haven't *imperilled* anything," Freddie insisted passionately. "I'm a private citizen running a successful and legitimate business. A member of the Fourth Estate."

"So you keep saying. I'm going to give you one final chance." The redness in Graham's cheeks receded gradually. "Retract your latest article and issue an apology." Remembering Laura's advice for situations with Freddie— and with everyone else, for that matter—he attempted an incentive. "It won't take a minute. I'll even put some tea on. You can use our Wi-Fi."

"No," Freddie said simply, like a child.

"You're certain?"

"Certain." The two men glared at one another, Freddie doing a creditable job of attempting to intimidate a man six inches taller than him. Thrusting his chin out, he defiantly held eye contact with the inspector. After five seconds, Graham blinked.

"Very well, Freddie. Constable?"

"Boss?"

"Would Mr. Solomon be more miserable in cell one with the air vent that perpetually rattles, or in cell two with that cold draft we can't pin down?"

"Weatherman said it's going to be a chilly night."

"Then get cell two ready, there's a good chap."

Freddie's panicked expression said it all. "You're *not* going to . . ."

"Yes, I am," said Graham. Barnwell jangled his keys and whistled contentedly; he had a new customer.

"Can I speak to Laura first?" Freddie asked brazenly.

Graham stood, his temper fast approaching a red line. "You can speak to a *lawyer* once you're charged."

Freddie sat stock-still. "I'm not retracting, and I'm not apologising."

Graham rubbed his hands together. "Glad to hear it. Now hear this. Frederick Solomon, I'm arresting you on suspicion of perverting the course of justice and for obstructing an officer in the course of his duties. You do not have to say anything unless you wish to do so, but it may harm your defence if you fail to mention something you later rely on in court."

"Are you *serious*?" Freddie followed this up with a highly colourful oath.

"Those cells have got *bars* on them. Isn't that right, Constable Barnwell?"

"Yep! Big, strong, steel ones, sir."

"Sounds serious to me," Graham said. He looked at his prisoner. "Come on, let's take a look at your accommodations for the next day or two."

"But I was being helpful!" Freddie complained, pressed forward by Barnwell's uncompromising knuckles against the knobbles of his spine. "I'm starting to crack the puzzle."

"You're the one who's cracked."

"And if those old guys in HMP Holbrooke open up to me some more, I'll know everything! I might even be able to help you iden—" Freddie tripped over his own feet.

"Mind your step," Graham said. "We don't want any loony theories propagating about how you nearly died in police custody."

"I want to talk to Laura!" Freddie begged fruitlessly.

"No."

"You talk to her then. She'll tell you that I was being helpful!"

"You're being a massive pain, and I'm dealing with enough of those already." With Barnwell ceremoniously holding open the cell door, Graham urged Freddie inside, then shut it with a convincing *clang*.

"Go to Hull!" Freddie cried through the door.

Graham opened the small, eye-level hatch in the cell door. "Same to you. Didn't your mother teach you any manners?"

"Hull, I said! H-U-L-L. Go to HMP Holbrooke. It's near Hull. You know, the big prison there?"

"Know it? I practically populated it to overflowing." Graham smiled through the grill, proud of his record. "I was instrumental in creating a thriving and diverse community at HMP Holbrooke."

"Really?" Freddie said, taken aback. Had he a major source of information on his doorstep this whole time?

"Yeah, it wasn't difficult. I just arrested, charged, and got convictions on a whole range of dodgy people who lived life in the fast lane. Anyhow, I'll be leaving you now. I do hope you enjoy your stay with us." Graham's face in the small slot disappeared, only to be replaced by that of Constable Barnwell.

"Would you like microwave lasagna or microwave butter chicken for dinner?" Barnwell asked him.

Freddie muttered something Barnwell pretended not to hear. "I think you should have something. It's gonna be a long time 'til breakfast."

"Butter chicken." Freddie was sullen.

"I'll be back in a bit. Don't have too much fun in there."

"George and Arthur Parnaby. Talk to them!" Barnwell closed the hatch just in time to see Freddie throw himself on the cell bench and sling his arm across his eyes like a grounded teenager.

His plaintive cries followed them up the stairs, but Barnwell and Graham exchanged smiles and carried on. They were freed for now from the pestilence of amateur news media. The only downside, the one that Graham was attempting to push from his mind, was that Laura wouldn't like what he had done one little bit.

CHAPTER THIRTY-SEVEN

EXHAUSTED AFTER HIS long day, Graham did his best to sneak in quietly, but removing his coat, setting down his briefcase, and levering off one of his shoes made enough noise to wake Laura and then some. She appeared at the top of the stairs. "Are you a burglar?" she asked, shining her phone at him, "or an overzealous policeman?"

"My zeal is legendary," he replied. "And yes, I am returned from the bounteous evidence buffet that was Bournemouth via a small detour to the station on my way back."

"It went well, then."

Graham nearly fell over trying to get his second shoe off. "Better than expected in some ways. Not so great in others. We're no closer to catching our murderer, but it was useful in ascertaining how our Mr. X came to be buried in Mrs. Taylor's attic."

"You still don't know his full name?"

"Nope, still stuck on that. I would have been home earlier but for your friend and mine, Mr. Freddie Solomon."

Laura turned off the light on her phone. "I saw his post."

It came out quickly; Graham's fatigue loosened his tongue. "He's interfered in police business for the last time."

"What do you mean?" Laura said as Graham slowly climbed the stairs. She didn't budge from her position at the top of them. "For the last time?"

"There are proper channels for submitting information about active or even closed cases. His blog is not the place for it. Still, he chooses again and again to press the 'publish' button."

"He has a large readership now, including outside the Channel Islands . . ."

"That makes things even worse. No one's *forcing* him to reveal sensitive information, love. He chooses to print salacious titbits that compromise our work and rubbish us in the process. It's a one-two punch, one he insists on consistently delivering. I've had enough. Someone has to hold him accountable. I've arrested him and thrown him in a cell for the night while he thinks about his actions."

Laura frowned, her hands on her hips as she stood defiant, sternly guarding the stairway. Only the moon-and-clouds night lamp on her landing dresser provided any light, and she appeared ghostly.

"What have you done?" she said. "What about the freedom of the press?"

Two steps short of Laura's guard post, Graham stopped. "If you'd been there, you'd have seen I had no choice. I don't like the idea of locking up journalists any more than you do."

"Good to hear you're not turning into a dictator." Laura stood her ground, barely contained fury radiating from her.

"Look." Graham wearily set his shoes down on the

stairs. "Say for a minute that we'd found solid DNA evidence connected to Mr. X's death—someone who's alive and known to us. If we arrested and charged them, I wouldn't be able to find a single juror who . . ." His words faded in the face of Laura's unyielding but quiet, fierce rage.

"Reach for the black grip underneath," she said, "to pull out the sofa bed."

"Laura, please. That's not very reasonable."

"You denied him his freedom, so now you get denied too. In your case, a comfy bed."

"Look, all I want is a shower and a good night's sleep." Wordlessly but firmly, Laura pointed back the way he had come. "I've only put Freddie Solomon in a nice, warm holding cell for the night. That's all. I should have done it ages ago. I didn't lock him in with anyone who'd beat his lights out. By breakfast, he'll be playing chess with Barnwell, you'll see."

"You forced Barnwell to suffer the consequences of your foolhardy decision?" Laura had the temerity to wag her finger at him. She folded her arms tightly, unimpressed. "You should have talked to me first."

"That's what Freddie said."

"Well, he was right! And he'll be right to publish an excoriating piece about Gorey Constabulary as soon as he gets out. I mean, he'll hang you out to dry, won't he? Investigative overreach, suppression of the media . . ."

"I'm not the KGB, for heaven's sake."

"What do you think the national press will make of it?"

Alarmingly, amidst this crowded, complex case, Graham had entirely forgotten to consider the wider impact of the arrest. "Ah."

"After your brilliant years here, that'll be all you're

remembered for: the policeman who lost his mind and started jailing journalists."

"He's only a bl . . ." Graham began but wisely killed the thought. Freddie had already established his credentials with Laura and the community. They didn't amount to anything as far as he was concerned, but that's not how others perceived him. Standing there on the step, feeling like he'd just run a marathon in the wrong direction, Graham sighed.

Only slightly softer, Laura said, "Go and let him out."

"Tomorrow," he offered. He looked at his watch. It was past one o'clock. "Today." He was exhausted.

"*Now*, please," Laura insisted, her tone's bite growing. "He needs to be rested so he can cover Janice's wedding at the weekend, for one thing. And not be threatening a punch-up with you across the aisle while he's at it for another."

"Alright. I'll call Barnwell and . . ."

"You'll go yourself. I won't have you outsourcing the job of solving your self-made problems to your subordinates."

"He's at the station anyway. He has to keep an eye on Freddie."

"Show some leadership and conviction for your decisions. Go."

"It's raining," Graham complained. Twenty hours awake, two ferry journeys, and multiple long drives had dulled him almost to insensibility.

"Just one of the many hassles that could have easily been avoided by talking to me *before* you made a silly decision," Laura said, tall and mighty on the top step.

Graham sighed again loudly. "Okay."

"And an apology to Freddie would be nice too," she said

as he slowly turned to go. "But it doesn't have to be in writing."

Graham took two steps down the stairs. "Is the condemned man afforded a last meal before dying of ritual humiliation at Freddie Solomon's feet?"

"No, he is not." Laura wouldn't even let him change his clothes until the wrong was righted.

Allowing his subconscious to handle the seven-minute drive to the police station, Graham worked to set aside his weary frustration with Freddie. But all too soon, he was interrupted by the nagging necessity of apologising to the man. Unprepared, he chose to wing it and keep it short.

"You're a contagious little sewer rat," Graham said to him, accompanying Barnwell as he opened the door to Freddie's cell. Graham handed the blogger his satchel. "And a continuing threat to my work. That said, I defend wholeheartedly your right to publish your opinion, provided you label it as such—an opinion."

"I'm not labelling anything," Freddie said boldly. He was surprisingly bolshie for someone woken from a slumber in the early hours, having fallen asleep on top of a plastic moulded shelf.

"And any established facts . . ."

"We might differ on what constitutes a 'fact.'"

" . . . that you publish must do nothing to prejudice any ongoing police investigations." Graham stopped and appeared to consider throwing Freddie back in the cell before continuing. "No more, Freddie, alright? I mean it. No interference, and no speculation when it comes to ongoing cases. Capiche?"

Instead of the crisp obedience Graham so obviously wished for, Freddie put down his satchel and rubbed his tired eyes.

"Think about it, Freddie. You're attending the wedding on Saturday. How will it look if you've just published a hit piece against the bride's boss and her constabulary?"

But Freddie was done with voicing his objections. "I want to thank you for reconsidering and for coming out so late." He checked inside his satchel to make sure everything was there—laptop, charger, phone, notebook, wallet—then hoisted it onto his shoulder and made for the door. "I have all that I need," he said rather cryptically, shaking hands with the bemused Graham. "Goodnight, Detective Inspector."

After Freddie left, Graham turned to Barnwell. "You go home too. I'm going to stay here to think through a few things."

"Are you sure, sir? Janice has Carmen, and I've still got to type up the statement from Neville Williams. Do you want me to keep you company?"

"Good lord, no. You can write that statement up tomorrow. Go and get some rest. We'll reconvene in the morning. Off you go."

Graham popped the kettle on and went to the kitchen for a cup and saucer. It was part of Barnwell's nightly duties to clean up, and he had left the washing up on the draining board to dry.

As he walked back to his office, Graham heard the kettle click off. The water had reached boiling point. The inspector idly wished he could do likewise. He, too, had reached his limit. He would like to turn himself off.

The Mr. X case with its interminable logic, its gaping holes, and its vintage nature was vexing. The complication that was Freddie Solomon was an unwanted bonus. Attempting to solve the case was akin to fixing some knitting that had gone haywire rows earlier without a pattern and the wrong size needles. They still did not have an identity for the victim!

Graham warmed his pot and spooned some organic yuzu tea leaves into it. They resembled dried grass cuttings but smelled divine—fresh, citrus, sharp. He hoped the tea would revive him. He brought the pot and the cup and saucer to his desk and sat down, setting an alarm on his phone for three minutes.

While he waited for the tea to steep, he sat back in his chair and stared at the ceiling, running through the interview with Neville Williams from earlier that day—correction, yesterday. It was Graham's view that Williams had been a young lad put in an impossible position by an older, malignant relative, one who had abused and exploited him. By enlisting Williams in a process to avoid the ruin of her own life, Emily Lovell proceeded to ruin the rest of his.

Graham shook his head. His mind ran to Laura and her displeasure. She was right. He had been petty, small-minded, and driven by his emotions. His normally sound judgment had left him, and he risked dragging his reputation and, inexcusably, that of his officers, through the crowded harbour of Freddie's complacency.

A ripple of gentle, tinkling notes massaged his inner ear, rousing him from his thoughts. He gripped his teapot and watched as the steaming, dark, honey-brown liquid plunged in a perfect arc into his china cup, tumbling and swirling before settling into a glassy calm. He would drink his tea black.

Desultorily, Graham picked up his phone and checked the home screen. There was nothing new—no texts or email updates. He tossed the phone gently onto his desk and raised his teacup.

Holding it to his face, the steaming tea tickled the fine hairs under Graham's nose. He inhaled, and hints of citrus —lemon, mandarin, possibly grapefruit—assailed his nostrils, captivating him. He closed his eyes and breathed in some more. This was what he so loved about tea, its restorative properties.

As the tea did its work, thoughts began to form. The uptick in transport between his synapses was marked. Abandoning his tea momentarily, Graham opened his computer and logged in. Inputting "Holbrooke" into the police database, he scanned lists of names before switching and logging into the Gorey charge sheets.

He picked up his phone again and checked the time, pursing his lips before coming to a decision. He dialled a number on the screen. The recipient answered immediately.

"Freddie? It's Graham. Let's talk."

CHAPTER THIRTY-EIGHT

"AY, AY, BAZZ. How're you doing?" Janice sped past Barnwell. She was carrying a cardboard tray laden with two coffees. "A decaf almond milk latte for you," she said, placing the cup on his desk. "And an iced caramel macchiato for me."

"Isn't that basically a bag of sugar mixed with cream and caffeine? Stress eating again, are we? I thought you'd had a 'reset.'"

"It's true. But that, Constable Barnwell, was before my mother woke me at five thirty a.m."

"What's she on about now?"

"I can barely remember. But let's just say a girl needs the occasional break. And a bag of sugar mixed with cream and caffeine is *just* what I need."

"That bad, eh? Nothing for the boss?"

"No, I didn't think he'd be in."

"He's not been out!"

"Huh?"

"He arrested Freddie when we got back from Bournemouth and threw him in a cell for the night. I'm guessing Laura gave him an earful because he came back almost immediately and let him go."

"What did he arrest him for?"

"What d'you think? Interfering with an investigation. Put some blog post up that got the boss's goat."

"Nothing new, then."

"Anyhow, I came in this morning, and he was still here! Fast asleep with his head on his desk."

"Do you think Laura threw him out? She likes Freddie. Well, perhaps not *likes* him exactly, but she sticks up for him."

"Dunno, but when he woke up, he was out of sorts. He looked terrible. He asked *me* to make him a cup of tea!"

Janice took a sip of her coffee. It was syrupy, succulent, sublime. "And did you? Make him tea?"

"Course I did, but none of that fancy-pants rubbish you and he drink. Straight up Tetley's, milk, and two sugars. Lovely jubbly."

"He doesn't take sugar. Not anymore anyway. Gave it up when he moved in with Laura."

"Doesn't he? He didn't say anything, and he drank it all up. Looked a lot better after it 'n' all. Set you up for anything, one of my cuppas will."

"Put hairs on yer chest, will it?"

"That it will."

"So where is he now? Has he gone home?" Janice giggled. Her mother had driven her almost to madness in the last twenty-four hours. Anything not associated with Rosemary Harding sounded wildly hysterical to her.

Barnwell's eyes widened. Behind Janice's back, Detective Inspector Graham appeared in the office area, wiping water from his face with a towel. "No, he hasn't. But he is focused and ready to work. I hope you are too, Constable. We have a trip to prepare for."

"Another one?"

"Yep, your turn again. I'm sure Sergeant Harding is tied up with last-minute wedding plans. Flowers, hymns, that kind of thing." Barnwell glanced at Janice worriedly and waited for her response. He had a feeling she wouldn't agree, despite Graham's good intentions.

"Oh, it's no trouble, sir. I'm happy to accompany you. Barnwell has only just come back from a visit and I'm sure he'd like a break. And Carmen missed him when he was gone."

"But don't you have things to do? I thought you'd appreciate staying put with just a couple of days to go."

Janice beamed, her smile unnaturally wide. "No, no. Everything's taken care of. And Jack can step in if there's a last-minute problem. He's very capable and fully involved, so he knows what's what."

"But your mother's—"

"Yes! Yes, I know. But she'll be fine by herself for a day. She's a grown-up. As am I, sir." Janice held eye contact with Graham fractionally longer than was necessary.

Graham hesitated. Barnwell stepped in. "I think you should let her go, sir. It's only fair. You know, *equal opportunities*." Barnwell's eyes widened. Graham raised his chin and lowered his eyebrows.

"Ah yes, alright. If you insist. It'll be a long day, Sergeant. Two interviews interspersed by a long drive, bookended by flights to the mainland."

"Perfect, sir. When do we leave?"

CHAPTER THIRTY-NINE

J ANICE DROVE THROUGH the narrow country lanes, tall grasses and hedgerows on either side obscuring her view on tight bends. "Phew, I'd forgotten these lanes were barely wide enough for half a car."

"Worse than Jersey, eh?" Graham replied.

"I'll say."

Graham looked at his phone. "We're nearly there."

"I've never been to this part of the world. Too upmarket for the likes of me. The villages are tiny, barely a few cottages and a shop."

"And a pub."

"Of course, always a pub."

"In fact, these villages are made up of enormous houses at the end of very long drives obscured by ancient trees. You just can't see them."

"You must need a pretty penny to buy one."

"Definitely. This is stockbroker belt. Quite a number of them here."

"Along with a few lords and ladies, the odd celebrity."

"Probably. An oligarch or two as well, I shouldn't wonder."

"A heaven for thieves."

"Occasionally, I'm sure. But these people hire private security. And dogs. Lots of dogs. And you know how the thieving fraternity like them." Graham looked at his phone again. "Turn right here."

Janice drove onto a tiny single-track road and followed it deep into woodland, eventually reaching a gate. Just as Graham had forecast, a man with a dog approached. "Here we go, sir." Janice let down her window and showed her police ID. Graham leaned over and held up his. The man with the dog leaned in and scrutinised them.

"Hang on a minute," he said, holding up a finger. He walked away and put a phone to his ear.

"He's calling ahead. Should we stop him?"

"No, this is a friendly visit. We're here to ask Angela Dillon if she has a missing relative, someone who disappeared forty years ago. If she's going to spend a minute hiding how she's gone from street prostitution to billionaire island in a remarkably short period, we don't need to know about it." The gate opened, and the guard waved them through.

At the top of the drive stood a huge, Georgian, red-brick house draped with purple wisteria. Janice looked up at the skylights as she climbed out of the car. "I always wanted a bedroom up in the roof with a window like that. Like something out of the books I read as a girl. A place where you could get away . . ."

"From your mother?"

"Exactly." Janice pressed the bell. The door opened to reveal a butler dressed in traditional black and whites. "We're here to see Ms. Angela Dillon," Janice said. She and

Graham held up their IDs again. The butler glanced at them and, obviously prepared for their visit, stood back to let them in.

"Please follow me." He led them to a sitting room. "Ms. Dillon will be with you shortly."

Janice regarded the room around her, the sage green walls lined with Georgian portraiture. "Am I in a stately home? These carpets are so squishy and thick, they're like trampolines. I can bounce."

"It's the padding underneath that gives you that. But these are undoubtedly high quality." Graham pressed the balls of his feet into the wool pile. A noise behind them interrupted their conversation and in walked Angela Dillon. Immediately Graham revised his estimation of her. Unrealistically, he had been expecting someone younger, a woman whose demeanour and appearance reflected her tough life on the streets and in jail cells. But Ms. Dillon defied this expectation.

An elegant, attractive woman with thick, bobbed brunette hair appeared in a shiny blue, paisley-patterned wrap-over dress, cinched in at the waist by a gold chain belt. She wore no makeup except for red lipstick and mascara that framed eyes so blue they were almost purple. She wore mules, although Graham wouldn't have known they were called that. He knew they weren't slippers though and suspected that the delay at the gate had allowed Ms. Dillon time to upgrade her appearance for her visitors rather than for any dubious reason.

She smiled broadly at them and held out her hand. "Angela Dillon. Pleased to meet you. Won't you sit down?" She gestured at one of two sofas that sat facing each other, separated by a walnut coffee table. "Can I get you some tea?"

Graham, sensing he might be in for a treat, replied. "That would be lovely, thank you."

"Would Darjeeling suit? Assam?" This did suit Graham to no end.

"Darjeeling would be exquisite, thank you." Angela looked at Janice for her answer.

"Same, thanks." Angela pulled a bell rope in the corner of the room and immediately the butler appeared. After a quiet word with his employer, he disappeared again.

Graham and Janice sat on a grey sofa with languorous curves and studded arms. It wasn't terribly comfortable, but it kept them alert. Angela sat on the opposite sofa, which appeared only marginally more agreeable. She smiled at them.

"Now, how can I help you? It's been a long time since I last had a visit from the police." Angela seemed unperturbed by their visit and smiled at them disarmingly as she crossed her legs and clasped her hands around her knee.

"We're from Jersey, ma'am."

"Jersey? The Channel Islands?" Angela pursed her lips and twisted her head to the side before turning to face them again. "I've never been there. What does Jersey have to do with me?" The door opened, and a young woman entered with a tray of tea things. She placed it on the table and quietly left the room, just like the butler.

Angela released her knee and uncrossed her legs. She poured the tea gracefully and with a steady accuracy that perhaps only Graham appreciated. "Milk? Sugar?" Graham declined both, but Janice accepted some milk. Picking up the cup and saucer, Graham took a sip. The Darjeeling was the delight he had suspected it would be. Hot, humid, refreshing.

As he drank, Graham searched for the right words.

"We're investigating a case that dates back some forty years. We're wondering if someone related to you went missing around that time?"

The woman stared back at him without blinking before slowly placing her teacup and saucer on the coffee table and interlinking her hands in her lap. "Inspector Graham, I am estranged from many members of my family. Over time, several have disappeared, sometimes reappearing after not being in contact for decades. Others remain missing, their whereabouts or situations unknown. We are that kind of family. Chaotic, messy, dysfunctional. We breed profusely without regard for love, friendship, or even acquaintance beyond a few hours. And we scrap our way through life, living on our wits or the dole, having benefited from very few advantages and even fewer expectations." Graham pointedly glanced around him, but there was no forth-coming explanation for the opulence in which Angela Dillon lived. Instead, she simply said, "I have very little contact with anyone I'm related to."

"Very well. Perhaps I may show you a photograph. I'm sorry to tell you that we recently discovered some remains on Jersey. Testing showed that you share twenty-seven percent of your DNA with this man. This would mean he may be a half brother, a nephew, or a cousin—someone not immediately related to you but only one or two steps removed. We estimate the man to be in his mid-twenties. He died in February 1982. We have prepared an image of what he may have looked like at the time. And I would like to show that to you now."

Seemingly unmoved, Angela said, "Very well. You want me to tell you if I recognise him?"

"Yes, please." Graham slipped out the image that Fiona had prepared for him. Angela took it and sat for several moments, staring at it. She briefly put her finger to her top lip before handing the image back to Graham.

"That's my half brother, one of many I may add. We share a mother. I have no idea who his father is. I doubt he or my mother knew either. I haven't seen him in decades."

"And his name, Ms. Dillon?"

"Dylan. My mother's little joke, I suppose. Dylan Dillon. We called him Dilly." Angela reached for her teacup. "So, he's dead, is he?"

"You didn't wonder what happened to him?"

Angela's nose wrinkled, two short lines appearing on either side. "Can't say I did. I had my own problems, and as I said, family members come and go all the time. I assumed he'd gone abroad, Costa del Sol or somewhere. That was all the rage in the eighties for ne'er-do-wells."

"Would you happen to have a photo of him?" Janice asked.

"Of Dylan?" Angela raised her eyebrows as though the idea that she had a photo of her half brother was a strange one. "I don't think so." Pausing for a second, she continued. "No, no, I'm sure I haven't. It's all so long ago. A different time." She scanned the room—the expensive art, the antiques, the plush furnishings. "I have a different life now."

"He had a suitcase with him when he died. Do you know anything about that?" Graham handed her a photo of the tomato-red Tourister suitcase.

A small smile crossed her lips. "Well, well, well, so that's who took it. I wondered what happened to it. I loved that suitcase. I got it off a secondhand stall on the Portobello Road. It was cute. Vintage. I got in an argument with my boyfriend over it."

"How so?"

"Because when I went to write the Valentine's card I

got for him, I found the suitcase in which I'd stashed it was gone. You had to do things like that in my family. Anything worth anything to anyone else, even a stupid Valentine's card, would go missing if you didn't hide it. It was too late to get another, and I got dumped over it." Her face fell, the light on her features changing so that the contours of her cheekbones became apparent, aging her in a second. "I was heartbroken. It was the start of a very dark path for me."

CHAPTER FORTY

"**Y**OU'VE GOT TO hand it to the Victorians," Graham said as he and Janice walked up to HMP Holbrooke's visitor's entrance. "They could certainly build to *intimidate*." As functional as it was unlovely, the prison loomed dark and ominous, a hulking stone and steel warehouse for men who had fallen afoul of the law, often many times.

Janice had only experienced the more modern facilities in St. Helier. "It's like a fortress."

At the front desk—a large, glassed-off office that resembled border control in some European airports Janice had passed through on her holidays—they signed in and were handed passes to attach to their jackets before being shuffled on to the next stage of their journey by a warder assigned to them.

As they walked along the corridors of the prison, Janice calculated their speed to be slower than that of a car during London's rush hour. This was mostly due to the number of doors that required unlocking and relocking as they passed through. She found their passage along the empty, echoing halls thoroughly tedious, the experience depressing her further with every stop and start as they made their way deeper into the bowels of the building. Eventually, they reached the governor's office.

Mike Tenbeigh was in charge of this fortress. He certainly looked the part. His tall, military bearing towered over even Graham, and Janice suspected that his wide, bristling, and greying moustache had seen sights not always savoury or wholesome.

"How many prisoners have you got here?" she asked him.

"Around a thousand or so. Changes every day, of course," Tenbeigh replied. "We're not max-sec. Maximum security," he added in response to Janice's frown. "We mostly take prisoners on remand, but we have a few long-timers—old boys like the Parnabys—the ones with a bad rap but limited energy and impact due to their advanced years. Over time, lower testosterone and poor health tend to age guys like them out of the criminal mainstream and they become less of a threat. I wouldn't have them if I thought they were still criminally active or influential. Too many young ones come through who might turn around with the right input. They're vulnerable, and I don't want them corrupted by old mobsters who think they've still got it, even if they haven't."

Now that they were walking through the admin wing, the painted, scuffed Victorian brick had given way to a refurbished interior that was all glass and chrome, replete with cameras and digital locks, a dizzying contrast to the earlier crumbling patched and austere stonework. "We've not had a serious incident in eight months," Tenbeigh added.

"Serious incident" meant that none of the inmates had

succeeded in murdering one of the others. Or attempted to do so. "Congratulations on that, Governor. Long may it continue," Graham said.

"Thank you. I pray every night that it will. I'm very proud of what we've achieved here. We're showing the world how to run a modern jail. Even if, from the outside, it looks like a legacy from the Dickensian era. We have a few bad lads here, but we keep them under control."

"You've got some 'whole-lifers,' I think?" Janice said. "Whole-lifers" were offenders with no prospect of release.

"Currently, we have seventy in the UK, with some housed here. Whole-lifers get moved around more than anyone else. Does nothing for their temper, I can assure you. And these lads know they're never getting out. This means they have nothing to lose if a situation flares. With no hope of release, they already exist in a floating state somewhere between life and death."

"But how does that square with your lower security designation? Do you keep your whole-lifers in solitary, away from the general population?" Janice wondered.

Tenbeigh showed them to the control room. It was bright and modern, with a bank of screens across one wall showing feeds from dozens of cameras.

"For a couple of years, whole-lifers are certainly kept apart. It's not ideal, but it's for their safety. We have to assess their mental state. Understanding you're never getting out, never having a normal life again, no hope of redemption or purpose in life is a challenge for the mind to contemplate and accept." Janice nodded. "And they often need protecting from other inmates. People naturally order themselves into a society, and inside a prison, it's no different. Aggravated murder or serial killing is the usual crime for whole-life orders, and people charged with heinous crimes like that are not appreciated. But we don't have new whole-lifers here, just ones that are deep into their sentences. We're talking about evil people often unable to reflect on their crimes or show any remorse."

Thus far, Graham had felt relatively mellow inside the prison, but he was becoming uncomfortable. Perhaps it was the tedious layers of security or some residual discomfort about the necessity of coming to an agreement with Freddie that had led to this visit. More likely, he decided, it was the thought of being surrounded by men he had put away, and the deeds that caused him to do so. The speech would have come out, regardless.

"'Evil' connotes something unchangeable, intrinsic to the self," he said to Tenbeigh, who immediately understood he'd walked into a philosophy lecture by accident. "Do you have children?"

"Megan's three," Tenbeigh answered, puzzled. His eyes narrowed. As the governor of a large prison, he didn't normally host visiting detective inspectors. He left that to his subordinates. However, he had heard about Graham and been curious. Tenbeigh now understood why Graham's reputation preceded him. He was no ordinary blokey DI.

"Is Megan capable of despicable criminal acts?"

"Of course not."

"Agreed. Now, imagine offering a girl access to only a failing school, and with parents who either can't read or just won't. Place her somewhere she's forced to choose between fighting bullies or teaming up with them to survive. Or maybe she decides her best bet is to hide inside a gang, hoping she's not chosen as a honeytrap charged with luring a rival gang member into an ambush." Janice opened her mouth to speak. "I realise, Sergeant, that some are not unwilling participants and play their parts with gusto and a lack of conscience, but hear me out." Graham kept his tone steady even as his temper rose.

"Then, *then*, when she makes a mistake or enough of them, slap a custodial sentence on her. Henceforth, the path to decent work will be shut off, but that's alright because she knows about crime now. She has something to fall back on. And so it continues. Limited options lead to even fewer options until there are barely any at her disposal."

The assumptive inference of his daughter notwithstanding, Tenbeigh was enjoying this tirade from a slight remove. Once he realised Graham was finished, he said, "Ah yes, the 'criminals are made and not born' speech. I see they weren't wrong about you."

"Who wasn't?"

"I spoke to a few people when I heard you were coming. Nigel Needham, for one."

"You did?" Graham wished that Tenbeigh hadn't bothered his old mentor. "He's not well, you know."

"Yes, it's sad," Tenbeigh said soberly. They moved from the control room to another part of the admin complex where a new suite of offices and interview rooms were in busy use judging by the number of people toing and froing from them. "He mentioned your performance at the Harrogate conference. Around nine or ten years ago, was it? Nigel said you tore a DCI to shreds for even *suggesting* compulsory lie detector tests for violent criminals."

Graham recalled the incident with crystal clarity. "It was a dangerously stupid idea. Got short shrift, thank goodness."

"It was only an informal brainstorm-and-biscuits session, he told me!" Tenbeigh laughed at the thought of the scene: a younger, angrier Graham ascending the moral high ground at a gallop while his older superiors hid behind their teacups, their cheeks reddening, speechless. Tenbeigh had been to plenty of similar meetings; they were tedious and rarely resulted in any positive action. "I'm sure you livened up the proceedings no end. Anyway, Needham says you wrote the book on interrogation techniques."

"Only one of the chapters," Graham said just modestly enough.

"So, I'm looking forward to seeing how you handle these two."

The crimes of George and Arthur Parnaby were serious: two armed robberies, the latter ending in the killing of a security guard by another of their gang. The Parnabys were convicted of manslaughter. They had been on the Met's "most wanted" list for years.

Evading capture, and consequently punishment, they had had the luck of cats with nine lives each, but the law finally caught up with them. While their cases had been difficult to prove, the judiciary had made certain that the sentencing for those charges that stuck compensated for the earlier difficulties by being the maximum allowed.

"Have they been behaving themselves?" Graham asked.

"They haven't stuck up any more armoured cars, that's for certain," Tenbeigh remarked. "In all seriousness, we've had no complaints lately. They've been on their best behaviour. We even let them do a couple of interviews for a book someone's doing. They were each given twenty-eight years, required to serve twenty-five, and are hoping to get out as soon as they do."

"Will they?"

"George, maybe. But Arthur will be here longer." They navigated a hallway that ended in three glass-walled meeting rooms. "A couple of years ago, he stabbed another inmate in a dispute over a pot of yogurt. The ones with the fruit in the corner."

"To death?"

"Almost. They're good, those yogurts, and they take on additional currency on the inside. I thought the stabbing a bit excessive though. The victim recovered, but Arthur got three more mandatory years. Since then, he's been good as gold. Almost helpful, you could say. The brothers support us in policing the younger ones. A bit of seasoned experience in the inmate ranks can be useful to us. Both men are nearly eighty and realise their stick-up days are over.

"George has been diagnosed with congestive heart failure so he's simply trying to hang on long enough to see the sun again. You might find them keen to strike a deal. They've got a parole board hearing coming up."

They had finally arrived at the interview suite—a dark room that Mike Tenbeigh had clearly passed over when allocating the facility's modernisation budget. Graham completed some quick paperwork, and then the guard radioed for the Parnaby brothers to be escorted to the room. "What's brought you up here, then? To speak to them?" Tenbeigh wondered. "Something from the eighties, I heard."

Janice briefly explained the discovery of the body in the attic and the powerful handgun. "We have evidence that our man was perhaps an associate of the Parnabys. There's a connection between them that we're following up."

"Oh?"

"The gun found with the body was used in a crime in which Arthur Parnaby was a suspect."

Just then, two elderly men with nothing but wisps of hair on their heads were led into the room by a pair of watchful warders. One of the old men rode a motorised scooter. They looked sallow and poorly fed but also strangely optimistic. Graham wondered if they thought this meeting might somehow be their ticket home. Or maybe it was just the break in their monotonous routine that had captured their mood.

Tenbeigh took his leave. "Well, have fun. If you need anything, you can call this number." He handed them a business card. "I have a meeting with the minister for prisons in five." Tenbeigh smiled and stuck out his hand. "Nice to have met you both. I do hope your journey will prove fruitful. Perhaps see you later at lunch."

"Thanks, Mike. Hope I didn't bend your ear off. I can get passionate at times." Graham shook his hand. Janice did likewise.

"Not at all. It was good to finally meet the man behind the stories, Detective Inspector Graham of Jersey, formerly Scotland Yard. Watch out for these two. They're wily fellas."

CHAPTER FORTY-ONE

"ARTHUR PARNABY," ANNOUNCED the elderly man who walked without assistance. It was just as well that he identified himself; the brothers were identical twins. Bald, stooped, and reed thin except for bellies that resembled footballs under their prison shirts. "At your service, sir!" He was mocking Graham, but there was an underlying truth to what he said.

Arthur and George Parnaby had agreed to this interview, not for the attention or for any service to humanity but for the "bennies"—advantages that were currency in prison and which they were keen to accrue. The Parnaby twins were there to do a deal.

Arthur pointed a thumb at the man next to him. "This is George." George's rounded shoulders suddenly straightened.

"'ow do." His voice was a ruined whisper, and he breathed with difficulty. A cannula connected to an oxygen cylinder on wheels that trailed behind him hung beneath his nose. He seemed confused, unsure why he was in this dark, windowless room with his brother and not watching prison life pass by in front of him, which was how he usually spent his hours. "'Oo are you, then?" he said, eyeing Graham and then Janice.

"I'm Detective Inspector Graham, and this is Sergeant Harding. We're from the Gorey police force. We're here to ask you a few questions."

"They're following up after that little fella, George. The journalist," Arthur said loudly. "Remember? Might be somethin' or nuthin.'" He raised his chin defiantly, then dropped it before winking at his brother. "They might be able to help with your art project."

George raised his head. "Yeah?"

"And more time in the garden for me."

Graham had handled this kind of sparring before. Brief feints to lay out their opening gambits. The Parnabys were in this for themselves. Freddie had warned him. . .

"Nothing is guaranteed. But if you're helpful, I'll make sure the authorities here know that."

"Sounds like a plan." Arthur grinned as his brother wrestled a chair out from the table and, supporting himself with one hand on the back, the other flat on the table, lowered himself into the seat. Arthur did the same, although considerably quicker. "Whatcha wanting to know about?"

Graham could have laid out the folder of evidence and walked the two inmates through what he'd learned, but he decided to keep things simple. "I'm writing the biography of a revolver," he said. "A three-fifty-seven, a ferocious piece. Goes missing for many years, then turns up in someone's attic on Jersey."

Arthur's old man's eye, its corner creasing ever so slightly in reaction to Graham's mention of the island, caught the inspector's attention. Hundreds of tiny muscles govern human facial movements. Children, adults, and the elderly use those muscles in different ways, and the nuances of these two identical craggy faces as the men processed 'Jersey' told Graham much. The island resonated with them in a way that they were keen not to parse. And if the word elicited such a response, there would be others. Graham watched for them while listening with a blazing intensity.

"Jersey's where they had all the Nazis and stuff. Superman lives there, the nerdy one."

"Uh, yes." It wasn't how Graham would have characterised the island. He would have described its beautiful scenery, beaches, and history. Not mentioned the bedevilment of the Nazi occupation during WWII or that it was the home of the local-boy-cum-Hollywood-actor best known for playing Clark Kent. Graham hadn't even understood the last reference. Janice filled him in later.

"The Smith and Wesson model twenty-eight. A rare firearm, and an unusual find, I think you'll agree. We did some comparisons, some testing . . ."

Arthur's face darkened, and he leaned over to his brother, whispering.

"Hey, hey!" Janice said urgently, her arm outstretched, her palm facing down. But it was too late. The message had been transmitted. Arthur, the healthier, fitter brother, stood up. "We didn't come here for this! It's a setup job, George. Careful what you say, alright?"

"Yeah," George answered. Graham, unsure if they were bluffing to force an advantage, stayed impassive.

"No one's setting anyone up. Look, we're being straight with you here. We're just trying to understand who owned the gun. Running it through our system provided a link with your good selves." Seeing his brother remain at the table, Arthur slowly sat down again.

Through the bubbling marsh of his lungs, George said,

"I've never used a gun personally. They make the most bloody awful noise."

"Ah, yes, it was your *accomplice* who fired the shot during the robbery that left a man dead, wasn't it? Nevertheless, it led to your arrest and incarceration here," Janice responded pointedly. She cast her eyes around the bleak room. She had read the Parnabys' case file on the flight over, and then again while waiting in the visitors' centre. The lives of the two brothers would make for an intriguing film.

George, despite his breathing apparatus, age, and dire prognosis, still possessed the confidence, some might say self-delusion, of a man far younger and healthier. He put one hand on his hip and leaned an elbow on the table, resting his chin casually on his thumb as he faced Janice. "Look, love, I wasn't told anything about guns. We just drove the van."

Graham also knew the case well. It was encapsulated in Metropolitan Police lore and his own untrammelled recollections of stories passed down to him from veteran officers. "Of course you did. You 'drove the van,' but you also scoped out the security company and tracked their armoured cars for days so you could plan the robbery in minute detail. You devised the plan, hired the team, and doled out the loot. Dumb getaway drivers you were not."

Laughing hard, an awful sound that conjured the image of air forcing its way through thick, black paint, George eventually found the breath and clarity to speak. "I'd never call it a 'plan.' We were a bunch of idiots trying to rob a van and screwing everything up. Your mate, that Freddie fella, wants to paint us as the mob, some kind of organised crime gang. Ha! Organised? We were more like Laurel and 'ardy."

"A man died," Janice reminded them. "It was more than a botched job."

Arthur shrugged. "Not our fault some numpty gets trigger-happy on his first job."

"That 'numpty' cost you nearly thirty years in the slammer, and he was a numpty you hired, but hear me out," Graham said. "You've spent your final years inside, and you may well spend whatever time you have left in here as well. But if you answer everything we put to you today, you can redeem yourself in part . . ."

Arthur snorted. "Redeem? Who cares?"

Janice leaned forward. "No one. You could spend more time with your roses though. Imagine that? You'll get more time outside in the sunshine, pruning, clipping, and mixing in fertiliser. The colours of the blooms you grow could really sing. You could pull carrots and potatoes from the ground and cover your raspberries with netting so the snails don't get them. It's annoying when the bugs destroy everything after all the hard work you've put in, isn't it?"

Janice peered into Arthur's blue eyes. They glazed over as he pictured what she described. "Maybe you could even win a few bets with the other men who work their gardens, build your status that way."

Seeing an opening, Graham followed this up with a metaphorical rapid right hook. "We've got a victim, someone who died a nasty, painful death. And it's not impossible you know who he is."

George laughed again, though everyone in the room wished he had not. Janice especially. His gurgling, phlegmy wheeze made her feel ill. "What, and you need our help? We've never been to Jersey. Either of us. Honestly, you'll be reaching for the divine next. Bleedin' miracles now, is it?"

"Look." Graham pulled out two sheets of paper from his folder. "Here's a slug fired from the gun by our ballistics expert just the other day. And here," he said, putting the two printed images side-by-side, "is one fired in 1976." The images looked roughly the same, small chunks of cylindrical metal, badly malformed and compressed by impacts.

"Miracles, I tell ya!" George repeated. "You two weren't even *born* in seventy-six."

Janice folded her arms. He was irritating her. He wasn't helping his brother get any closer to spending more time with his beloved roses either. At this rate, she was hard-pressed to believe Arthur would even lay any atop George's coffin when the time came. Which, judging by his cough, wouldn't be long now.

Arthur made a dismissive noise. "Two bullets fired from the same gun, years apart. So what?" He tipped his head to one side and languidly glanced around the bare, peeling, plastered walls.

"Remember this chap?" Graham slipped out another image from his folder, turning the mugshot photo so Arthur could see it.

"Bloody hell, we really are off on a jaunt down memory lane, aren't we?" Arthur leaned over to study the image, then he sat back as George reached over to pick it up, the flimsy paper shaking as he tremulously studied it before lapsing into a long chuckle that sounded like a traction engine suffering an oil leak.

"Well? What do you say?" Graham said.

Arthur Parnaby flicked a speck off his trousers before replying. "Yes, for cryin' out loud, I recognise him. It's Potty Patty. Right loon, 'e was."

"Also known as Patrick Havers."

"What's he got to do with this?" Arthur added. His eyes lit up. "Is he dead?"

"Oh, he's been dead for years," said Graham. "But sometime in October 1976, he was seen by two friends of yours in the car park of the Angel and Greyhound in Clapham, enjoying overly friendly relations with your then-wife."

There was no restraining his guffaw, so George let it all out. "Overly friendly . . . relations . . ." Janice shut her eyes and wished she could shut her ears as George coughed into a white handkerchief and then heaved once again with laughter. "That's . . . a good one . . . " he wheezed.

"Shut it," his brother said, his cheeks blooming as his anger grew. Arthur snatched the photo from his brother's hands and looked at it again. "Ask what you're here to ask and be done with it. Did I have him killed? Is that what you want to know?"

CHAPTER FORTY-TWO

"WELL, YOU CAN see why I might think that, but no, he died of natural causes. And a few years before he did, you chased him, threatened his life, and fired several rounds at his car as he tried to flee."

"Maybe, maybe, but I missed the bugger completely," said Arthur. "'E was alive and kickin' when I last saw him."

"Hit his car three times though. Which was later impounded following Mr. Havers's arrest two days later for dangerous driving."

"He always was a dozy sod. He should have dumped the old thing. Would've saved us all a ton of bovver." Arthur growled and pushed his chair away from the table, folded his arms, and looked down at the floor.

"The bullet fragments found in the car were logged," Graham continued, "and carefully photographed. Comparisons with the gun we uncovered on Jersey were possible. The testing proved that it was the same one that fired at Patrick Havers's car, the person who was having an affair with your wife, Arthur. At the time, it was suspected that you fired that gun, but the case was dropped for insufficient evidence and probably a host of other reasons that law enforcement often employ in relation to rolling up serial offenders like yourself."

The two old cons were sufficiently experienced to understand when silence was golden, especially their own. They let this snooty, overeducated detective inspector say his piece, hoping it would soon be over and there wouldn't be too many long, fancy words.

"So this gun, the one you used, Arthur, was on Jersey in early 1982," Graham told them. A subtle fluttering of recognition crossed the men's faces, but they said nothing. "What I want to know is—who did you give it to after you shot up Patrick Havers's car?"

Within moments, the two men were huddling to discuss the question.

"Oi," Janice objected, "none of your secret conspiracies in here, thank you. Just tell the detective inspector what he wants to know."

It took time and more assurances. "One hour *every afternoon* on the allotment," Arthur clarified. "And I get to have the rain days roll over."

"I'll see what I can do. No promises though," Graham said.

"And George Van Goff here can have as much paint as he likes to throw at the art room wall provided he cleans it all up after."

"I don't *throw* it," George rasped, offended. "I *liberate* it."

They had a deal. Graham would do his best. Arthur swung into gear. "I gave the item in question to a man who I employed now and then. I'd used him as an odd jobs man and labourer."

"Why? Why would you give an odd jobs man a gun?"

"As payment in kind."

"You paid a bloke for some odd jobs with a firearm?"

Arthur nodded solemnly. "At his request, yes."

"A firearm which had been used, in public, to attempt some rough justice." Arthur pressed his lips together. When it was clear he wouldn't answer, Graham continued. "So, Arthur, to whom did you give the gun? Give me a name."

"Dylan Dillon," came the reply. "'Dilly' for short. It got too complicated otherwise. Stupid the things some parents do to their kids. Practically grew up together, we did. We were a bit older though."

"A lot older, bruv. Ten years. Always had his nose in a book, did Dilly."

"And what became of Dilly?"

Arthur cracked a smile. "Nah, mate. I've given you what you wanted—a name. If you want more, you have to pay. What's he say in that flick? The one with the bloke who's chained up in a glass cell?"

His brother helped him out. "*Silence of the Lambs*. 'Annibal Lecter."

"Yeah, yeah," Arthur said. "When he's working things out with the FBI girl, right, he says . . . you know . . . if there's something for me, then there'll be something for you."

"A *quid pro quo*," Janice said. "Is that what you're reaching for?"

"Yeah, exactly. Squid provo. You want more? What's in it for us, eh?"

Outwardly, Graham's expression remained inscrutable, but his mind, which had been huffing along with the efficiency and velocity of a high-speed train, hit a speed bump. Efficient negotiating was hard when his opponents had absolutely nothing to lose or in their calendar.

"Now," Arthur explained, "the currency is *time*."

"If either of you tells me something that leads to a conviction . . ."

"An *arrest*," Arthur countered. "Not a conviction. That'll take way too long. No good to me nor 'im."

"If you tell me something that leads to a *conviction*, then I'll make a case and remind the parole board that twenty-six years is not that much different from twenty-eight." The old men glared at their opposite number across the table.

"And the extra thing?" Arthur asked eventually, a little less confrontational. "I'm seventy-nine. Shaving a year or two off my stretch doesn't mean much when I've got another six to go."

"You mean the violent assault which put an inmate in hospital?" Janice said.

"Lost my temper, didn't I?" Arthur Parnaby grumbled. "Paid the price in solitary, day after day, for *three* months."

But Graham wouldn't be drawn. "These decisions depend on people higher up the chain. I can't promise what I can't deliver. It's not down to me."

"No promises from you, no insider intel from us." George lifted his chin as he spoke before dropping it low and looking out from under his eyebrows. "We're putting ourselves on the line here. We could be looked at as grasses. That won't make our lives easy in this place."

Graham highly doubted that the brothers telling him about a case that occurred over forty years ago would dent their inmate reputation in any way. "I can't make promises," he said, "and you're not well placed to demand any, but I'll ask them to consider releasing you as a pair."

"Alright, but no new charges, okay?" said George. "Immunity from self-immolation."

"I think you mean incrimination."

"Yeah, incrimin . . . Yeah, that.

"It depends on what your role was."

"Then we're not saying anyfin'."

Graham had already ascertained that the brothers could not possibly have had anything to do with the death of Dylan Dillon. In February 1982, they had been under surveillance by Met officers for a bank job. On February 14th, undercover cops observed the Parnabys meeting two men in a park at eleven o'clock at night. They hadn't been there to play on the swings, but neither had they been involved in a killing on Jersey. But Graham wanted to hear from the Parnabys' own mouths what they knew about what had happened to Dillon.

"Alright, you give me everything you know about Dillon, including names and dates, and there'll be no charges with respect to the case we're investigating. *If* I get an arrest that leads to charges and a conviction, I'll ask them to release you as a pair at George's next parole board meeting. How about that?"

The two brothers turned to one another. Some silent twin language must have passed between them, because when they looked back at the two officers, Arthur said, "Squid provo. You ask us the stuff. We'll do our best for you."

Finally.

"So, let's start again," Janice said. "When did you last see Mr. Dylan Dillon?"

"Dilly?" George said. "Phew, ages. He's long gone, isn't he?"

"I'm afraid so," Janice said. "On Valentine's Day, 1982, he was found dead on Jersey."

Graham saw it again: those tiny flickers of movement around the eyes. They were never entirely meaningless, but their hidden nuances required interpretation.

"His body, along with his belongings, was discovered in his hotel room."

The Parnaby twins furrowed their brows and turned down the corners of their mouths but remained silent.

"Forensics found traces of average-purity powdered cocaine on his shirt," Janice continued.

Neither man suppressed a guffaw, and after coughing extensively, George added a phlegmy bark of congratulation: "Good old Dilly!"

"Died as he lived" was Arthur's assessment. "He always was a rascal. Way to go, man! Fair play to the lad. Bit young though. I'd raise a glass if they'd ever let us have one in here."

"We found something else on his shirt too."

"Chicken tikka?" Arthur guessed.

"Spilled scotch? Ash from his B&H?" George chuckled.

"When did you last see him?"

"Hmm, let's see," Arthur said. "Early 1982. We told that other fella. 'E went to Jersey and never came back. Last we saw of 'im."

"Do you know of anyone who might have wished Mr. Dillon harm?"

It was a key question, and Graham's focus grew more intense. It was their eyes again. Arthur seemed to look down and away, blinking; George's eyes narrowed a smidgen.

"I suppose you wouldn't bother coming up here if he'd just keeled over from a drug overdose," Arthur said.

"Someone did him in, then?" George added.

"You haven't answered my question."

"About what?"

"Who might have wanted to spike Mr. Dillon's cocaine with rat poison?"

Graham watched them carefully. There was a pause as the two men stared straight ahead, their faces a carbon copy of the other, blank and unreadable. He noticed a minuscule twitch of a muscle. Were they processing this information and what it might mean? Did they actually know anything worth knowing?

"You're talking about forty years ago," Arthur said eventually. "We're not young men anymore. Things slip away, you know?" He raised his hand to touch his temple before letting it drop in a broad arc, mimicking the journey of a memory leaving his mind, becoming forever lost.

Graham tried a different approach. "Do you know why he was on Jersey, then?"

"For his holidays?" Arthur replied. "To read a few books on the beach, drink a couple of afternoon pints. Sounds alright to me."

Graham wrote in his notebook with his custom short-hand and soon saw that neither brother cared for this. They both watched him silently. Arthur shifted in his seat and passed a hand across his face. "Did he regularly take breaks on his own? Disappear for the weekend?"

"We were his mates," said Arthur. "Not his wife."

"No," George said simply.

"When he travelled was it typical for him to bring a handgun? *Your handgun*, I should say?"

"How should we know?" Arthur said. "I figured he'd sell the gun. I didn't want it no more. Bloody great thing was too heavy anyway. Good for nuthin'."

A phone's jingle sounded. The prison officer stationed

in the room, who had been quiet up until now, stirred. With the tension broken, Graham pushed himself away from the table. Arthur Parnaby smacked his lips. George coughed. Janice watched the two men intensely.

"Lunchtime!" Arthur stood, straightening slowly. "Oof," he moaned, his hand pressing the small of his back.

"It's fettuccine alfredo or meatloaf if I remember correctly," George said. He shifted to his motorised scooter but was soon wracked with coughing again. He followed Arthur out, his oxygen tank trailing while his older brother wore a knowing, high-handed smirk that bothered Graham intensely.

CHAPTER FORTY-THREE

W HEN THE BROTHERS left, Graham stretched his arms to the ceiling. He squeezed his eyes tight and made fists with his hands. Janice walked over to the tiny, reinforced glass-and-barred gap in the wall that barely deserved the title of window. She looked outside. In the distance, she could see men in the exercise yard.

"They're hard work, aren't they, Arthur and George? Slippery characters. All matey to your face, but you know underneath they are for no one but themselves. Wouldn't even stand up for each other if push came to shove, I shouldn't wonder. Their mere presence exhausts me. There's simply no part of them that is likeable or that isn't self-serving," she said. "And they're people who you would think would share everything they knew in case all they have to look forward to is the privilege of dying in one of the best-run all-male prisons in England. I mean, it's a very amenable facility Governor Tenbeigh has here, but it is, let's not mess about, a *jail.*"

"We need to be on high alert with them. If I don't watch

it," Graham said, "I'll end up agreeing to support their release just because I added some interesting case notes to the file. We need to understand *why* Dillon was on Jersey. Without knowing that, we can't move forward."

"Do you think that they know? Apart from the gun connection, we don't have anything else to connect them. Not to Dillon's trip to Jersey anyway."

"No, but they told Freddie that two members of their gang disappeared after they visited the island. Never saw or heard of either of them again. They gave him no names though. Clammed up, he said, when he pushed them."

"You don't think they're stringing Freddie along, do you? Making up stuff in exchange for painting supplies and seeds?"

Graham rolled his eyes. "I sincerely hope not."

A prison warder appeared at the doorway. "Governor Tenbeigh asked me to tell you that lunch is this way."

"Smashing," Graham said to him before following Janice out of the dreary room. He was looking forward to a cup of tea. Any kind would do. He wasn't, at this point, fussy. "They'll try to make a little look like a lot, that's for sure. They'll offer details which seem helpful but lead nowhere, or tell us things we already know, like the name of the guy whose car Arthur shot up in seventy-six. Like," he pointed out, "them telling us Dillon enjoyed reading. All of those small elements *seem* significant, somehow, but none of them take us closer to solving the case or an arrest. At least Arthur admitted giving the gun to Dillon, but even that isn't game-changing."

When they got to Governor Tenbeigh's office, they found lunch laid out for them. Nothing fancy, just a few sandwiches, crisps, and biscuits. There was a pot of tea though. "We heard you liked a good cuppa, Detective

Inspector," Tenbeigh said, suddenly appearing. The tea was a bog-standard brew, but to Graham, at that moment, it was like the elixir of life, immortality, and eternal youth all rolled into one. He closed his eyes as the piping-hot, brown liquid grazed the soft flesh at the back of his throat, warming it and soothing him.

With nothing helpful to add, and with Graham's tone and body language signalling he was ready for a "big think," Tenbeigh wordlessly invited Janice to leave the inspector to it. When the governor pulled the office door closed, Graham was muttering to himself and scribbling in his notebook.

"Why don't we get our lunch in the senior prison officer's section of our newly refurbished staff canteen?" Tenbeigh said. "I imagine you've earned it this morning. Must've been an early start for you."

"Very early," Janice replied. "Four a.m. to be exact." She stifled a yawn. "That seems a long time ago now."

"I believe salmon en croute and Eton mess are on the menu today."

"Sounds lovely. Reviving."

Back in the governor's office, his eyes closed, Graham sighed and set his notebook on Tenbeigh's desk. At first, the lunch break had felt like an imposition, but he needed time to consider his game plan.

The cautious sparring with the Parnabys would endure until Graham played a weak card. Then they'd see his notebook held nothing to boast about. There were worrying limits to his inquiry. The passing of time meant he needed to build an ironclad case. A confession backed up by forensic findings, ideally. He was a long way from achieving that.

Graham had a victim but no witnesses. He had a means

but no motive. He lacked both a suspect and any discernible reason why anyone might risk poisoning Dillon. He didn't even know why Dillon was on Jersey and why he had taken a weapon with him.

"Someone got into his hotel room," Graham muttered at the office walls, "and switched out a portion of his cocaine for rat poison. Two types for good measure. It wasn't elegant, but it was near certain to succeed provided Dillon had dependable, consistent cocaine habits. Like, you know he's going to roll up a tenner and break out his stash. That would require intimate knowledge, someone who knew him well."

Graham couldn't pace properly in Tenbeigh's office, so he strode out into the hallway, smiling briefly at the handful of staff he encountered. They stared at him curiously before their eyes glazed over and they lost interest in him, returning to their work or their phones.

"The chosen murder method was highly personal," he said to himself in a low whisper. "A substance the victim rammed up his nose, entered his bloodstream, and travelled to his brain and then, fatally, his heart. Something that was *supposed* to make him feel *great*. But because the poison was self-administered, the method was one step removed. It required intimate knowledge but no direct hand." He turned around and returned to Tenbeigh's office, where he stood looking out of the window with his hands clasped behind his back until Janice found him some minutes later.

"Enjoy your lunch, sir?" Janice looked at the table. Nothing had been eaten. Even the tea was cold.

"Our killer was the victim's buddy, someone he knew quite well," Graham told her.

"Huh? Wait, how did you get there?"

"The drugs. Dillon was poisoned. There's something *intimate* about it."

"Not just a cold mob hit, you mean. Not just business."

"No, it was too messy for that. A mob hit would have made certain—a gun preferably, or strangulation, a beating. They wouldn't leave until they knew he was dead. This is less certain. It was less efficient. And it wasn't foolproof by any means. Have you managed to get anything on him yet? This Dylan Dillon." On the way up to Holbrooke, Janice had liaised with her opposite number at police headquarters in St. Helier.

"Yes." Janice pulled out her tablet. "He doesn't have a record surprisingly, given his associates, but he was known to the law as a teenager. Petty stuff, nothing significant. But one thing stands out. He had his tonsils removed at nineteen."

"Why is that interesting, Sergeant? So do around thirty-seven thousand other people each year."

"He listed his next of kin as one Charles Cross from Mile End. I guess they might have been school friends, but strange, no? You'd put your mother or a family member down, especially at that age. Who do you think Charlie Cross might be?"

"I'm not sure. These Parnaby guys were never my patch. I don't know them or their mates," Graham admitted. "They've been in jail since I was in middle school. I don't know their accomplices, their methods . . . but I have an idea whom we might ask." He pulled out his phone. "My only worry is that he won't remember any of it."

Janice continued to read the report from St. Helier. Her voice rose in volume and register. "Listen to this, sir. A Dylan Dillon left Jersey on February *fifteenth*, 1982. He reentered Jersey in *October* 1982. And since then, according to records, he's never left."

CHAPTER FORTY-FOUR

A FTER WHAT FELT like an entire morning of pedalling through Jersey's rural areas, Barnwell pulled his bicycle over to the lane's grass verge to catch his breath. He was almost certain he'd already searched this section. It was easy to recognise—again—the big, almost unruly copse which sprang out of the farmland, surrounded in part by a centuries-old stone wall.

As he took a breather, Barnwell once more brought out the note he had made of the address he was hunting down: 4 St. Julian's Road. Fiona had alerted them to the scrawl in blue ballpoint on the inside back cover of the paperback copy of *The Hitchhikers Guide to the Galaxy* found in Mrs. Taylor's attic, and Barnwell had taken it upon himself to undertake some sleuthing. Originally a BBC Radio 4 comedy science fiction series, the novel the radio show spawned was unfamiliar to Barnwell, but he had occasionally watched popular old repeats of the TV show of the same name and knew of its cult-like status.

Barnwell had called Graham as he drove north on his way to interview the Parnabys to tell him of his lack of success in locating the address. The sun's rays beat down, and even Carmen, normally as energetic as a hummingbird, dragged a little.

"Keep trying, Constable. I know it's just a note on the back of a book, but however unconnected to the case, we must find that address, if only to eliminate it. It's a discrete, straightforward piece of evidence, and as such, a rarity. And you're at St. Julian's Wood, aren't you? It must be there somewhere."

"Doesn't explain why no one's even *heard* of it," Barnwell grumbled when he got off the phone. He wiped beads of sweat from his brow and untucked his white police shirt from his trousers. The internet was almost no help, pointing him only to a collection of trees, a two-acre stand of hawthorns which offered no help or comfort.

Barnwell pulled out a collapsible dog bowl from a pannier on his bike and popped it out with his fist. He filled it from his water bottle, and as Carmen drank, he pulled up a map of the area on his phone, spreading his second and third fingers across the screen to magnify the destination to which he was being guided. Looking up, he raised his head and surveyed the surrounding countryside, trees to one side, open fields to the other.

Once Carmen had drunk her fill, Barnwell threw the remains of the water into the hedgerow. He swung his bike around and, laboriously pushing off, got going again. He headed into the trees, more relieved than ever to have changed his diet and slimmed down.

"Imagine pedalling along like this," he said to himself as he heaved the bicycle back up to speed, "while weighing twenty percent more." Each time he stood on the bathroom scales, a shiver of achievement rippled through him. Briefly, it would be tempered by regret—*why did I wait so long*—

before he would be buoyed further by newfound confidence. For one thing, he looked *a great deal* better in his uniform. And for another, he could keep up with Carmen who, lithe, young, and always game, galloped along beside him.

"But more importantly," he muttered through gritted teeth, "where the blinkin' heck *is* this house?" Emerging from the canopy of trees into green fields on the other side of the wood, he put his foot down and once more turned his bike around to retrace his route. This time, he found a rough turnoff excavated by tire tracks but partially covered by brush. It led deeper into the woods in a different direction.

With no better ideas, Barnwell headed down the track, navigating channels of dried mud and leaves through the brush and trees, disturbing nothing but the odd bird and perhaps other wildlife. As he travelled along, he thought he heard voices, but the path ended in a silent, open, dry, flat stretch flanked by vegetable allotments. Beyond them was a row of neat hedging. "Can't make head nor tail of this place," he complained to Carmen, bringing out his phone. "Will we even have reception? We're miles from anywhere civilised."

A year ago, Carmen's stigmatism caused her to be rejected from police dog training. The eye disorder was inconvenient but nothing more. The diagnosis hadn't affected Carmen any, but the threat to the local squirrel population diminished substantially. She couldn't catch anything, but she had a happy time trying.

Now she was Barnwell's—and by extension the Gorey constabulary's—pet, living a life of canine indulgence: regular walks with Barnwell on his beat, plenty of treats, and snoozes in the station. In return, she accompanied him to his "Dog and Doughnut" sessions at the local primary

266 ALISON GOLDEN & GRACE DAGNALL

school. Sitting quietly, acting as a therapy dog, Carmen showed remarkable tolerance as young children took turns to cuddle her while Barnwell gave road and child safety talks to classes of twenty.

"Are you stuck in the maze?"

Barnwell turned to see a woman in her thirties smiling curiously at him. She wore a loose red dress, her hair braided in a halo around her head. Under one arm was a basket full of what looked like leaves, and a sleeping baby lay swaddled against her chest.

"Ah, well, I'm not exactly sure," he said. "Looking for St. Julian's Wood. Is this it?"

The woman rolled her eyes good-naturedly. "It certainly is, Detective!"

"Just a constable, ma'am."

"Well, Constable, we call it Julian's Wood these days."

"We?"

"There are a few of us living here. Five families, no pollution, no problems."

"All recycled and what have you?" Barnwell asked, interested. "Low carbon footprint and all that?"

"Zero, if we can."

"Great. Well, I'm looking for number four St. Julian's Road. Do you know where that is?" He peered behind her, only now noticing a row of semicylindrical steel huts. Painted a shade of light green, they blended perfectly with the surroundings. Barnwell eyed them curiously.

"They're Nissen huts," the woman informed him, noticing his interest. "We've restored them. They look good, don't they?"

"Yeah, yeah, they do. Must've taken a bit of work." The cylindrical corrugated metal huts lined up in military formation, their entrances facing out across fields.

"We've completely rebuilt them but kept the original footprint and shape. We used environmentally friendly materials and installed solar energy for power. There's even underfloor heating and a wood burner."

"Blimey, you've got better facilities than I have in town."

"We love it out here," the woman said, smiling and gazing at her sleeping baby. "So, you're looking for number four? We don't really go by addresses out here. Do you mean the fourth one to be built?"

"No, I mean house number four. Like on a residential street. And back in the early eighties." The woman frowned and turned down the corners of her mouth. "Oh, never mind." He knew he sounded delirious.

Strewn around, Barnwell could see strollers, potted ferns, barbecues, and bikes. A few yards away, a pile of logs, neatly stacked, fenced off a children's play area, and beyond that, half a dozen goats grazed quietly.

As he spoke to the woman, Barnwell noticed the intrigue and curiosity his arrival incited. First out of the huts appeared a young child around the age of two, three fingers in her mouth. She stared at the dog and the stranger, who wore an even stranger costume. A tall, stringy man dressed in faded jeans and a work shirt followed the child. More people emerged from the huts, gazing intently at Barnwell, around twenty-five in all—men, women, and children of all ages and sizes.

They didn't seem threatening, just curious. It was weird. Barnwell wondered if he had somehow stepped into another world.

A slight sheen appeared on his upper lip. Suddenly acutely aware of his push bike and lack of backup, he searched for something to say as he glanced around. Each vegetable patch was well-tended; some families kept chickens. It seemed idyllic, especially with the children running around.

"Are you a commune?"

The woman smiled again, and a chuckle rose from deep within her throat. "Some would say so."

"I thought a commune would be a bunch of sticks and a tarpaulin strung between branches," Barnwell admitted, "or, you know, people living in broken-down caravans. But you've got a nice little thing going on here."

"We got permission, gave it a go, and made it work," the young woman explained, making soothing sounds as her baby fussed. "I'll get Rory. He might know about number four."

CHAPTER FORTY-FIVE

WARY AT FIRST, Rory wiped his hands on dirty jeans as he walked up to Barnwell and looked through dark hair that needed a trim. "What's all this, then? Trouble with the law, is it? We're all legal, like."

"No trouble," Barnwell promised, and briefly explained his afternoon assignment.

"Ain't got numbers, only names," Rory replied. "The two newest ones are *Bluebell* and *Foxglove*."

"How do you support yourselves out here?"

"I'll do anything, but I learned as a carpenter. Some of us work locally in the community. The others digitally, software engineers and the like, working for all sorts. All remote now. Good broadband service. We've got good throughput out here."

"So, you're only slightly off-grid, then. I mean just a bit, falling off the edge kind of thing." He smiled but the man looked at Barnwell uncomprehendingly. "Never mind," he said again. "How did you come to choose this site?"

Rory hitched up his jeans and looked around him. "Ah,

well. Scouts used to camp here and such. I was one of them. We used to call it Fort Feathers 'cause of how soft the pine needles are around here. There's some buildings through the trees. All run-down like. They were put up for sale, what, ten year 'go? Nobody besides us made an offer. We just wanted the land and these huts. We left the buildings for the animals, did up the huts, and moved in. Thankfully" —he laughed, exposing a couple of missing teeth—"several other families had the same idea, and here we are."

Barnwell scribbled words in his notebook. He was glad to have left his iPad back at the station. It would have appeared out of place in this idyllic, eco-friendly paradise. "Buildings? You mean"—Barnwell looked at the curved huts —"bricks and stuff?"

Rory nodded. "Like I say, the scouts had them before. We never bothered with them."

"And before that?"

The carpenter puffed out his cheeks. "Before? Well . . . it'd have been . . ." He scratched his sandpaper beard. "Just . . . a *wood*, I expect!"

Others in the community were able to offer more help, or at least hearsay. As the men had been talking, adults and children, like timid wild creatures, had slowly crept closer to within earshot. "My nan used to say it was, you know, um, they used the buildings for, like, seminars," said one of the younger women. She was perhaps of upper school age, although Barnwell suspected she hadn't seen the inside of a school of any kind in some time.

"Meetings, conferences, that kind of thing?" Barnwell thought the idea strange in such a remote location.

"Dunno, really. She said, like, they ran out of money or something and, like, closed everything down."

No one else knew anything about house numbers. "Did

they do wrong, then? Someone?" one elderly man wanted to know. It was a reasonable suspicion given Barnwell's uniform. "Late on their taxes, is it? Or they not got the proper permits?"

"Permits?" Barnwell asked. "What kind of permits?"

"To be here in the woods living our lives this way 'n all that. Needs permits, permissions from the council."

"Why?" Barnwell asked. He thought it best to keep the questions short.

"'Cos they have to come and have a look every now and again, make sure we're not growing anything we shouldn't or selling the kids into slavery."

The young woman from earlier piped up while breast-feeding just yards away. "I tried that already with this one, but they told me to come back when he's old enough to wash dishes." Everyone got a chuckle except Barnwell, who still didn't understand why an address from forty years ago had yielded a community created only recently and a rather unexpected one at that. Still, no laws were being broken that he could see, and the place had a pleasant balance of the relaxed and industrious. It was a little bit glorious in fact.

One of the oldest members of the community, "Grandma Pam," told Barnwell, "We like to live our lives at a slower pace than most. Folks come to take photos of us sometimes, as though we're eco-warriors or something." She cackled, showing off yellowing teeth and old, dark fillings. "But we're just here to find ways of living sustainably, giving our kids a better childhood and chance at life."

Barnwell thought that *did* make them eco-warriors, but he thanked her for her input. Feeling he had got as much as he could from this visit, he made his way back out to the path he had come in on. As he went, he reassured the crowd that followed him, apparently unwilling to let their novel visitor go. "Just trying to chase down an address for an enquiry."

"Someone who lived here before, eh?"

"Not sure. All we've got is the address."

"Did something awful, did they?" Rory's concern grew again. The crowd was still following. "Are you lot going to be out here with mechanical diggers and what have you, tearing up the place looking for bodies?"

"Almost certainly not."

"'*Almost* certainly not.' I like that," Rory said, unimpressed.

"We're investigating a case, and the address might relate to it. It also may be absolutely nothing."

The carpenter laughed again, saying as he stepped away, "Hard for it to relate to much of anything if it ain't real!"

Privately, Barnwell was forced to agree. Then Grandma Pam caught his elbow. "Did they show you the ruins?"

Images of sacred standing stones and cavorting druids troubled Barnwell immediately, but as Pam took him a hundred yards through the woods, he made out some unnaturally straight lines ahead.

As they drew up, Pam pointed. "It was a cottage, someone said, but a man passing through once told me it used to be a chapel."

"Looks like it caught fire," Barnwell said. Only ruined blackened beams and tumbledown walls remained, half grown over with vines dotted with white flowers.

"Probably kids mucking about one night, letting things get out of hand. But not since we've been here. It was like that when we arrived."

"What are those over there?" Barnwell wondered. To

the right of the burned building and through the trees were more broken-down walls of brick.

"A few more cottages, old and dangerous to my mind. We don't let the children go anywhere near this place."

Barnwell left her to tramp through the brush and nettles, focused only on the piles of brick ahead of him. Almost completely buried beneath weeds, more vines, and undergrowth, he found a row of semi-detached cottages and some outbuildings, not burned but partially fallen down and certainly derelict. He counted them before walking back to Pam, Carmen, as ever, by his side. "Well, I think I've found number four."

CHAPTER FORTY-SIX

"I KNOW MIKE Tenbeigh was in touch recently, and I'm sorry if he . . ." His brow furrowed, Graham brought every ounce of courtesy he possessed to his request. Veronica Needham was taking her duties as the wife of a retired superintendent suffering from early dementia with the intensity (and potential bite) of a guard dog. "I'm sorry Nigel was so tired afterwards, and I promise I won't take more than two minutes of his time." Graham listened patiently as Veronica laid down the ground rules for his conversation with her husband and reflected that for the second time that day, he had to accept someone else's terms of engagement.

A few seconds later, a different voice sounded on the line, at first gruff and impatient, then cordial. "David?" Nigel Needham sounded in fine fettle at least.

"Good afternoon, sir. Sorry to bother you."

"Not a bit of it. Happy to hear from you. Veronica makes a fuss over every last little thing, but she means well. What can I do for you?" Graham could hear Needham shuffling into his study and closing the door on his maddened and maddening spouse.

"George and Arthur Parnaby," Graham said.

"Bad boys!" Needham said immediately. "We nicked them for that armoured car job in Shoreditch in . . . ninety-nine I think it was. The guard shot in the back. Only a lad. Didn't make it through surgery." Needham sighed. "That's the curse of this bloody disease. You forget the good stuff and remember the upsetting bits."

"Who are these guys, sir? They act like they were nothing but a couple of minor players." Graham knew the brothers' criminal careers amounted to much more than that but wanted to hear Needham's telling of their story.

"Bloody *menace*, they were. Four of them, originally going right back to the seventies. We put people in there, got close a couple of times, but the more dominant one—Arthur, if I recall . . ."

"That's right."

"He got suspicious, and we had to close the operation down both times. He was an all-round nasty piece of business. We wanted him for a string of other serious crimes but couldn't pin things down."

"What was their setup?"

"Originally in their twenties and thirties, the brothers ran a builder's merchant with the help of a couple of younger lads. It looked legit on the outside, but there was some 'import-export,' pills, dodgy paperwork, this and that. The other two moved on in the early eighties and the brothers went solo, bringing in people for different jobs as and when. They did everything from beating up a grass or two and running a protection racket right up to armed robberies. Did a few bank jobs and all. No one killed though, until the Shoreditch fiasco. A thoroughly unpleasant pair whom everyone knew and steered clear of if they had the chance."

"Who were the other two?" Graham asked. He wished now that he had contacted Needham earlier, despite the awkwardness of depending on an exhausted mind. Graham imagined Needham's rheumy eyes unfocused, his mouth gaping slightly.

"Eh?"

"Who made up the band of four? The younger two?"

"Dillon and Cross," Needham said without pause, as though naming his own dogs. "Suspects in a couple of post office jobs, and I fancied them for an odd, rural burglary in Northamptonshire."

Gears turned for a couple of seconds, then the file popped up in Graham's brain. "Planned a hostage-taking . . . affluent young couple?"

"That's the one. Then the dozy buggers realised they'd forgotten the rope and tape. Ended up running off with whatever they could carry."

"Sound like amateurs to me."

"Oh, they were appalling, incompetent criminals. Should have gone straight while they had the chance. But they were influenced, led astray by older, harder men looking for patsies. And they were lucky they never got caught." Needham rattled off a list of the Parnaby jobs he could remember.

"Arthur and George gave genuine mobsters a bad name. They did what a lot do when they don't have the intelligence. They compensated with menaces and ultimately violence. And as time went on, their crimes depended on it. But Dillon and Cross were involved fairly early. By the time of the Shoreditch job that sent the Parnabys down, those two lads were long gone."

"What happened to them?"

"Vanished, as far as I can remember. They never crossed my path again, that's for sure."

"Well, I can solve one-half of that mystery. Mr. Dillon's just turned up dead on Jersey."

The assumption was instant. "Murdered?"

"Looks that way. In 1982. We found his body bunged in a block of concrete in a hotel attic—the White House Inn where you stayed when you came over for that conference a few years ago." Graham waited for some murmur of recognition from his former boss, but none was forthcoming.

"Some bright spark cut his cocaine with rat poison. The owner of the hotel was running a drugs racket while dying of cancer and wanted to avoid a scene. So instead of raising the alarm, she blocked him up. His remains were found by accident some days ago." Graham hoped his words would spark something in Needham's memory.

After a pause, the former DCI said, "You like rock'n'roll, don't you, Dave?"

"Who doesn't?" Graham responded tentatively, afraid the *non sequitur* signalled an abrupt and unwelcome change of topic.

"Think of your classic rock band. Usually," Needham said, "one band member lives hard and checks out early. Overdose, suicide, that kind of thing. Two of the others keep on rocking as a duo, reliving their heyday until age catches up with them. And the fourth one, often the brainiest of them all, what does he do?"

"Well, if he's smart, he makes his millions while he can and goes off to live on a farm in the Wiltshire countryside."

"Exactly."

With thanks for his help and good wishes to his wife, Graham ended the call with Needham and immediately placed another.

"Freddie? I have a question for you."

CHAPTER FORTY-SEVEN

J ANICE AND GRAHAM were huddling, talking quietly, when the two Parnaby brothers returned to the interview room.

"Dylan Dillon went to Jersey to murder Charlie Cross, didn't he?" Graham said as soon as they resumed the interview.

Arthur blinked at him. "Afternoon to you 'n' all. How was your food? I thought the meatloaf was a bit dry."

George rubbed his stomach and licked his lips, grinning widely to reveal a couple of missing canines that seemed to have gone AWOL during lunch. His volcanic lungs rumbled into action. "I had the pasta with the creamy sauce. Very nice, it was."

Graham ignored these comments. "Did the two of you order him to do it? Or was it Dillon's idea to go to Jersey? I mean," he said, turning to Janice as if to explain, "he must have been incensed at the way Cross ripped you all off."

Janice blinked in amazement. "East End, low-end, dead-end mob lackeys ripping each other off?" She gasped. "Whatever next?"

"Shove it where the sun don't shine, lady," George rasped.

"Cool it, George. She's only trying to understand what the good detective inspector is saying. And frankly"—Arthur turned to Graham—"so am I."

"In 1981, I put it to you that Mr. Cross decided, on reflection, not to pursue a career as an aimless hoodlum any further. He felt his talents might extend beyond nicking bikes, threatening village postal workers, and jemmying back windows. As law enforcement officials, we normally welcome this kind of revelation, don't we, Sergeant?"

"With open arms," Janice agreed.

Graham paused. He was extemporising. He pulled together everything he had learned, made some educated guesses, and lobbed a theory to test the brothers' reaction. "But this new convert's erstwhile brethren, during their grief and anguish at their friend's abrupt departure, made a highly incriminating discovery."

Hand under his chin as though thoroughly engaged in story time, Arthur said, "Eh? Oh, no, please don't stop. It's great, this. Quality entertainment."

"Nothing like watching coppers try to prove a crime they just made up," his brother said. "Go on, don't let us stop you. Is there any popcorn?" George turned to Janice, whose mild, almost disinterested expression gave him no satisfaction.

Graham stood. After hours in a car, then more hours trying to lever information out of this miserable pair, he'd lost all feeling below his left knee. "Carry on, Sergeant," he said, flexing his ankle.

"This discovery was an unpleasant one," Janice said. "Mr. Cross likely fancied setting himself up for a life of luxury . . . Well, a few years of it anyway. Whatever third-hand safe, or space beneath a squeaky floorboard, or back bedroom mattress had become the resting place of your loot, Mr. Cross found it."

"Sounds like it must have been annoying," Graham added, "to find that your former mate has summarily slinked off with most of the takings from your post office jobs."

"I mean," Janice added, "it must have wound you up something terrible."

"If I'd known you were going to waste my time with fiction, I'd have gone to the library after lunch. They have better stories." Arthur sniffed.

"I'd have hung out in the canteen a bit longer, maybe blagged an extra pudding," said George. "There's always someone with a fresh face you can snatch one off of."

Graham took over again. "Was it on your orders that Dylan Dillon went to Jersey to find Charlie Cross?"

"Orders?" Arthur scoffed. "It wasn't the bleedin' army or anyfin'. We worked together in the building trade is all."

"'The building trade'," parroted a sceptical Janice. "Threatening shop owners for protection money." She checked off a list on her fingers. "Collecting on payday loans from young single mums, intimidating a local councilman to—"

The two brothers interrupted her with a synchronised routine so smooth she suspected they had rehearsed it. "No charges were ever brought," Arthur intoned.

"And we have nothing to add to our earlier statements."

"Okay, fine. Thanks for all your help," Graham said, his hands on his hips. "Sergeant Harding, if we hurry, we can grab that earlier flight." He made a note with a final flourish and folded away his notebook. "And it seems I won't have to make any phone calls in support of these two after all. They've decided to wither in HMP Holbrooke in one final gesture of defiance. Will they deem it worth it in the final analysis? Ah well, not our concern. You know what they say about old dogs, new tricks? Defying the police is a lifelong pursuit for these two. Seems they can't change even when it's in their best interest."

Graham took a moment to glare at the brothers as he spoke, regarding them like decrepit museum pieces, destined for dust. Graham found George's eyes, and they were those of a sick man, veined and yellow. "You've got months at best, I'd wager, not years. Why spend them in here miserably?" He opened the door for Janice.

The pain of confusion involuntarily curled George's fists into tight balls. "Stop him," he growled to his brother. "We ain't finished here yet."

CHAPTER FORTY-EIGHT

I N THE CAR on the way to the airport, Janice helped
Graham note down every last detail the Parnaby
brothers had eventually told them, and then on the
flight back to Jersey, she played devil's advocate as they
reconstructed events as best they understood them. By the
time the inspector was done, they were on the final
approach, the journey passing in a flash amid the blur of
work, fuelled by an overpriced but gloriously caffeinated
double-tea-bag cuppa.

"So, now we have Cross's life story," said Graham. "An
everyday one, really. Bloke grows up surrounded by stub-
born, middle-aged men who never taught him to control his
impulsivity and anger. He gets in with the wrong crowd and
ends up among the Parnabys and their lot, thieving and
threatening. But he sees the way the wind's blowing—the
Parnabys, his older brothers and cousins, other associates—
and decides he won't end up like them."

"It takes time, but he plucks up the courage," Janice
guessed, "gets himself set, and absconds with all their loot in
the middle of the night."

"More options that way. Gave him a head start, the means to disappear."

"But Dillon tracked him down to Jersey." Graham paused, jutting out his chin. "Dillon arrives on the island full of fury at being double-crossed, whipped up by the Parnabys. He ferrets out his prey. But before he can take action, someone, maybe his target, gets to him first. Kills him."

"But, sir, the timeline. According to passport records, Dillon travelled from Jersey to France immediately after his death, then returned in October 1982. After that, we lose him. He, or someone posing as him, must still be on Jersey." They had landed and were taxiing down the runway when Graham's phone picked up a cell tower and delivered an avalanche of texts.

"Not necessarily, Sergeant. Dillon was a British citizen. Did we need our passports for our jaunt to the mainland?"

"Ah, no. So, Dillon wouldn't use his passport if he's traveling to and from the British mainland. Only if he's crossing a country border."

"That's right. He could have reentered Jersey from France, then gone back to mainland UK and we wouldn't have known. I assume the flight and ferry manifests are long gone?"

"Yes, I checked. So, Dillon could be anywhere in the UK?"

"Yes."

"But he was dead, sir."

Graham blew out his cheeks. "Yes. I'm thinking that he must have had his passport with him when he arrived on Jersey, perhaps because he had plans to go to Europe and hide out for a bit. Then someone, perhaps his murderer, used it, and that's who we're seeing travel to France and back."

"Charlie Cross, do you think?"

"Maybe. Did you get anything back on him?"

"Yes and no. There's another puzzling thing. There are no records for Cross at all after 1981 when the Parnabys said he disappeared . . . And that means . . ."

"Yes, Sergeant?"

"He could also be anywhere in the UK."

"Or he too is dead." It was Janice's turn to blow out her cheeks. Graham looked at his phone again. Barnwell was calling.

"Phew, I'm already wishing we were back in the air, uncontactable for a bit longer." Graham pressed the "accept" button. "Yes, Barnwell?" Chatter and laughter filled the background.

"Hope you had a fruitful day, sir. Just wanted to let you know that I had another go at finding that address in Julian's Wood, and I think I found it. Four cottages, some outbuildings, and another building, perhaps a chapel. The story, ah, let's say the folklore, is that someone ran courses there, seminars. Can't imagine in what—bushcraft? When that stopped, the scouts took over. At some point, a fire came along and burned part of it down. The buildings were abandoned. But now the area's a thriving eco-warrior commune with gardens and such. It was all a bit strange, to be fair. But that's all I got. Doesn't seem like it had anything to do with our case. Dead end if you ask me."

"Hmm, okay. Thanks for doing that. Pity it wasn't more informative."

"No problem, sir. Me 'n' Carmen are having a rest in the Foc'sle. Good crowd tonight. Beer's off though. Bad barrel. I'm drinking tonic water."

"Good man. We need your clear head first thing, Barnwell. Have a good rest of your evening. We'll see you tomorrow." The seat belt sign turned off, and Graham helped Janice bring her laptop bag down from the overhead compartment. "Here, let me. You need to look after yourself. After all, you've got that small thing in a couple of days."

"Hallelujah," she muttered.

"Hmm?"

"Nothing."

"Jitters are natural, you know. My wife was like a cat on a hot tin roof just before our wedding."

"Oh?" Janice arched her eyebrows. Graham caught himself and stared straight ahead. Sensing his discomfort at this slip of personal information, Janice said, "I can't wait to marry Jack."

"Glad to hear it."

"It's my mother."

"She doesn't like him?"

"No, no, she'd marry him herself if she could. She'd just do it her way."

Even without years of detective work, Graham would quickly have made the deduction. "You came on this trip to get away from her, didn't you?"

"Something like that."

"Janice," he said. "Tenbeigh runs an efficient joint, but . . . it's Holbrooke. Not exactly Saint-Tropez. As far as jollies go, it was hardly worth it."

"Oh, you'd be surprised. Holbrooke had at least one feature that made it an attractive destination," she said as they walked past the baggage carousels and looked for a cab.

"The thrill of the case?" he said.

"Great title for your autobiography." Janice smirked.

"Or just a getaway from your mother."

"How about a little of each? Like pie and ice cream for pudding."

A taxi pulled up. "Don't forget, Laura and I are here if you need us."

The heavens burst as Graham opened the car door for his sergeant. "My only advice is to remember to turn off your phone during the ceremony," he reminded her, "because your "Stayin' Alive" ringtone isn't going to do justice to the acoustics at St. Andrew's."

"Don't worry, it's on my 'List of Things to Do Before Getting Married.'"

"What else is on it? Your list," he said. The rain was coming down harder now.

"Exile my mother to the Outer Hebrides!" she shouted before the door slammed shut.

CHAPTER FORTY-NINE

C ARMEN'S EARS TWITCHED. She trotted
out from under Barnwell's desk as the doors to
the station opened.

"Mornin', all."

In unison, Barnwell's and Janice's heads popped up.
Delighted smiles spread across their faces, their eyes
shining.

"Roachie!" Janice cried. She hurried around the reception desk, her arms outstretched, ready to give a big hug to
tall, lanky Detective Sergeant Roach, formerly of Gorey
Constabulary, now a member of Homicide and Major
Crime Command based at Scotland Yard.

After they hugged, Janice stepped back, clutching
Roach's arms and scrutinising him, just like his mother had
done an hour earlier. "Look at you. I swear you've grown
two inches since we last saw you." Janice punched him on
the bicep. "And so muscly. Bet all the London girls are after
you!" Yeah, exactly like his mother.

"Ah, not really. At least not at the moment. We'll see."

Roach raised his eyebrows. "How's Jack? All ready for tomorrow?"

Janice smiled. "He's well. And we're as ready as we'll ever be."

Behind Janice, Barnwell stirred. "Hiya, mate," he said shyly.

"Wotcha, Bazza." Roach smiled. They shook hands.

"Aw, c'me 'ere," Barnwell said after a tiny pause, and he too pulled Roach in for a hug, a manly one, their hands clasped between their chests and accompanied by a hard, rough mutual pat on the back.

When they separated, Roach looked across and saw Graham standing in his office doorway, leaning against the frame. He was smiling. "Hello, sir." Graham pushed himself off.

"Detective Sergeant Roach, good to see you." They vigorously shook hands, but there was no hug in the offing this time. Telepathically or by osmosis, they both understood that simply wouldn't do. "How's it going up there in London?"

Jim Roach had certainly matured in the ten months he had been away. It showed in his chiselled cheekbones and square jaw, both more angled since he was last on Jersey. In his eyes, a confidence, an assuredness that reminded Graham of his younger self, bloomed. Stubble and an up-to-the-minute haircut, replete with gel, completed the makeover. Roach had never been a slouch, but now there was a slight air of danger about him, an edge.

"Great, sir. I'm enjoying it. Bit of a culture shock at first but getting an arrest or two under my belt helped a lot."

Hearing this, Graham's heart swelled. His cheeks reddened and his heart kicked up a beat or two. "Good man." He looked at his watch. "Well, I think it's time for an early lunch, don't you? Why don't the three of you go and have yours? I'll man the fort here. I'll call you if I need you."

Janice and Barnwell didn't need telling twice. Immediately, they grabbed their jackets, shut down their computers, and marched out into the sunlight. Janice grabbed Roach's arm and, linking his with hers, chattered away, updating him on all the news, clearly delighted to have him home as she bounced along next to him. Barnwell trailed behind, Carmen trotting alongside him, a familiar sight.

Alone in the office, Graham's phone chimed. It was Laura. "Yes, love. How's your day going?"

"Not bad. Bit quiet for a Thursday, but the old boys are asleep with the *Racing Post* and *Daily Mail*. St. Helier has just delivered a huge pile of requested books. And I have an enormous backlog of returns to shelve. You?"

"Ah, just mulling the Dillon case, not getting very far. Jim Roach has just arrived for Janice's wedding. I've sent the three of them off for lunch, so I'm here by myself."

"Aw, poor you. I'd keep you company if I didn't have all these books to shelve. I was ringing to tell you the amount of work I have to do this afternoon is all down to you."

"Me?"

"Yes, I've spent this morning doing some research on your behalf."

Graham paused. "Research?" Graham was relieved that it wasn't something serious, something perhaps to do with Freddie Solomon and his involvement-slash-interference in the Dillon case.

"Julian's Wood. What you told me last night. Barnwell was almost right about the seminars."

"Almost?"

"Back in the day, the place was a seminary, a small one. As far as I can tell, just a dozen or so theological students.

Its funding dried up, and it fizzled out, eventually closing." At the other end of the phone, Laura smiled, pleased with her sleuthing.

Graham pushed his lips out as he considered this. "Hmm. And when did it close exactly?"

"The mid-eighties—1983 to be exact. Is that helpful?"

"Not sure. Seems odd."

As Graham ended their call, loneliness and disappointment swept across him. He had no idea how the address of a long-closed seminary written on the back cover of a novel found at a crime scene was relevant to his investigation. He tossed his pencil on his desk as he sat down, leaning forward and rubbing his face with his hand.

The case reminded him of a mug of tepid, weak, milky tea. When making tea with a tea bag, if you add the milk first, before the tea, the hot water cannot extract the flavour from the leaves. It doesn't matter how much you stir, the tea will not steep. The fundamentals are wrong.

Graham couldn't escape the idea that he was missing something fundamental about the case of Dylan Dillon. It didn't seem to matter how much evidence they gathered; none of it added up.

Graham deliberately cleared his mind and reviewed what he knew, rhythmically tapping his pencil on his desk, hoping that a flash of insight would pop into his head. But nothing struck him. The inspector leaned back and sighed, resting his hands, fingers interlinked, on his head.

He had hit a wall. And with Janice's wedding tomorrow, he had to put the case aside. Laura would expect it of him, and she would be right. He stood to make another cup of tea. Perhaps that would help. He would make sure to put the tea bag in first.

CHAPTER FIFTY

G RAHAM STRAIGHTENED HIS narrow, black tie before shrugging on his uniform jacket and buttoning it. He stood back from the mirror, tugging at the jacket's hem. He checked everything was in order: the two pips on his epaulettes, silver now (they had been gold when he was in the Met); his three medals for bravery and honourable conduct; the position and arc of his whistle chain that stretched from between his first and second buttons to his breast pocket. Upside down on the bed, a pair of new white gloves sitting inside, lay his uniform cap, the black band on the peak denoting his status as a detective inspector.

"How do I look?" he asked Laura as he pulled on his cuffs. She looked him up and down.

"Devastatingly handsome, I'd say." She leaned forward on tiptoes, her lips puckered for a quick kiss. A notification came through on Graham's phone, and it pinged. "I'm glad you resolved your differences with Freddie in time for today. I'd been anxious about the two of you bumping into each other. I thought it might overshadow the occasion and spoil Janice's wedding."

"Her mother's doing her best to achieve that. And resolving our differences is going a bit far, I think. A temporary truce is more like it. And he better not write anything else about the case. That was our agreement. We're making progress, albeit slowly, and I don't want him prejudicing any court proceedings that might occur in the future. He can have his day in the sun later."

"Well, whatever you want to call it, I'm pleased. And today is a good day, a happy day. Finally, Janice and Jack are getting married, despite her mother's efforts, and we get the chance to dress up to celebrate it." Laura leaned toward the mirror to smear her lips with gloss. Still in her dressing gown, her fair, shoulder-length hair piled high on her head, she looked like a model posing for an impressionist painting. *Woman in Mirror* or some such.

"I'm disappointed the case is still hanging over our heads, though. I had hoped to have it resolved by the wedding. It is such a baffling case." Graham sighed. "Are you coming with me? I have to leave now." Graham, along with Roach and Barnwell, were ushers. His phone pinged again, and he picked it up.

"I hope that's nothing important," Laura said.

"No, not a number I recognise. So, are you coming?"

"I'm not quite ready yet. You go, and I'll catch you at the church."

Graham picked up his hat and gloves. He breathed in deeply through his nose and out through his mouth, relaxing his shoulders. "I'm going to do my absolute level best to forget about work and enjoy today."

"Woo-hoo! You mean like a normal person?"

"Yes, like a normal person." He pecked her jauntily on the cheeks and smiled. "See you later!"

Laura watched him stride down the short path through her cottage garden to the car parked outside. She looked at her watch. A frisson of panic shot through her. "Oh, my gosh! I'd better get going!" Bounding up the stairs to the bedroom, she plugged in her hairdryer and started wielding it like a weapon, rolling her hair into big curls with a thick, round brush. Eight minutes later, she turned off the dryer, and as she leaned over to stuff it in a drawer, she glanced out of the window.

She straightened slowly. Something was wrong. David should be at the church by now, but his car idled at the curb.

Inside it, the detective inspector sat in the driver's seat, frowning. He was staring at his phone.

In the photo, the two boys looked like brothers. Same light brown hair, short wide noses, and pointed chins. Their eyes crinkled at the outside corners as they posed, their arms around each other's shoulders, the faded black-and-white colours and long, pointed shirt collars hinting at the photo's age. It had been sent to Graham by Angela Dillon.

Found this. Dylan is the one on the left.
Don't know the other boy. Taken early 70s.

Graham guessed the boys were around fifteen. Dillon grinned broadly, revealing familiar metal tramlines that were the bane of pubescent teenagers the world over and which almost completely obscured his teeth. The unidentified boy next to him grinned a gappy-toothed smile, his lips stretched thin and wide as he cheekily raised a two-fingered peace sign. Graham thoughtfully tapped his phone with a fingernail before sending a text of his own.

> Thanks for this. Your brother had braces?

Graham knew of the organisation, time, and effort required for this type of dental treatment, and it didn't jive with what Angela Dillon had told him about her family. Almost immediately, he received a text back.

> We all had them. Free on the NHS. It was out of character for our mother, but she had terrible teeth herself and insisted. She was a huge fan of the Osmonds.

Graham glanced at the clock on the dashboard and sprung into action. He scrolled through his contacts and, finding the pathology lab's main number, he placed a call. Then, switching his phone to vibrate, he quickly fired up the engine. He was running late. Dylan Dillon and his braces would have to wait.

"Yes, yes, I can do that," Fiona said. She paused as she listened to Graham on the other end of the line. "Um, ten minutes?" She paused again. "'Kay, I'll send it straight away." The call ended, but almost immediately her phone's screen flashed, accompanied by a familiar peal of notes.

"Take a break, Fiona, it's the weekend." It was Tomlinson. He was on his way to the church too. Francine, resplendent as always, today in purple, sat next to him. She was driving.

"I know, but I'm waiting on the bone DNA results. In respect to the Dillon case. I still haven't received them."

"But they won't tell you much more than we already know. Go home and relax."

"Oh, alright. I'm not very good at relaxing, but since you insist. Inspector Graham just called and asked for another aged photo, but after I've done that, I'll leave."

"Are you on your own there?"

"Yes, Aidan left a little while ago."

"Do you know if he called the funeral directors? About Dylan Dillon. The body will be released to his next of kin soon now that we've finished our tests and know who he is. He needs to be moved and prepared for his service."

"He said he'd do it on his way home."

"Okay, thanks. Are you going to Janice and Jack's evening do?"

"Yes. It was nice of them to ask me. I can meet the rest of the team. I'm looking forward to it. I'll see you then. Have a lovely time. Bye, Marcus."

Fiona hung up. Comfortable among drawers of dead bodies, five currently, she opened the software she needed to complete the task Inspector Graham had asked of her. Taking the photo of the two teenage boys he had sent, she isolated Dillon on the left and set about aging his face fifty years as he had asked.

When it was done, she texted the image to Graham and prepared to leave. Looping her bag over her shoulder, Fiona walked to the bank of light switches and turned them all off. Darkness descended, and she paused for a moment, appreciating the peacefulness of the mortuary, the only sound the buzzing of the refrigeration system.

Shutting the door as she walked out, her phone began a steady, rhythmic tinkle that repeated twice before she answered it, listening carefully. Seconds later, Fiona rushed through the mortuary door, rapidly switching on the lights, the room suddenly ablaze as she powered her computer back on.

CHAPTER FIFTY-ONE

J ACK WENTWORTH, HIS younger brother Toby, and his best man Dexter arrived first, all roguishly handsome thirty-somethings in their grey morning suits and top hats.

"Cool," whispered Toby, looking around him at the ancient stonework, the soaring arched ceiling, and the dramatic flower arrangements at the end of every pew. He spoke as though the church were half-full, not empty. It was still early, an hour to go.

Dexter's contribution was a loud clap, hands above his head, followed by a graceful C-major arpeggio in his light-opera baritone. "I have to hand it to you, Jack, mate, it's a fine venue," he said in his broad Geordie accent. Jack and Dexter had been at university together.

"We searched for an acoustic that would make your voice soar while me and Jan sign the register," Jack said. "First order of business, that was. Promise." Dexter wandered off to the front of the church. There, the four members of the string quartet that would accompany him were setting up underneath the large, colourful stained glass window of a mournful St. Andrew holding a cross and surrounded by fish.

A year before, Jack and Janice had almost everything planned for their wedding when Janice was kidnapped and nearly drowned. They postponed the wedding until things had settled and they could think again.

When they were ready to proceed, they had slightly different priorities. They had wanted something smaller, personal, intimate. Something that reflected their wishes whilst also meeting the needs of their family members—salt-of-the-earth types, steeped in tradition, who held strong views on the milestones of life being taken in the "right" order. No babies before marriage for Janice and Jack! Living together had been as far as they had pushed it. Even that had been met with tight lips and stiff backs, both eventually relaxing once the older generation realised that the effort required to maintain the tension wore them out and was utterly ineffective.

St. Andrew's, though, was a keeper from the original plans. Jack's priorities had been to find a church that didn't feel too big, wouldn't insist on a huge fee, and would satisfy Janice's mother. On the sunlit morning Janice and Jack attended a service, they had felt warmth emanate from within its stones. Perhaps it had come from hours of bathing in the sun's heat—it had been a hot day, even at the 11 a.m. Sunday worship service—but they'd felt comfortable committing to a date.

Tipping the scales for Jack had been its spaciousness, despite it being a relatively small church. He had appreciated the unique way the church wrapped him in a timeless calm each time he walked in. He thought his future mother-in-law might like it.

Jack was a simple guy, easygoing with respect to most

things. At one point, he and Janice had considered a beach wedding somewhere nice and warm. But the explosion of fury that would have emanated from Mrs. Harding if they had chosen the heat of sand beneath their feet instead of that radiating off the sixteenth-century church stone filled him with horror.

As he reassured his fiancée many times during the preparations, the most important consideration was that they be married. The details of how and where were unimportant to Jack. They could wed in a cow barn and he would be happy.

The same couldn't be said for Janice. And certainly not her mother. Jack anticipated trouble and resolved to be the bulwark, a commitment that had tested him many times over the previous months.

"And what did Mrs. Harding think of the church?" asked Toby.

Jack savoured a fleeting moment of calm, sure that the day would later be full of opportunities to be otherwise. "She thought this was an annexe to the main building," Jack recalled, his eyes closing in discomfort. Rosemary's comportment during her tour of the church had been one of poorly restrained disappointment. As she'd expected, Janice later received a fulsome chronicle of her mother's objections in the form of six very long and detailed voicemails.

"I feel guilty," Janice had said to Jack after finally pressing "delete." "I want you to know that. But, sweetheart, this is self-preservation."

"From the way she talked up your wedding last night at dinner," Dexter said, returning from his chat with the musicians, "I'm expecting nothing less than a Royal Air Force flypast." He turned to the brothers; one was a shorter, stockier version of the other. Jack cringed.

"That's Rosemary for you. This is a significant moment in her life. Maybe the most significant. I suppose it is for all mothers of a bride. Rosemary is . . ." Jack tried to explain, "really enthusiastic about this wedding." For a moment, he and Toby privately appreciated their sisterless existence in silence.

"Will she have you waving at the crowd from the balcony like the royals?" wondered Dexter. "So nice of you to come." The best man partnered a royal wave with the accent of landed gentry, his voice falsetto, feminine, and ludicrous. "Paupers and the other unwashed may watch in silence from the back," he added, dropping his voice and mocking the prim, high-handed elocution of the privileged.

"Leave her alone. She's not that bad," Jack said, regretting not shutting down the subject of his soon-to-be mother-in-law the moment it had arisen.

He allowed himself a laugh. If he could manage not to take Rosemary Harding too seriously, not to let her meddling bother him, there was a decent chance he might enjoy his own wedding day. "Alright. I'm going to find Reverend Bright. You two stay here and wait for the ushers to arrive. They should be here any minute."

"No problem, mate. It's your wedding day. Your wish is my command," Dexter said, saluting.

"Thanks, pal. That's what I need today." Jack left them and headed through to the vestry.

Reverend Bright was there, but he wasn't alone. Jack slowed his pace and prepared to wait. Bright had so many responsibilities in the community, from arranging funerals to scheduling bake sales, that he could have been doing anything. As Jack got closer, Bright ushered someone to the door.

It was Rosemary, here at the church much earlier than

planned. Why wasn't she at the house with the bridesmaids? Perhaps Janice had got shot of her.

"I really wish you'd speak to them again," she was
saying. "It's short notice, but there must be several organists
on Jersey."

"I've long since learned," Bright said, his patience still
intact but beginning to drain, "that musical choices are very
personal. It would be wrong of me to intervene."

"It's just . . . the spectacle of it. I think they're losing out
on so much." It was then, as the reverend closed the vestry
door behind them and they emerged into the sunshine, that
Rosemary noticed Jack. Far from embarrassed, she tried
once again to recruit him to her cause. "That huge sound,
Jack! It'll fill the place! Let's get the organist to play
"Widor's Toccata" as you walk out together and really lift
the roof! What do you say?"

CHAPTER FIFTY-TWO

JACK'S BRAIN CLENCHED like a vice. His expression said, "We've been over this a million times." His mouth said, "Morning, Rosemary! Great day for it." He nodded to Bright. "How are you, Reverend?"

"Jack, you lucky lad! Best day of your life, this is!"

"It's highly promising, that's for sure." Jack smiled. "Are you, um, with the bridesmaids, Rosemary?"

Before she could answer, the reverend's mobile phone rang—always jarring and tricky to find given it had to be retrieved from within his cassock. "Joshua Bright," he answered affably. He turned away from them but not before his face darkened and his mouth fell open.

Jack caught the vicar's reaction and tracked Bright's responses to the caller, searching for clues, worrying they might be related to the wedding. "Yes, of course, but . . ." Bright said.

Janice's mother seemed unconcerned about the call and the vicar's reaction. She watched the groomsmen's tails flutter in the breeze as Toby and Dexter approached. "I trust your best man has the ring?" Rosemary said. "He didn't seem completely with it during the rehearsal dinner. Are you sure he is up to his responsibilities?"

Jack defended his best man. "Dexter was vice-chairman of the Durham University Debating Society and he's been my friend for nearly fifteen years. He's on the case, don't worry."

Not in the least reassured, Rosemary caught Jack's gaze and joined him in watching the now-pacing vicar. She tried to lip-read but had to settle for interpreting his body language. "Now he's distracted," she said. "Humph."

"Everything all right, chaps?" Dexter said as he and Toby reached them.

"Bigger churches assign you a liaison," Rosemary claimed, "because they're dedicated to making sure the . . ."

Jack whirled around to look at her. "Rosemary!" he said through clenched teeth. "Will you—"

"Of course!" said Reverend Bright cheerily, turning back to them as he ended the call. He smiled at the wedding party and waved at them, telegraphing all was well and narrowly preventing Jack from losing the temper he had so carefully kept in check for so long.

"Is there a problem?" Rosemary inquired.

"Not at all." Bright beamed and clapped his hands. "How's everyone feeling?" he asked, smiling broadly, injecting into the group the warmth and energy for which he was generally admired by his congregation, small and elderly as it often was. "Jack, when did you last see the blushing bride?"

"Not today, obviously!" interjected Rosemary. "Worst kind of luck to see her before the organ strikes up."

"I saw her last night at the end of the dinner," Jack replied calmly. "And speaking of lifting the roof off, four choristers plus Dexter and a string quartet are going to perform during the processional and at the end of the service, Rosemary. They'll do us proud. They may well lift the roof off. Perhaps you'll consider paying for the repairs, eh?"

Rosemary's body language was tortured and dissatisfied, like a child offered jelly when she craved ice cream. With thirty minutes to go, she seemed to be finally accepting that things were not going her way. "Singing. Yes, you said."

Rosemary flounced off to await the arrival of the brides-maids whom she'd left at Janice's home. They had been giggling with the bride, glasses of champagne in their hands, and Rosemary had been unable to bear their gaiety and complete unwillingness to listen to her remonstrations. Bright took her departure as his cue to leave and also vanished, although rather more elegantly, his cassock skirts flowing.

In the distance, Rosemary noticed Marjorie Taylor walking down the lane to the church, her forefinger and thumb delicately holding in place a spaceship-size pink hat wrapped in mesh. She was early, but finally, here was a mature, sensible woman with whom Rosemary could hold a decent conversation. She raised her hand and called out to attract Marjorie's attention.

Toby turned to Jack, a hand on his arm. "And you, lucky boy, get to call her 'Mum' for all eternity."

"Yeah, but Jan's got her number. There's a reason she lives on a small island hundreds of miles and a large stretch of water away." Rosemary may be proving to be the most irritating mother-in-law in history, but Jack was keeping his eye on the prize. "Shortly," he told his friends, "I get to marry the single most amazing woman I've ever met."

"And someone who can arrest your neighbours if they're noisy in the small hours," Dexter said. "Win, win."

"It'll be Rosemary getting arrested if she's not careful," warned Jack. "Jan won't stand for it. Tampering with a police officer's sanity on her wedding day sounds criminal to me."

Arriving alone at the lychgate, Graham stopped to hear the curious mix of words floating across the green, sunlit churchyard: sanity . . . police officer . . . criminal . . . "Uh-oh," he laughed as he opened the creaking gate. "Don't tell me I'm needed!"

"Only if you think slinging Rosemary in a holding cell for three hours while I marry her daughter would help," Jack said, then saw the attraction. "Actually, is that a real crime? 'Tampering with a police officer's sanity'?"

"Just one in a long list of offences still awaiting their place in the statute book," Graham replied. "Jack, my lad, you look fantastic. And these two ruffians must be Dexter and Toby," he said, quickly introducing himself. Graham rubbed his hands together. He felt his phone vibrate in his pocket.

"Morning, all." The lychgate creaked again, and Graham quickly glanced at his phone as he turned to see Roach and Barnwell, also in full dress uniform, walking towards them. As usual, at Barnwell's heel trotted Carmen, a spray of baby pink roses to match the groomsmen's button-holes attached to her collar. "Here's the rest of the gang. Are we all set? Tell us what to do and we'll do it."

"Yep, you're to be stationed at the door," Toby said. Dexter groaned and rolled his eyes. "What?"

"Stationed, geddit?"

It was Toby's turn to roll his eyes. "Yeah, yeah, wagster. Come with me, guys. I'll show you where to stand."

Inside the church, the warm, musty air elicited comforting childhood memories for Graham, and the three officers looked in awe at the enormous stained glass at the opposite end of the church as they listened to their instructions.

"Welcome the guests as they arrive. Hand them an order of service. Ask them if they're with the bride or the groom, and then lead them to a pew on the appropriate side."

"The what side?" Barnwell whispered to Roach.

"If their connection is to the bride, they sit on the right side as the vicar looks from the front. They're on the left side if they're with the groom," Roach whispered back.

"The first two rows are for family," Toby added. "Now, where are those orders of service? They should be on that table." He looked around him. "Hmm, wait there and I'll find the vicar. He'll know where they are."

Dexter walked up and spoke in Toby's ear. "Your parents have arrived. I think you should speak to them. They're by the war memorial."

"But Dex, we don't have the order—"

"Don't worry, you see to your parents. I'll find the vicar," Graham said, taking charge. "It's no problem."

Dexter clicked his heels. "Excuse me while I attend to the potential natural disaster that is Mrs. Harding, as tasked to me to prevent the fraying of the groom's already shredded nerves. She needs constant management such that we avoid a meltdown of nuclear proportions. I'm sure you understand. The vestry's that way." He pointed to a side door at the front of the church.

"Understood," Graham said. He turned to his officers. "Right, lads, I'll be back in a minute."

As he walked up the side aisle, his phone vibrated again.

He pulled it out and glanced at it. It was Fiona. She had sent him a text and copied Tomlinson. As he read it, his heart turned over.

> Massive development. Bone DNA just in. Does not match with hair. I repeat, DNA from bones does not match hair DNA. Mr. X is not Dylan Dillon.

Graham paced the back hallways of the church, still attempting to track Reverend Bright down. The place was immaculately neat, its offices bright and clean, the hallways spotless. According to the poster on the noticeboard exhorting sign-ups, there was a "Godly Play" after-school program on Thursday afternoons. Graham could imagine the tumble of schoolchildren filling the ancient space with fun and noise, and his mind briefly wandered to Katie.

At other times, so the noticeboard told him, the church held coffee and cake mornings, popular with the elderly in Graham's experience, and baby yoga classes. Then, three evenings a week, support groups created a more sombre atmosphere. Focused as they were on bereavement, addiction, and mental health, they provided for those who attended an indispensable service. Reverend Bright had certainly created in St. Andrew's a busy, thriving cornerstone that underpinned the Gorey community.

Graham was about to go outside to explore the cemetery when he checked the vestry for a third time. He discovered Bright standing in the middle of the small room, the door ajar. His back faced the door, his head bent.

"Ah, just the man," Graham said, knocking on the door to announce his presence.

Quickly burying his mobile phone among his cassock folds, Bright turned to greet the detective inspector. He eyed the inspector's uniform and waved him in. "Come in, come in." With a dramatic flourish, Bright lifted his wrist to check his watch. "Can I help you? I haven't much time. I'm about to . . ."

"I'm here about the orders of service, Reverend. We're missing them at the door." Graham smiled. "I'm one of the ushers. And the bride's boss."

"Ah, of course. Hold on, they're around here somewhere." Bright walked over to a small table by the wall and opened a drawer. "Yes, here they are. Sorry, they should have been waiting for you."

"No problem. Thank you." Graham waved the pamphlets in salute. Bright smiled broadly.

Graham turned to leave, shutting the door behind him. The first guests who had been milling around outside chatting entered the church. It would be a race as to whom would reach the ushers first—Graham or the guests. The inspector briskly strode through the church to reach Barnwell and Roach anxiously waiting for him by the door. And then his stride faltered.

Avalanches of information converged in Graham's mind. At first, they were barely more than wisps of ideas nudged by memories, but they gained momentum and stature to form a roiling torrent, eventually converging into a wild, powerful river of ideas and theories into which the inspector, his investigative intellect overwhelming his instincts for decorum and tradition, now plunged.

Barnwell and Roach watched as Graham drew to a halt midway down the aisle.

"What's he doing, Roachie?"

"I'm not sure, Bazza."

"He's got the orders of service in his hand."

"I can see that, but he's turning around. Where's he going?"

"I dunno, but those guests are going to get here in around ten seconds, and we'll not have the orders of service to hand them."

"Stall them with Carmen. I'll go get them off him." But Graham had disappeared, and Roach, like his former boss earlier, began traversing the back hallways of the church looking for him.

CHAPTER FIFTY-THREE

"REVEREND BRIGHT?" GRAHAM had knocked on the vestry door and tried the handle. Inside, he found the reverend sitting in an armchair, his hands clasped in his lap around his phone. He looked mildly at the detective inspector. "May I come in?" Graham said.

Bright gestured with his hand, inviting him. "There isn't much time, Inspector."

Graham closed the vestry door. "I know, but I have a few questions I thought you might know the answer to. Now seems as good a time as any. Won't take long."

Bright sat up in his chair. "Okay, fire away."

"St. Julian's Wood. There's a small commune there now, but they tell me it used to be a seminary. Does that ring any bells with you?"

Reverend Bright paused, a thumbnail to his teeth, considering it. "St. Julian's." He said the name as if drawing the memory from a deep well. "Yes, yes. Back in the day, it was a small theological seminary. Just a handful of people."

"And it closed in, what, the mid-eighties?"

"Something like that. It ran out of money, as these things often do. I think some local people have set up in the woods as some sort of eco-friendly community now." The vicar blinked quickly and smiled. "Hard even to remember the way it used to be. But why would the police be interested in St. Julian's? Trouble with the people there? Surely not."

"We're investigating a murder," Graham said, reluctant to bring gravity to a such joyous day.

"Oh, I see," Bright said, quickly catching onto the seriousness of Graham's enquiry. "Is this about the man discovered at the White House Inn? With the gun? How awful for the poor soul to have been up in the attic all those years."

"I see you've been perusing Freddie Solomon's latest."

"Of course. As a local vicar, it's always a good idea to keep an eye on the community's comings and goings. Even if they are, er, at times, a bit extreme. But I'm still not following you."

Graham glanced at the large antique wall clock; there were only minutes until Janice's wedding ceremony was to start, maybe a few more if she was late. He could hear the hubbub in the sanctuary building as the wedding guests arrived, and their low but animated chatter burbled through the cavernous space. "The seminary's address was among the physical evidence."

"The poor soul's belongings?"

Graham saw no reason to avoid sharing. "Written on the cover of a novel."

"Well, who was he?" Bright added quickly, "You'll forgive some professional concern when a seminary, even a long-closed one, finds itself embroiled in a murder enquiry. And as it happens, I've just been asked by our local funeral directors if I would conduct a service for him.

I understand his remains will be released to his next of kin soon."

"We believe a man named Dylan Dillon came to Jersey to carry out a hit. Freddie Solomon has theories about East End skull-breakers coming to Jersey to do dirty work, and honestly, I still consider them to be mostly fantasy, but I do think he's right here. Dylan Dillon was a small-time crook who was either ordered or incited to murder his former friend and accomplice by his criminal bosses."

"And was the planned killing carried out?"

"Doubtful. Certainly no gun-related death was recorded on the island at the time."

"I see, Inspector." Bright stood. "That's all very interesting, but, well, I'm sorry, don't you have a wedding to attend? I certainly do."

"Why would Dylan Dillon have that address written down, do you think, unless he was following a lead on the whereabouts of his target?"

"Well, I . . . You think he was looking to kill someone at the seminary? But it was just a group of young men devoting themselves to a godly life! The idea that they were involved in any criminal activity is ludicrous."

"But it would be the perfect place to hide out, wouldn't you say? Especially if you had been part of a criminal gang engaged in activities that brought you in contact and relationship with people you'd now rather not know or be associated with."

Bright blinked and raised his eyebrows. "Maybe, but I—"

"At the risk of derailing my sergeant's wedding, I'm hoping you can shed some light on the matter so that we can get things over with and back on track without delay. It would be enormously helpful if you could. Because you see, we followed the trail to the Parnaby twins. They're a couple of hard nuts currently serving twenty-eight years for an armed robbery. They told us about a lad called Charlie Cross. Dillon and Cross were childhood friends, inseparable until one day in the early eighties when Cross did a runner with a pile of loot. The Parnabys' loot. They weren't best pleased. They still aren't."

"I can imagine. But I'm sorry, Inspector. What does that have to do with me?" Bright made for the door, but Graham swiftly moved to place himself in front of it. Bright attempted to go around him. Graham stood firm. Bright huffed. "Inspector, look, we really should be going. It's not good form for the vicar to arrive *after* the bride." Graham cast his eye over the desk in the middle of the room.

"There's no computer in here. You don't use technology?"

"Not too much. There's little need for it except for admin, and my secretary does that from home. And I find it gets in the way of God's work. Puts up barriers. It's rather unhelpful."

"In police work, we use it a lot. And technology has moved on since the eighties. It's amazing what you can find out." Bright stared mutely at Graham, his eyes fierce, penetrating. "We can trace DNA from the tiniest of samples, old ones too. We can track down relatives of our victims even if we don't know their identity. We can dredge up images from long ago. And we can age the people in those images too. Fascinating stuff."

"I see."

"I wonder, Reverend Bright, if you would look at a photo for me?"

"Why?"

"To tell me if you recognise anyone in it."

The vicar shrugged. "Okay."

Graham pulled up a photo on his phone. He turned it to Bright. "These boys. Recognise either of them?" Bright looked at the old, faded black-and-white photo booth picture of the two fair-haired teenagers with cheeky grins, short, stubby noses, and pointed chins. Bright regarded the boys impassively and then said, "No, sorry. Can't say I do. But that looks like an old photo. How am I supposed to know them?"

Graham didn't reply but scrolled to another photograph. It was the image he had shown Angela Dillon, the one Fiona had modelled from the facial remains of Mr. X. "This is one of those boys as a twenty-five-year-old man. Perhaps you recognise him now?" Bright shook his head.

"No, Inspector. Are you sure you don't want to return to the wedding? The groom will be wondering where you are. And I really should be preparing."

"Just one more." Graham scrolled to another photograph. "How about this one?" This time, he showed the vicar a photo of an elderly man. It was the image that Fiona had sent him earlier. Bright sighed. He hesitated before speaking. "No. I have never seen any of these people."

"Really? Are you sure? Because, to me, the man in that photo looks exactly like you."

Bright looked over Graham's shoulder at the picture of Christ on the wall. He muttered silently.

"What's that, Reverend?"

The vicar cleared his throat. "I said that's impossible."

"What is?"

Bright nodded at the phone. "That that's me."

Graham turned the phone around and looked at the photo. "Looks like you to me." Bright gazed past Graham's shoulder again.

"We need to go. The bride will be here soon."

"It's too late for that, I'm afraid."

"What?" Bright's eyes darted between Graham and the door and back again. His cheeks bloomed. His chest rose and abruptly dropped. "Look, I have a lot of things to do. I need to get the readings ready. Set my sermon out. Oversee . . . everything. I need to get things back on track. Now, please!"

"If you think I'm going to let you go out there and marry my sergeant only for the full story to come out later and sully the memory of her wedding day, you can think again. Now tell me, is this you?" Graham showed him the picture of the schoolboys, then swiped left to the image of the elderly man.

Bright sat down, and trapping his soft, fleshy inner cheeks between his teeth, he pursed his lips in a mew before closing his eyes, his lips moving in silent prayer. As he muttered, his body seemed to diminish, shrivelling as Graham watched.

Eventually, Bright opened his eyes. His pupils dilated, appearing as deep, black holes. "Very well, Inspector. I'll tell you."

"Good." Graham pulled up a chair and sat down facing him. "Now, tell me, who are you, exactly?"

Reverend Bright crossed his legs and brushed his cassock skirts, smoothing them. He took a deep breath. "I'm Dylan Dillon."

CHAPTER FIFTY-FOUR

"THEN WHO IS the man in the mortuary?"

"I suppose it must be my old friend, Charlie Cross."

"Arthur and George Parnaby, two lowlifes I interviewed recently, said that one of their crew absconded with over a hundred thousand pounds' of loot. Tore their gang apart overnight. Nothing was the same again, they reckoned."

"They were right about that last part," Bright said simply.

"So, you admit to knowing the Parnabys?"

"I do. I did."

"They say Dylan Dillon, you, came here to locate the absconder and recover the money. You checked into the White House Inn, formerly known as The Grange, under the name of John Smith on the thirteenth of February 1982. Records show that you entered France two days later. You returned to Jersey in October of that year."

"You've done your homework, Inspector. That's right, although a small quibble. I was *compelled* to come here to track down Charlie, believing he had stolen money, money that I thought, in part, I was owed. I had been given an address: 4 St. Julian's Road."

Graham closed the door to the vestry. The noise from the sanctuary was getting louder as the wedding guests got restless. But he couldn't afford to be distracted. For the first time in this case, two plus two suddenly made four without any irregular, inelegant remainder. As he listened, Graham graduated to higher-level maths: the cold calculus of conspiracy, and the convoluted algebra of death.

"It is the most terrible weight being party to a violent death," Bright said, resplendent in his vestments, minutes shy of a much-anticipated wedding ceremony. "But I felt that I had to bear it, that there was simply no other way."

"You killed Charlie Cross?" Bright shifted in his seat.

"Not exactly. Do you think I killed him?"

"It did cross my mind. But if you didn't, what happened?"

"It's important that you understand. You see, it was him or me. Brutally simple." Joshua Bright/Dylan Dillon uncrossed and recrossed his legs and rearranged his cassock skirts so they fell evenly over his knee, the wedding forgotten, forty-year-old memories taking its place in the vicar's mind.

The calculations changed again, and Graham found he could complete all three sides of the investigator's classic, triangular geometry: method, motive, opportunity.

"Robbed blind by one of their own," he said. "The Parnabys exploded."

"Charlie didn't rob anyone, blind or otherwise. That was just the story the Parnabys bandied to discredit him, cover their backs, and incite me to murder. They hadn't lost any money. But they had lost Charlie. And he knew too much."

Graham drew back like a shrewd, patient, investigative bird of prey gaining altitude for a clearer view. "So, what did he do? Charlie. Left the gang, the family, the life?"

"You never leave people like the Parnabys," said Bright. "You can't even take holidays."

"But Cross tried. And the Parnabys couldn't allow that. They couldn't just . . ."

"Leave him floating around, a potential witness to dozens of crimes? Never. That's why they set me onto him. They gave me a gun and told me to deal with him."

Bright sat back. The clock ticked onward. Graham was acutely aware of the growing clamour in the church. The guests were getting fidgety.

"I don't suppose you'd still let me . . . ?"

"Not in two months of Sundays," Graham said. "I won't have Janice and Jack joined in matrimony by someone I'm about to arrest. Just tell your story and be quick about it so we can sort all this out without too many tears." Privately, he thought they were way past that point. He glanced at his watch. There was no time for a long expository. Janice would arrive any minute.

"Very well, Inspector." Bright began his story. "In 1981, Charlie was at a loose end, let's say. He'd always daydreamed about joining the clergy. Strange, I know, given his earlier life, but thieving and criming were never him, not really. It was more my kind of thing. He just came along for the ride. When he arrived on Jersey to get away from all that, he hid inside the seminary, passing himself off as a theology student."

Graham had a quiet respect for the humble toil of the priestly life. "Some people have a calling. I've watched some turnarounds in my time."

"You're a brilliant detective, Inspector Graham. Gorey is lucky to have you."

Graham frowned. "Just tell me what happened."

"I came to Jersey planning to shoot Charlie. He had reinvented himself as a do-gooder, a theology student. He was thinking of becoming a vicar. We met up. He told me he lived under a false name, Joshua Bright, because he didn't want his past catching up with him. I thought I'd be able to get him to tell me what he'd done with the money, but he convinced me he hadn't stolen anything. We ended up doing some coke together in my hotel room just for old time's sake, as you do . . ."

"Quite."

". . . when he suddenly keeled over." Graham squinted. "I panicked. Left the hotel immediately, abandoned my stuff, and walked around all night. I got myself on the early morning ferry to Calais first thing."

Graham spent a moment piecing together the timeline of events. "So, the body found in your room was Charlie Cross."

"Must've been."

"And the people who found him believed him to be you."

Bright shrugged. "We looked very similar. We were always being mistaken for brothers. The only difference was a gap between Charlie's front teeth. I had the same gap as a child, but my mother insisted on braces."

The clock was ticking; perhaps two-thirds of the guests were now seated in the wooden pews, an odd few mingling in the aisle, catching up with friends not seen in a while. Graham opened the vestry door and peered out.

He spotted Mrs. Taylor taking a seat, leaning forward, pinching the bridge of her nose in a moment of quiet prayer.

Of Rosemary Harding there was no sign. It occurred to Graham that perhaps her absence wasn't necessarily the mercy it seemed; if she wasn't causing trouble that he could see, she was probably causing it for Janice.

"So, you left in a panic and went to Calais. What did you do then?"

"I hid out on the continent for six months or so. I kept checking the papers expecting to see something about Charlie's death, but there was nothing. It was confusing. I didn't know what to do."

"So, in October 1982, you returned here? To Jersey?"

"Yes. I wanted to find out what had happened. And, like Charlie, I didn't want to go back, not to the Parnabys. I thought they would kill me."

"But you never left the island?"

"Yes, I stayed here. In my efforts to understand what happened to Charlie after I left him on that bedroom floor, I went to the seminary and knocked on the door. When they opened it, they welcomed me in like a long-lost friend. It was bizarre until I realised they thought I was Charlie. I was bewildered at first, but I quickly saw my opportunity."

"Stuck between a rock and a hard place, you assumed his identity."

"As Joshua Bright, yes. I got to escape my past and the Parnabys. Dylan Dillon effectively disappeared in that moment."

"And no one suspected? Really?"

"One person at the seminary appeared suspicious. But I just said I'd had some dental treatment while I'd been away."

"And how do you think Charlie died?"

"I assumed he overdosed, although he didn't use much

that night. He brought two bags of coke with him, small ones. He had one, I had one."

Graham tapped his phone against his mouth, thinking. "And if I told you his coke was cut with rat poison?"

Bright's eyes grew big. "No!"

"Yes." Graham leaned forward. "And why should I not believe that you did that?"

Bright tucked in his chin. When he spoke, he sounded affronted. "Because I planned to shoot him. Why would I risk bringing a gun to the island if I was going to kill him with rat poison?"

Graham sat back, considering this answer. "And what did you think all these years? Years that you assumed the identity previously assumed by Charlie Cross, who you left for dead on the floor of your hotel room for other people to find?"

"I didn't know what to think. After a while, I just got on with life." Bright regarded Graham coolly, his legs still crossed, his cassock skirts smooth, his hands placed one on top of the other in his lap.

There was a knock at the door. Roach appeared around it. He was red-faced. And breathless. "There you are, sir. Um, we're in dire need of the orders of service." Graham stared at him. "The wedding, sir?" Roach hesitated before plunging on. "Janice's . . . wedding?"

Graham shook himself and swatted away an imaginary fly. "Roach, get Barnwell, then arrest this man and take him to the station."

CHAPTER FIFTY-FIVE

L AURA LOOKED AMAZING as she walked up the church path, past the war memorial, in a silky, shiny, emerald satin wraparound dress—tall, just a little shy, and the only woman at St. Andrew's who was in danger of upstaging the bride. As she approached though, she slowed a little as Graham's knitted eyebrows conveyed a distinct warning. "Problems, dearest?" she asked quietly when she reached him.

Graham didn't answer at first. His hand found hers, and with the other, he leaned for a second against the wall of the church. It appeared to offer support, and after a moment more, a trickle of energy.

"Laura, would you honour me with a peculiar favour?" he said, his tone amenable but his brow terraced like a rice paddy. "Stroll on into the sanctuary and oblige the groom in the direction of the front entrance, would you?"

Laura did some pointing and figuring out of things. She glanced at her watch, then at the lychgate. "That's where . . . the . . . um, bride is going to be very shortly, isn't it?"

"Yes, the bride and the groom need to talk. And we need to be there when they do."

"You mean, now?"

"Yes. And, um, one more thing," Graham said, coming closer. "This is going to be the strangest day you and I have spent in a while."

Hands on hips, Laura retorted, "David Graham, you took me on a hot date in London three months ago . . ."

"I remember it well."

". . . where we both attended the London Ambulance Blood Spatter Conference for six hours."

"That's not what it was called."

"No, but that's what it *was*. Today can't be stranger than that!"

"You were unlucky. The second day was compelling. Anyway, aren't you friends with Councillor Jenkins? She was the one who invited me."

"I know her. She helped us out, gave a talk at the library to open the . . . She's the wife of a bishop, you know."

"Great! Give her a ring, would you? We might need her help," Graham said as abruptly as the moment demanded. "We'll be needing some paperwork expedited."

Laura blinked, half affronted by his tone, half curious as to the reason for it. "What's going on, David? Is it anything to do with Rosemary?"

Graham's eyes closed at the mention of Janice's mother's name. "Not yet. But brace yourself." He was away, pointing for Laura to head back into the church as he walked to the lychgate to await Janice's wedding car.

Inside the church, Laura elegantly sashayed up to the front and, as discreetly as she could, she parted the confused groom from his groomsmen and began guiding him down the aisle to the doors. "Just doing some photos," she said, beaming at those in the aisle seats as she and Jack zipped past. At the door, fresh from traumatising a flower girl, they encountered Rosemary Harding.

"What's *he* doing back here?" she demanded. "He should be at the front."

"There's been a change of plans," Laura told her, confident that this was the case but unsure as to what they might be and certainly unsure of the reason for them.

"But Janice will be here at any moment!" Rosemary's voice was increasing in volume and register in line with her alarm.

"Yes . . ." Laura sensed an emotional outburst incoming. She put her palm up. "Wait there."

Laura left Jack and Rosemary staring at one another in the south porch while she nipped back inside the church, returning a few seconds later with Marjorie Taylor still resplendent in dusty pink and mesh. "Mrs. Harding, Mrs. Taylor will keep you company while we sort this out. Jack, you come with me." Laura grabbed Jack's upper arm and pulled him down the gravel path to the lychgate.

"She is coming, isn't she? Janice?" Jack said.

"She's in the car, and you are getting married today. I'm just not sure under what circumstances."

Panicked, Jack looked back at the church. "Is the place on fire?" Just as they reached Graham and he made to explain, Janice's black limousine rounded the corner. The door opened, and Janice's father helped the bride gather her skirts.

The lychgate creaked, and as Graham opened it ahead of her, he said, "Janice, you look absolutely beautiful."

"Inspector, thank you! It's lovely to see you." Janice glanced over his shoulder. Jack opened his hands and shook his head, his lips turned down in confusion. "But what are you doing here?"

Dragging her eyes from the huddle under the lychgate canopy, Rosemary Harding turned to Marjorie Taylor. "Now's the time when organ music would have been so very wonderful. And . . . what's that Mr. Graham doing?" she complained.

In the distance, but within earshot of Rosemary's piercing voice, Laura turned. Her eyes and those of Mrs. Taylor met. Laura winked. Marjorie acknowledged her signal with a minute dip of her head. Cluelessly, Rosemary continued her ranting.

"I knew it! This is very bad luck, and quite extraordinary, and I can't imagine for a moment why—Ow!" Pulled sharply by the elbow from behind, Mrs. Harding deflated like a sandcastle meeting seawater.

"If Michelangelo is in the middle of painting the Sistine Chapel, you don't scale his ladder and witter at him," Mrs. Taylor said through gritted teeth as she all but heel-dragged Rosemary around the back of the church.

"How dare you . . ."

"Mrs. Harding, Rosemary," Mrs. Taylor said, pulling up, her eyes flinty, her cheeks unusually red. "People sometimes underestimate the detective inspector, but I've learned to trust him, whatever he's doing."

"Even if he's in the middle of ruining the . . ."

Mrs. Taylor's eyes flashed. They burned. Her voice, full of controlled rage, trembled. "Mrs. Harding, you have a beautiful daughter who is about to marry a wonderful, charming man. Their union will be blissful, and in time, you will have equally beautiful, wonderful grandchildren running around your ankles. Do you know how lucky you are? Now stop your moaning, stand down, and enjoy your good fortune in whatever form it takes!"

Rosemary Harding's eyes grew larger than her gaping mouth. "Wha—H-How dare—Wha—!" Taking advantage of her disarray and knowing that she had only moments to act, Mrs. Taylor grabbed Mrs. Harding by the wrist and bundled her into the vestry through the back door, proceeding to lean her entire body weight against it, so trapping Mrs. Harding inside.

Rosemary banged furiously on the ancient oak until it dawned on her that her efforts were fruitless and quite possibly blasphemous. On the other side, Mrs. Taylor folded her arms and settled in to wait, pressing her back against the door. It was in this position that Graham, Laura, Janice, and Jack found her five minutes later.

"She's in there, Detective Inspector. She's quietened down now. Would you like me to step away?"

"I would, Mrs. Taylor. Thank you very much."

"Mother, cool it!" Janice shouted through the door, her wedding dress skirts gathered in her arms. She reached out to open the door as carefully as one might when releasing a feral feline from a cat carrier. "You can come out now," Janice said more quietly.

Rosemary appeared, ruffled and out of sorts. She glared at Marjorie Taylor in the sunshine. "Mum, there's an excellent reason why we're breaking with wedding protocol established across millennia. Right, boss?"

"Yes, indeed," said Graham. He straightened his jacket and smoothed his brown hair into an unusually formal side parting. For the first time, he missed his cap. He couldn't remember where he left it. "And that means I've got good news and bad news."

"Is he already married?" Rosemary said, glaring at Jack. He suppressed an eye roll that would have had him viewing his brain stem. He opted instead to beam at Rosemary with a smile that even she considered to be conceivably sarcastic.

"The good news," Graham said, cutting across her, "is that Janice and Jack are getting married."

"Hooray!" said Janice, her voice conveying no confidence at all.

"The bad news is the vicar has vacated the vestry."

Rosemary sputtered into life again. "Well, I know that. I've just been in there for goodness knows how long and he wasn't with me."

"What I mean is that we've identified the man involved in the death of Mr. X in 1982. And since, in the circumstances, it would be inappropriate for him to conduct the ceremony . . ."

"The vicar murdered Mr. X?" Jack cried.

Janice smirked. She looked around. "Where's Freddie when you need him?"

Laura walked up, pulling the phone from her ear. "She can't do it," she said simply. "Councillor Jenkins."

"What?" Graham said. "But I . . ."

"She's not on the island, and she's the only person with the authority to extend your wedding officiant licence to the Bailiwick of Jersey. The wedding wouldn't be legal if you did it."

There was silence from Jack, a hysterical giggle from Janice, and an "I knew it!" from Rosemary, words quickly stifled when she caught Mrs. Taylor's ferocious eye.

"What are we going to do?" Janice said to Jack. "We

have guests in their finery, you in your posh togs, me in me posh dress, flowers up the wazoo, oranges galore . . ."

Laura continued. "So, there's been a change of plan. Councillor Jenkins spoke to her husband, the bishop, and he's sending a new vicar. Someone who's here on holiday celebrating their wedding anniversary."

"Excuse me, excuse me! Yoo-hoo!" They all turned. A woman in a T-shirt and shorts opened the lychgate and walked up to the wedding party with confidence and purpose. Behind, a man accompanying her stayed outside the gate, looking slightly less confident and with a lot less purpose. He looked vaguely familiar to Graham, and the detective inspector searched his memory banks for some recollection.

"You're looking absolutely divine, my dear," the woman said to Janice, taking in the bride's full-skirted ivory dress with ruched bodice and lace, three-quarter length sleeves. "Now, I hear you're in a spot of bother over a vanishing vicar. But you're not to worry." The woman stuck out her hand. "Reverend Annabelle Dixon. Perhaps I can help?"

CHAPTER FIFTY-SIX

"**P**HEW, THAT WAS close." Jim Roach wrestled his way through the crowd, narrowly avoiding spilling the beer in the glasses he clutched tight above his head as he made his way over to Barry Barnwell. His erstwhile colleague, who sat by himself quietly feeding Carmen scraps from the buffet, lit up when Roach came into view.

"Ah, lovely jubbly, mate. Thanks." Barnwell sipped the foam off his drink, then took a good swig and smacked his lips. "Just the ticket. All the wine and champers is nice 'n' all, but you can't beat a good pint of Jersey ale."

"That you can't," Roach agreed, following Barnwell's lead. "I miss it."

"What, the beer?"

"Yep, and all the rest. The people, community, my mum. You, Jan, even the boss."

"Feeling a bit homesick, eh?"

"A bit. I mean, I'm as busy as heck, and I'm learning loads. It's just fast-paced. So very different from here. It's a nice change to come back."

"Must be dangerous, is it? All that knife crime and drugs."

"There's more opportunity for it there than here, for sure. But, you know, there's lots of backup. You're trained for it. I wake up every morning and have no idea what the day's going to throw at me. One minute I could be called to a suspected trafficking, another an armed raid. It's exciting. Right now, I'm trying to decide if I should specialise. They're always looking for people in the different units. We even have one dedicated to cold cases."

"Feel like I could apply for that one after this case. It's been like pulling teeth." Barnwell gazed across the dance floor. "Would you look at that? Rosemary Harding enjoying herself."

"Who's that dancing with her?"

"That's the archaeologist Tomlinson brought in to help us extract the body from the concrete. Papadopoulos. Greek. Top man."

"Must have been a bit of a shock finding a finger poking out like that."

"Gawd, I'll say. Shook me right up, it did. But, as you say, all in a day's work."

"Thank you so much for stepping in, Vicar." A few feet away, Marjorie Taylor chatted with Reverend Annabelle and Laura. "You quite saved the day."

"You did a wonderful job at such short notice," Laura added.

"Oh, I was delighted to be asked. I got to spend my first wedding anniversary on the island where we honeymooned marrying someone else. What could be more fun than that? Heavenly. And they seem such a lovely couple."

Janice was laughing with one of her bridesmaids, while next to her, Jack put an orange quarter in his mouth. The look of surprise on his mother-in-law's face when he opened his orange-filled mouth to smile hideously at her from the edge of the dance floor was almost worth all the earlier kerfuffle.

When, in response, Rosemary threw back her head and laughed while jigging around to the music opposite an equally jiggy Dr. Papadopoulos, Jack knew everything would be alright.

Outside, Graham and Fiona sat across from one another on a pub bench, both grateful to be away from the flashing lights, darkness, and loud music inside. "Do you still keep in touch with Bert Hatfield? He was a fine pathologist."

"I do! He's still doing the same old thing and still loves it."

"And is he still having his heart broken on the regular by Charlton Athletic?"

"He still is."

"Thanks so much for putting in the extra time today. It changed everything."

"No problem. The DNA results were confounding, weren't they?"

"They truly were. And I couldn't believe it when I looked at Reverend Bright and saw the man in that aged photo of Dylan Dillon staring back at me."

"That must have been some surprise. Changed the trajectory of the day, that's for sure."

"You can say that again."

"When did you know you were barking up the wrong tree?"

"The first sign was the photo of the boys. It showed Dillon with braces, but our body in the block had imperfect teeth, so I knew there was a possibility that things weren't as they seemed."

"There *was* a gap between the two front teeth!" Fiona exclaimed. "I remember now."

"That's right. Then you sent through the DNA results and confirmed my thoughts."

"You know, I took another look at the DNA." Graham glanced at her quickly. "I compared the DNA from the hairbrush, which we know was Dillon's because of the match with his half sister, and compared it to the bone DNA. There was a match there too."

Graham leaned forward. "Oh? Was it strong?"

"Pretty strong. It was as strong between Dillon and Cross as that between Dillon and his half sister. It's perhaps why they so closely resembled one another."

"You mean they were half brothers?"

"Or maybe cousins. It's also perhaps why they gravitated to one another. They shared a close relative and maybe personality traits."

"They lived on the same estate. And Dillon's sister said family members were promiscuous to a fault." Graham leaned back. "Wow, blood relatives, perhaps brothers, intent on killing one another. That doesn't happen very often."

"Do you think the boys knew they were related?"

"I didn't get that impression." The pair sat in silence as they comprehended this new information.

"So, it was death by misadventure, you think? Cross administered the poisoned drugs to himself?"

"Looks like it, by mistake. At least that's Dillon's story. At this distance, it'll be difficult to prove otherwise. Everyone's dead or long gone. But there were enough crimes surrounding this case to keep us busy for a month of Sundays." Fiona stirred her gin and tonic.

"Do you like it here?" she said.

"On Jersey? Yes, I love it."

"You don't miss the hustle and bustle of London, the strategic, far-reaching cases that involve networks of criminals all over the country, sometimes the world?" Fiona grinned.

"Not at the moment. I appreciate the discreet containment of individual crimes. It's very satisfying. In many ways, I've had a broader experience here than in London. I get involved in all aspects of the policing. And I enjoy working closely with my team. I get a lot of pleasure out of their development. It's made me a more rounded person. Balanced." Fiona nodded. "What are your plans?"

"Well, I've had great fun working on this case. It's given me the chance to try lots of new things. Have more responsibility, you know?"

"This was an unusual case. They're not all like that."

"No, I get it, but as you said, I've the chance to get involved in aspects of forensic pathology that I wouldn't normally. And Dr. Weiss has offered me the opportunity to cover for people on her team from time to time. It's all grist for the mill. I can see myself staying here for a while. Plus, I get to live in my very own castle!"

Graham glanced at Fiona quizzically. "Dr. Tomlinson rented me a flat in Elizabeth Castle. It's just about the best commute I can think of. And it's eerie at night. So many spooky noises and weird lights." Fiona's eyes gleamed as she raised her hands and contracted her fingers like claws.

Graham smiled uncertainly and took a sip of his drink. "Not your average experience, that's for sure."

They glanced over to see Tomlinson sitting in an armchair on the terrace, animatedly talking to Freddie Solomon.

"Freddie looks pale. Perhaps it's the light," Graham said.

"Nah, Marcus is probably educating him on the finer details of postmortems and the assist, if complicating factor, corpse wax can provide."

"Corpse wax?"

"Another word for it is 'adipocere.' It forms when fat on a body turns into a hard insoluble substance under conditions of high moisture and an absence of oxygen, like wet ground or mud or . . ."

"Newly mixed concrete."

"Precisely. It's what helped our Mr. X stay in as good a condition as he did."

"Interesting."

"I've had so much fun on this case, Inspector. The spectrometry, DNA tracing, ballistics, using software and AI to build the man's face from the remains. It was all new to me. It was an experience I couldn't have anywhere else. In bigger labs, I would get stuck with photographing and weighing brains and such. Every day. It quickly gets boring."

"Boring? I hope you're not talking about my lab, young lady." Tomlinson walked over.

"I was saying the exact opposite," Fiona replied. "Are you finished talking to Freddie?"

"Yes, it took some time, but I think I finally managed to utterly repulse him. He was looking quite green by the time we were done. I invited him to drop by the lab, told him he could view my collection of anatomical oddities that I've saved over the years, but I don't think he was interested. I doubt we'll be seeing him anytime soon. He told me you'd granted him an exclusive on the case for his book, David."

"Yes, I promised him, as long as it doesn't go out before sentencing. He helped me, I helped him. Squid provo." Graham grinned ruefully.

"But how was he helpful? I thought he was a lightweight, meddling troublemaker with nothing useful to add," Fiona said.

"The Parnaby brothers told him two of their gang had gone to Jersey and disappeared. I think Freddie thought, hoped maybe, that they'd been murdered on gangland business. That turned out to be wrong, but it gave me a wedge I could use to get information out of them. Do you want to sit down, Marcus?"

"On one of those hard benches? No thanks. I'd never get up again. I came to tell you they want us inside. I think the bride and groom are doing something. Going away on honeymoon perhaps."

They traipsed in to find the wedding guests outside the front of the venue. From deep inside the grounds came the sound of tins being dragged along the tarmac. An Aston Martin rolled into view. It seemed almost entirely filled with Janice's ivory dress, the bride squeezed into the middle of it, white silk and net petticoats puffed up all around her like a marshmallow.

Next to her, Jack beamed in the driver's seat. A cheer went up, and Janice waved, shaking her bouquet high in the air above her head. Barnwell whistled while Roach whooped, both delighted to see their sergeant making this personal milestone, one she had longed for in what seemed like forever.

With Francine by his side, Dr. Tomlinson clapped as Fiona stood next to him, the old pathologist and his new assistant standing next to one another. Graham found himself across from Freddie, and as the car drove between them, they caught each other's eye, a small nod passing between them, an acknowledgement that despite their differing opinions and objectives, tonight there was a truce, some element of mutual respect and a "squid provo."

The Aston Martin drew up alongside Graham, and Janice, her happiness and joy radiating from her so force-fully it was catching, waved furiously at him and then tossed her bouquet into the air. As was Janice's intention, Laura had no choice but to catch it.

Janice laughed, waved, and leaned in to kiss her new husband's cheek. The car drove onward into the Jersey darkness, the tin cans dangling from the bumper continuing to rattle even after the car had long disappeared into the night.

CHAPTER FIFTY-SEVEN

Extract: *Murder Island: The Mob on Jersey*
by F. J. Solomon

If you talk with Gorey's vibrant community of senior citizens, you'll know the greatest gift of retirement is more time with family. Two acquaintances of mine, Arthur and George, had the same expectations—to play with the grand-children, maybe enjoy a bit of sunshine, and indulge in some hobbies. Greying and, in George's case, ill, they kept their big dates firmly in mind, determined to get there and enjoy the fruits of their patience.

Except these two men weren't about to draw their first pensions. Arthur and George Parnaby, convicted armed robbers, each received a twenty-eight-year prison sentence in 1999. When I first met them in the visiting suite at Holbrooke prison, they were just completing their twenty-fourth year. I interviewed them several times for my forth-coming book, *Murder Island: The Mob on Jersey*.

During those interviews, I gained information that I handed over to the States of Jersey police as they processed an inquiry into the death of a man whose body lay undiscovered for over forty years in the attic of Gorey's White House Inn. As we now know, it was an investigation with a remarkable outcome.

Through interviews with the lead investigator, the proprietor of the hotel where the body was discovered, the person arrested in connection with the death, and anonymous but dependable elders who were in Gorey at the time, I have successfully reconstructed the events of February 1982 and their lead-up like never before.

Charles Cross was a little different from those around him. Growing up on a sink estate in London, unemployment, poverty, and that scourge of the underclass—drugs—surrounded him daily. His environment offered little in the way of a stable upbringing, and being a sensitive boy, the bullies made Charlie suffer. Being the "wussy kid," it was hard for him to make friends, and Charlie cherished those he had: a cluster of dropouts without a grain of ambition between them.

But when one of them left a corner shop without paying (again), Charlie and his best friend, Dylan, were suddenly "in" with two older boys, and Charlie's life of exclusion and ignominy ended.

These two older boys had a reputation already, but to Charlie and Dylan, the Parnaby brothers became instant family. From them, the younger boys learned to drink and smoke and do drugs. They coveted the latest gadgets, technology we now consider "quaint" but which were transformative at the time.

Those pastimes required money, and gaining it became

an ongoing challenge. While his friends had few qualms, Charlie found dishonesty discomforting. And he hated violence. Lashing out at victims in the street, outside the pub, or at each other after consuming too much drink disgusted Charlie. But he seemed unable to loosen the gang's grip on his life.

As time went on, the violence grew. A menace growled at someone in the street. A brawl in the pub. A knife an inch from a commuter's face. They all figured in Charlie's life, even if his role was a passive, observant one. These offences could be but one of a string on the same evening. Eventually, inevitably, blood would be drawn, the older, drunken Parnaby brothers pivotal in the act and unquestionably to blame.

But a shroud of silence between the four held strong, and understanding grew. Charlie remained quiet but low-key participatory in the group's endeavours. He wouldn't turn his back. Nor, as time went on, could he.

"I was under the Parnabys' spell from start to finish," recalled Dylan Dillon the first time I interviewed him in La Moye prison, St. Helier. Dillon is better known to Jersey residents as Reverend Joshua Bright, vicar of St. Andrew's Church, Gorey. "Charlie, less so. He did everything he could to fit in, to make sure he was available and willing, but his reluctance was noticeable."

Charlie read books, including the Bible, often in secret. "I didn't understand, and I'm sure his family didn't," Dillon says. "My half sisters and half brothers and I grew up in a chaotic, disorganised fashion. Our parents, who were a bewildering array of people, floated in and out of our lives regularly. The churn was extraordinary. There was no structure, no expectation, no education.

"Charlie's family was more normal, poor but decent. He

gravitated to anything that provided stability. He couldn't afford Boy Scouts. The youth centre closed. So, he mostly went to church. It was his way of sitting out the experience of the chaotic estate life around us. Can you imagine? I suppose it gave him belonging.

"The Parnabys already had me down as a foot-soldier type, someone who'd jump up and do any mundane job he's told to—passing a message, leaving a dead drop, or making a collection. They wanted Charlie to do the same. But Charlie was quieter than me, less impulsive, with no stomach for the rough stuff. The Parnabys found him frustrating but kept him on. He was useful. You'd never look at him and think gang member. He was good cover.

"But one day in 1981, he had enough. He went to church and then witnessed another awful beating outside a pub. Charlie and me fell out. I was into partying, all the club drugs. I was using a lot. It puffed me up, had me thinking I'm a kingpin, a stud.

"I fancied myself as a criminal mastermind, running my own patch, raking in the money. I was a regular drug user, cocaine being my preference. It was the eighties, and it was everywhere. I had illusions of grandeur; that I could achieve anything. But all cocaine does is make you sound like an idiot.

"Charlie was no angel though. He was right alongside me, using, petty thieving, occasionally menacing. It was just that it was an act with him. One he put on but didn't really live into. He wanted to go straight. He had ambition. And he needed to find some peace."

Eventually, Charlie made his choice: he packed his things and fled. We can judge the Parnaby brothers' reaction from their interviews with Detective Inspector Graham of Gorey police and the senior officer in charge of the case.

"They were black with fury when I raised Cross's disappearance with them," the DI said. "They told the world that they were 'well shot,' implying his disappearance was the end for them. But it was far from it."

Caught between the Parnabys and his friend, Dillon attempted to tread the line between them. "I knew everything the Parnabys had done. Ten years of petty crimes, big crimes, and stupid, nonsense, pointless crimes. They had done them all, sometimes just because they were bored. They became paranoid. I tried not to get involved, but eventually it ate them up, and they executed a plan for which I was the fall guy."

Arthur, George, and Dylan would face lengthy stretches in prison if Charlie grassed them up. "They saw only one course of action open to them," DI Graham told me. "Charlie Cross had to be hunted down and the threat he posed eliminated."

But there was a problem they had to overcome. The Parnabys were menaces and meat-headed thugs, but they weren't about to put themselves on the line. Dylan Dillon would need to do the job.

But Dillon was Cross's oldest friend. How would Dylan be persuaded to kill Charlie? They convinced Dylan that Cross had ripped them off.

"They sold me this story about their haul being raided by Charlie," Dillon told me. "That a hundred thou had gone missing. They implied that a significant part of that money was mine, although, with hindsight, it's unlikely that they would have shared it with me. That just wasn't their style. They weren't honourable gangsters."

Dillon, abandoned by his friend, was confused, then furious. He came to believe that Charlie had betrayed them and needed to be taught a lesson. "The Parnabys manipu-

348 ALISON GOLDEN & GRACE DAGNALL

lated me like a pawn, a useful idiot, to get rid of Charlie and remove the threat he posed to them. All while keeping their hands clean. They modelled themselves on London gangsters—the Krays, the Richardsons—but really they were small-time and pathetic."

"Small-time and pathetic" the Parnabys may have been, but they were successful in turning Dillon. It seems the young man had made up his mind—he would do the job.

Over to Inspector Graham: "The Parnabys gave Dillon the gun and the address. When I interviewed them, the brothers maintained their story of the stolen money. Later, they told me it was Dylan who visited Charlie's sister, roughing her up and demanding information."

Dillon countered this version of the story. "No! That wasn't me. I wouldn't do such a thing. I'd known Lou since we were kids. It was Arthur Parnaby who threatened and beat her. He broke her wrist, blacked her eye. He deserves every second of his sentence, however long it is, just for that." Louise Cross, who died in 2001, never brought charges, and the true nature of the incident remains a mystery.

DI Graham commented, "This is endgame stuff for dysfunctional gangs on the verge of breakdown—they accuse one another."

At first, while on the run from the gang, Charlie Cross found exactly what he most needed: peace, quiet, and a clean slate. "When we met, he told me he wanted to help other people. To find his place in the world. And after everything," Dillon added heavily, "he felt the need to atone."

But all that changed in February 1982. For months after his arrival on Jersey, the quiet seclusion he had found at St.

Julian's seminary gave Charlie Cross the life he was looking for. But then, he made a devastating choice.

"Everything told Cross that his life was on the line," said DI Graham. "His sister was begging him to be careful, warning him the gang wanted his blood. Meanwhile, Dillon was raging, egged on by the Parnabys, who made up the story of Charlie as a 'Judas,' a 'grass.'

"Remember, Dylan had been with the Parnabys for ten years, since he was fifteen, an impressionable teenager. These people he trusted completely were warning him of an existential risk—his childhood friend. They permitted him to act on the gang's behalf and empowered him by handing him a gun."

Dillon now says, "I was completely mad with anger and fear. I was determined to kill Charlie. It was how I planned to become a truly 'made man' in the Parnabys' small, ad hoc, but demanding organisation."

"The Parnabys treated Dillon like a chess piece. One who could be manipulated," continued Graham. "They showered him with responsibility, comradeship, and cocaine, then sent him into battle."

Dillon: "I think Charlie knew I was coming. His sister probably alerted him. He told me he staked out the ferry terminal, meeting the boat from Poole and Portsmouth daily. He knew I hated flying and would be unlikely to arrive that way." As it was, Charlie spotted Dylan Dillon the minute he stepped off the big, blue car ferry from Portsmouth.

"He walked right up to me. Imagine it, me thinking I was on a secret mission to kill an enemy turncoat, and he greets me like a long-lost brother. He suggested we meet up the next day and I agreed, unsure what to do. I wasn't an experienced killer."

But Charlie Cross had not yet completed his transition to Joshua Bright, theologian and man of the cloth, not entirely. The plucky East End scamp who had struggled through school bullies and jaded, disinterested teachers, who had pulled free of a gang culture that would have seen him jailed in the end, now faced the possibility of a fate so terrible it was absurd.

To those who know him, "Reverend Bright" is a generous and decent man, and so the next part is difficult to relate.

"The second I saw Charlie, my plans to kill him, such as they were, fell into disarray. I couldn't take the chance of sitting down with him in public," Dillon said. "So I invited him to my hotel room. I intended to learn more about his life so that I could plan the hit in a way that I wouldn't be caught. I could hardly take the risk of splattering him all over some nice Gorey tearoom.

"I suggested we do some lines. I wasn't sure he'd be up for it, not now he was living clean. But he surprised me. He was hopped up, spurred on. Seemed really into it. From what I know now though, I realise he fully intended to kill me before I killed him. It was a dog-eat-dog situation.

"He came to my room with a bottle of whisky that night. We downed it all and then another. It was like old times."

Inside the room, Cross pulled out two small bags of cocaine and gave one of them to Dillon. "There wasn't much, just enough for a few lines. It was all over quickly. I had barely laid mine out before he keeled over. I couldn't believe it. There I was, on Jersey, tasked with a quick kill, and before I'd even the chance to use my gun, my target had died. I didn't know what to do. I could barely think. My only thought was to get out of there. I took my passport and the cash I'd brought with me, and I ran.

"I must be the most hapless criminal ever. I don't know what I was thinking, really. The whole plan was nuts. And my friend died."

Inspector Graham concludes this part of the story. "We suspect Cross adulterated one packet of cocaine with rat poison at the seminary, intending to supply Dillon with it, killing him. Perhaps he was nervous, or disorganised, but in his drunken state, he got the packets mixed up and took the compromised batch himself. It was a murder plan that went awry."

Dillon continues: "What I didn't realise, obviously, is that there would be a cover-up. Lady Luck was protecting me. After travelling through France and spending months in Spain, not knowing what happened was driving me mad. There was nothing in the papers, so I took a risk and returned to Jersey. I went to the seminary where, to my astonishment, one of the students mistook me for Charlie. He took me inside, and they genuinely believed I was him. That was when I realised something odd and unusual had happened.

"I saw their acceptance of me as a sign, one telling me to leave my old life behind. Over the next days, I mingled, observed, and followed the others' lead. It wasn't hard. They lived a simple life, far less complicated than the one I was used to.

"I did my chores and learned my Scripture, ate and

slept, and let the world turn. I didn't talk too much. I was terrified I'd be exposed, but it never happened.

"Eventually, the seminary closed. By then, I had successfully created an identity as Joshua Bright. I could barely remember the old me. I spoke differently, walked differently, and most importantly, I believed differently. I didn't want to go back to being Dylan Dillon. For the first time in my life, I felt safe, weird as it might seem, and I wanted to do good.

"And so I stayed here, blocking out memories and questions that I didn't want to confront. If ever my mind wandered to what happened that night, I would busy myself with my parish work and my thoughts would go away. I could say that I felt troubled, that I experienced nightmares or panic attacks, but that would be a lie. Conducting my life as a local vicar is, I hope, some atonement for my sins in the eyes of God.

"The actions of the hotel owner helped me enormously. I see that now. Throughout the years, I wondered why I heard nothing about Charlie's death, but I pushed my questions away. For me, it was dumb luck that he was buried in concrete and lay undiscovered for over forty years. The downside is that I've been waiting that long for the authorities to arrive.

"Charlie Cross was my oldest friend. What happened to him was tragic, outrageous. I hold the mendacious, rapacious Parnabys responsible. I rue the day we ever met them."

The science of Charlie Cross's death is best explained by

Dr. Marcus Tomlinson, Jersey's senior forensic pathologist. He agreed to discuss the case with me.

"The three substances—the cocaine and the two poisons—were almost the same colour," said Tomlinson, showing me side-by-side analyses derived from a sophisticated UV spectroscope. "The two adulterants are used in commercial brands of rat poison. Probably purloined from a garden shed, perhaps at the seminary.

"Adulterants are highly dangerous," Tomlinson told me. "'Spiking' someone's drug supply like this is a rare and risky method of murder, not at all foolproof. It's possible Cross knew this and so made extra sure by adding two different poisons to the cocaine. Unfortunately, he signed his own death warrant in the process. His death would have been quick, near instantaneous, the poison inciting a massive heart attack."

"Once we found Charlie Cross's body," Inspector Graham told me, "we faced the challenging task of identifying him." Tomlinson and his assistant Fiona Henson were herculean in their efforts to examine and identify the remains. "It was like completing a very complex jigsaw puzzle—each piece leading us to the next one until we built up a picture of who our guy was and what happened to him. For the longest time, we thought Dylan Dillon was the murdered man."

The men looked remarkably similar, and an image generated from the remains confused both the inspector and Dillon's half sister. However, persistence eventually paid off and uncovered two pieces of vital information. Ultimately, it was this evidence on which the case turned.

"First, we received a photo of Charlie Cross and Dylan

Dillon as teenagers. Dillon wore braces, yet the man in the concrete had a gap between his two front teeth. If the body had been Dillon, I'd have expected his teeth to be perfect.

"I began to suspect that the remains were not those of Dillon. I tasked Fiona in our forensic pathology lab with taking the photo of the teenage Dillon and aging it so that I could see what he would look like today. The confirmation of my suspicion came when the DNA samples taken from the body and the effects found with it didn't match. We knew for certain that the DNA from the effects was that of Dillon because it matched with his half sister."

This, then, begged the question: Who was the body in the block? And then, as it is wont to do, luck intervened.

Inspector Graham again: "Imagine my surprise when, a few minutes after receiving this information, I met Joshua Bright and found myself looking at the face in that aged image of present-day Dylan Dillon. My questioning of Reverend Bright led to him revealing his true identity.

"Eventually, we were able to match Cross's DNA with family members and confirm the remains were his beyond a reasonable doubt. Extraordinarily, we found that Cross and Dillon, although they didn't know it, shared a close relative, which may account for their similarities in physical appearance and personality."

In 1982, when Mr. Cross's body was originally discovered, Miss Emily Lovell and her grandson, Neville Williams, prevented the crime scene from being secured. According to DI Graham, "Nearly everything needed for a conviction—fingerprints on the bag of cocaine, powder left sprinkled on a coffee table or the floor, footprints, the exact position of the body—all would have been available to the police at the time. I'm sure they would have established the situation quickly."

"The scene was likely to be rich with toxicology evidence," Tomlinson agreed. "Right up until the hotel proprietor involved herself."

Police interviews with hotel staff revealed a disturbing truth. Long before Mrs. Marjorie Taylor took over the hotel, its previous owner, who, let me be clear, was neither a business partner of, nor any relation to, the present proprietor, sought to shield herself from justice. It has been claimed that Miss Lovell ran a drug-dealing operation out of the hotel. She dealt in small amounts of drugs for the casual user. According to interviews, Miss Lovell, who had been diagnosed with terminal lung cancer and had only a few months to live, attempted to conceal the death of her guest to avoid being implicated in it. She wanted to avoid spending her last months under investigation.

DI Graham is slightly less generous. "She opened the door on a crime scene, worked diligently to destroy the evidence, including the concealment of a body, contaminated the rest, and left it in a dusty attic for forty-odd years, telling no one."

He added, "She did not want her last weeks and months on earth spent embroiled in a police investigation, her reputation tarnished, and her liberty jeopardised. So, she sought to hide not just the circumstantial evidence but the body, with the help of her grandson Neville, only a young lad at the time.

"This was another case of an older person who should know better preying upon and manipulating a younger person to do their bidding at significant risk to themselves. Neville was a builder's apprentice on the island and, as part of this investigation, eventually faced charges relating to his involvement back when he was seventeen.

"At Miss Lovell's behest, he lugged the materials to mix concrete up the back stairs and built a brick coffin, filling it with concrete." Neville Williams disappeared to the mainland soon after the incident. Miss Lovell also departed Jersey soil a few weeks later.

The gravity of Miss Lovell's actions was not lost on DI Graham. "If Miss Lovell had been caught disposing of a body in this way, she would have been convicted and jailed until at least 1988. As it was, Charlie Cross was only discovered when the storm that lashed the Jersey coastline also damaged the attic in which he had been buried."

DI Graham understandably takes a very dim view of this action, not least because of the long-term consequences of the behaviour exhibited by those involved in this case. "Charlie Cross, Dylan Dillon, Emily Lovell, and Neville Williams all sought to evade justice. But in so doing, they provided cover for perhaps the most heinous people of all— the Parnabys. The brothers continued their activities, which, as is the nature of crime that is allowed to go unchecked, escalated in severity. Perhaps if any of the aforementioned had done the right thing at the time, a young security guard killed in a Parnaby-led armed robbery seventeen years later would still be alive."

Even now, many of us who live in Gorey find it hard to believe that our beloved, longtime local vicar once sought to end the life of another, harbouring so many secrets for so long. The question I was left with was: did he, Joshua

Bright/Dylan Dillon, truly believe in the Word of God, or was it all an act to escape justice?

There was no outright confession. At least, not to this author. "I confessed before the court, just as I confess every day, in my own way, before my Maker. His Word transcends laws or prisons and frees every sinner," was his enigmatic reply.

Dylan Dillon received an early draft of this book and approved it without changes, except for saying one thing: "DI Graham coming to see me like that was God's gift. He offered me the chance to be honest, almost by luck, and thank God, I seized it. I accept my punishment and will repay my debt to society and God." Dillon faced a criminal trial, with his confession to DI Graham the crux of the case for conspiracy to murder Charlie Cross.

The future for Dillon is uncertain, but his forty-year investment in religious life gives Detective Inspector Graham some hope, and for Dillon, a chance at redemption. "Dillon has received a custodial sentence, and I've requested that his skills and experience be put to good use at whichever prisons he finds himself incarcerated. Most prison sentences are a complete waste. I hope that isn't the case here.

"He planned to take a man's life, then covered up his death—there can't be a 'but' after that," said Graham at the end of our interview. "He must pay the price. While he's doing that, he has the chance to help those who need it."

Dylan Dillon should see the sun outside that of a prison yard again in his lifetime. The two men who betrayed him and Charlie Cross, though, will never see it again. "Their prior cases and their involvement were revisited. With Dillon's help, additional evidence came to light, and Arthur and George Parnaby were reinterviewed."

With a small lift from my research and Dillon's recollections, a team of Metropolitan Police detectives, many of them former colleagues of Detective Inspector Graham, made progress on a dozen cases. Twenty-four arrests were made, and sixty-eight charges were submitted to the Crown Prosecution Service in London and Eastbourne as a result.

Inspector Graham had an interesting take. "Despite his apparent insignificance, Charlie Cross acted as the moral centre of the Parnabys' little gang. They didn't realise it, but Cross's reticence for violence and more serious crimes had prevented the gang from radicalising further. Without him, the Parnaby brothers, Dillon, and whoever else they initiated into their gang spiralled quickly into increasingly violent crimes and, eventually, the chaotic, deadly robbery in Shoreditch.

"The Parnabys cooperated well enough to avoid curtailment of their privileges inside prison and earn themselves some points with the powers that be in Holbrooke," Graham said. "But when convicted, their sentences were extended. In court, we showed they ordered the murder of Charlie Cross to protect their own hides. They incited Dylan Dillon to perform the hit. The Parnabys must share responsibility for conspiracy to murder." Dylan Dillon testified against the Parnabys in respect of charges related to this case and many others.

Two elderly men, longing for freedom and family time, were denied both. And another, someone who served

Gorey's Christian community and brought new life to St. Andrew's Church, will have to continue his work from within the ugly confines of a British prison.

And where does this leave Gorey as it recovers from a major investigation?

Proud of the constabulary, for certain.

Proud also of the unsung heroes, including the tireless Laura Beecham, whose research connected Dylan Dillon to St. Julian's seminary, where the guilty, terrified "Joshua Bright" found refuge.

Proud of Detective Inspector Graham, who I interviewed exclusively for this book and who put ego aside and spoke to me about what I knew to bring two old gangsters to justice.

Proud of my friends in the senior community, who are both a trove and a treasure.

Proud of Doctor Tomlinson and his assistant, Fiona Henson, who took no time at all to prove her worth. They undertook technological wizardry under what were sometimes the most unpleasant conditions.

Proud of Mrs. Taylor, owner of the White House Inn where the body of Charlie Cross lay undiscovered for so long, and who gave the police every assistance, all while her hotel seemed in danger of collapse.

Proud of Gorey for coming together in a spirit of light and honesty, for facing an awkward past, and never flinching from the truth.

As a journalist, I am proud to have helped the investigation identify the "body in the block" and have a small hand in bringing to justice those who did harm.

I first interviewed the Parnaby brothers when I was merely doing research for this book, and they told me something I shared with the constabulary as soon as I was able. Little did I know at that interview that those words would later set off an investigation the likes of which Gorey has never known. From the lips of Arthur Parnaby and endorsed by his brother George: "You're from Jersey. We did a bit of work on Jersey. Sent one of our boys there in the early eighties looking for another one who'd done a runner with some loot. Dunno what happened. Never heard from either of them again. Good riddance. Useless eejits."

This is an edited extract from *Murder Island: The Mob on Jersey* by F. J. Solomon, to be published by Smithson Collingwood on 13 April.

EPILOGUE

Arthur and George Parnaby were convicted of conspiracy to murder and asked for nineteen other charges to be taken into consideration. Each had seven years added to his sentence. George's condition worsened, and he passed peacefully a month later. Arthur moved to a lower security prison where he grew prize runner beans and supplied the prison kitchen with potatoes. His penchant for yogurts with the fruit "in the corner" has not waned.

Dylan Dillon was sentenced to seven years in prison for conspiracy to murder, failing to report a body, and the perversion of the course of justice. While incarcerated in prison, he serves as a mentor and counsellor to the neighbouring young offenders' institution. He hopes to one day return to the clergy in some capacity.

· · ·

Further DNA testing confirmed the familial relationship between **Charles Cross** and Dylan Dillon, although the exact nature of the connection is unclear. Charlie's remains were cremated and eventually claimed by his family. The Parnabys continue to maintain that Charlie Cross stole £100,000 from them. Yet, despite a forensic bank audit, no money was ever found.

Angela Dillon disappeared from the village of Leeslake. A man of Middle Eastern appearance now lives in the house with his teenage daughter. Ms. Dillon's half brother tried to contact her from prison, but his efforts were not reciprocated, and her whereabouts are not known.

In light of his age at the time, the influence of his grandmother, and his lack of a police record in the time since the offence, **Neville Williams** avoided prison and was given a two-year suspended sentence. He was required to work in the community with "at-risk" teenagers. He enjoyed the work so much that he studied for a degree in social work and was eventually employed full-time in the field.

Janet Northrop retired from her long-time position at the White House Inn but still visits often. It was determined that it was not in the public interest to bring charges against her, but she has arranged for a monthly subscription of Scilly Isles narcissi to be delivered to the White House Inn as a form of apology for bringing unwanted attention to the hotel.

. . .

Freddie Solomon's book, *Murder Island: The Mob on Jersey*, was serialised in the *Daily Mail* and hit the *Sunday Times* bestseller list in the United Kingdom. His publisher sent him on a promotional book tour, the pinnacle of which was being interviewed on the BBC's *The One Show*. Freddie was last seen in the Orkneys talking to a crowd of around twenty-five in the local library.

Jack whisked **Janice** off on honeymoon to a private island, where they relaxed on their own white sandy beach and slept in a luxury villa serviced by a dedicated butler. They kept the destination a secret until their return to avoid the possibility of an ambush by her mother.

Graham and Laura returned to the Bangkok Palace on several occasions, but Graham decided that one entry into the Order of the Perfumed Jewel was enough. At Laura's behest, he restricted his menu choices to pad Thai, tom yum soup, and other "cooler" dishes for the next several visits. The Palace staff were relieved to be able to leave the fire and chemical extinguishers in their usual spots.

Barnwell and Carmen continue their regular runs around the streets of Gorey and Sunday walks with **Melanie Howes and Vixen**. After a stilted, awkward conversation, Barnwell and Melanie agreed to leave the dogs at home one evening and go to the pictures together.

. . .

Marjorie Taylor was delighted when, on the Monday after the Wentworth's wedding, repairs to the roof of the White House Inn began. The hotel eventually reopened after six weeks of almost total closure, the repairs assisted by a vigorous, local GoFundMe campaign. Business is brisk, and the hotel is booked to near capacity for the next two months.

Fiona Henson continued to stay in the apartment on Elizabeth Island, although she found the crossing a bit choppy in bad weather. Much to **Marcus Tomlinson**'s chagrin, **Miranda Weiss** offered Fiona a job in Southampton, but she decided to stay on Jersey for at least another year.

Rosemary Harding returned to the mainland after her daughter's wedding, exhausted but satisfied. She wasted no time regaling at length the unfortunate members of her local Ramblers club with tales from the wedding. This ultimately spawned a rebellion by a few of her fellows who, on one weekend, met at a different car park from usual and did not tell her.

After their experience travelling to Jersey for Janice's wedding, her nan and step-grandad became members of the Youth Hostels Association. They became avid budget travellers, visiting countries across Europe and beyond. They harbour particularly happy memories of Jersey fish and chips.

Thank you for reading *The Case of the Body in the Block*! I will have a new case for Inspector Graham and his gang soon. To find out about new books, sign up for my newsletter: https://www.alisongolden.com.

If you love the Inspector Graham mysteries, you'll also love the sweet, funny *USA Today* bestselling Reverend Annabelle Dixon series featuring a madcap, lovable lady vicar whose passion for cake is matched only by her desire for justice. The first in the series, *Death at the Cafe* is available for purchase from Amazon. Like all my books, *Death at the Cafe* is FREE in Kindle Unlimited.

And don't miss the Roxy Reinhardt mysteries. Will Roxy triumph after her life falls apart? She's sacked from her job, her boyfriend dumps her, she's out of money. So, on a whim, she goes on the trip of a lifetime to New Orleans, There, she gets mixed up in a Mardi Gras murder. *Things were going to be fine. They were, weren't they?* Get the first in the series, Mardi Gras Madness from Amazon. Also FREE in Kindle Unlimited!

If you're looking for something edgy and dangerous, root for Diana Hunter as she seeks justice after a devastating crime destroys her family. Start following her journey in this non-stop series of suspense and action. The first book in the series, Snatched is available to buy on Amazon and is FREE in Kindle Unlimited.

I hugely appreciate your help in spreading the word about *The Case of the Body in the Block*, including telling a friend. Reviews help readers find books! Please leave a review on your favourite book site.

Turn the page to read an excerpt from the first book in the Reverend Annabelle Dixon series, *Death at the Cafe* . . .

A Reverend
Annabelle Dixon
Mystery

death
at the café

ALISON GOLDEN
JAMIE VOUGEOT

DEATH AT THE CAFE
CHAPTER ONE

NOTHING BROUGHT REVEREND Annabelle closer
to blasphemy than using the London public transport
system during rush hour. Since being ordained and sent to
St. Clement's church, an impressive, centuries-old building
among the tower blocks and new builds of London's East
End, Annabelle had been tested many times. She had come
across virtually every sin known to man, counselled
wayward youths, presided over family disputes, heard
astonishingly sad tales from the homeless, and still retained
her solid, optimistic dependability through it all. None of
these challenges made her blood boil, and her round, soft
face curl up into a mixture of disgust, frustration, and exas-
peration. Yet sitting on the number forty-three bus to Isling-
ton, as it moved along at a snail's pace, was almost enough to
make her take her beloved Lord's name in vain.

On this occasion, she had nabbed her favourite seat: top
deck, front left. It gave her a perfect view of the unique
streets London offered and the even more varied types of
people. Today, however, her viewpoint afforded her only a

teeth-clenchingly irritating perspective of a traffic jam that extended as far as the eye could see down Upper Street.

"I know I shouldn't," she muttered on the relatively empty bus, "but if this doesn't deserve a cherry-topped cupcake, then I don't know what does."

The thought of rewarding her patience with what she loved almost as much as her vocation—cake—settled Annabelle's nerves for a full twenty minutes, during which the bus trundled in fits and starts along another half-mile stretch.

Assigning Annabelle, fresh from her days studying theology at Cambridge University, to the tough, inner-city borough of Hackney had presented her with what had been an almost literal baptism of fire. She had arrived in the summer, during a few weeks when the British sun combined with the squelching heat of a city constantly bustling and moving. It was a time of drinking and frivolity for some, heightened tension for others. A spell during which bored youths found their idle hands easily occupied with the devil's work. An interval when the good relax and the bad run riot.

Annabelle had grown up in East London, but for her first appointment as a vicar, her preference had been for a peaceful, rural village somewhere. A place in which she could indulge her love of nature, and conduct her Holy business in the gentle, caring manner she preferred. "Gentle" and "caring," however, were two words rarely used to describe London. Annabelle had mildly protested her city assignment. But after a long talk to the archbishop who explained the extreme shortage of candidates both capable and willing to take on the challenge of an inner-city church, she agreed to take up the position and set about her task with enthusiasm.

DEATH AT THE CAFE   371

Father John Wilkins of neighbouring St. Leonard's church had been charged with easing Annabelle into the complex role. He had been a priest for over thirty years, and for the vast majority of that time had worked in London's poorest, toughest neighbourhoods. The Anglican Church was far less popular in London than it was in rural England, largely due to the city's disparate mix of peoples and creeds. Father John's congregation was mostly made up of especially devout immigrants from Africa and South America, many of whom were not even Anglican but simply lived nearby. The only time St. Leonard's had ever been full was on a particularly mild Christmas Eve.

But despite low attendance at services, London's churches played pivotal roles in their local communities. With plenty of people in need, they were hubs of charity and community support. Fundraising events, providing food and shelter for London's large homeless population, caring for the elderly, and engaging troubled youths were the churches' stock in trade, not to mention they provided both spiritual and emotional support for the many deaths and family tragedies that occurred.

The stress of it all had turned Father John's wiry beard a speckled grey, and though he knew his work was important and worthwhile, he had been pushed to breaking point on more than one occasion. Upon her arrival, he had taken one look at Annabelle's breezy manner and fresh-faced, open smile and assumed that her appointment was a case of negligence, desperation, or a sick prank.

"She's utterly delightful," Father John sighed on the phone to the archbishop, "and extremely nice. But 'delightful' and 'nice' are not what's required in a London church. This is a part of the world where faith is stretched to its very limits, where strong leadership goes further than gentle guidance. We struggle to capture people's attention, Archbishop, let alone their hearts. Our drug rehabilitation programs have more members than our congregations."

"Give her a chance, Father," the archbishop replied softly. "Don't underestimate her. She grew up in East London, you know."

"Well, I grew up in Westminster, but that doesn't mean I've had tea with the Queen!"

Merely a week into Annabelle's assignment, however, Father John's misgivings proved unfounded. Annabelle's bumbling, naïve manner was just that—a manner. Father John observed closely as Annabelle's strength, faith, and intelligence were consistently tested by the urban issues of her flock. He noted that she passed with flying colours.

Whether she was dealing with a hardened criminal fresh out of prison and already succumbing to old temptations, or a single mother of three struggling to find some composure and faith in the face of her daily troubles, Annabelle was always there to help. With good humour and optimism, she never turned down a request for assistance, no matter how large or small it was.

When Father John visited Annabelle a month after the start of her placement to check on a highly successful gardening project she had started for troubled youth, he shook his head in amazement "Is that Denton? By the rose bushes? I've been trying to get him to visit me for a year now, and all he does is ignore me. You should hear what he says when his parole officer suggests it," he said.

"Oh, Denton is wonderful!" Annabelle cried. "Fantastic with his hands. He has a devilish sense of humour—when it's properly directed. Did you know that he plays drums?"

"No, I didn't know that. He never told me," Father John said, giving Annabelle an appreciative smile. "I must say,

Reverend, I seem to have misjudged you dreadfully. And I apologise."

"Oh, Father," Annabelle chuckled, "it's perfectly under-standable. You have only the best interests of the commu-nity at heart. Let's leave judgement for Him and Him alone. The only thing we're meant to judge is cake contests, in my opinion. Mind those thorns, Denton! Roses tend to fight back if you treat them roughly!"

To get your copy of *Death at the Cafe* visit the link below:

https://www.alisongolden.com/death-at-the-cafe

"Your emails seem to come on days when I need to read them because they are so upbeat."
- Linda W -

For a limited time, you can get the first books in each of my series - *Chaos in Cambridge, Hunted* (exclusively for subscribers - not available anywhere else), *The Case of the Screaming Beauty, and Mardi Gras Madness* - plus updates about new releases, promotions, and other Insider exclusives, by signing up for my mailing list at:

https://www.alisongolden.com/graham

TAKE MY QUIZ

What kind of mystery reader are you? Take my thirty second quiz to find out!

https://www.alisongolden.com/quiz

BOOKS IN THE INSPECTOR DAVID GRAHAM SERIES

The Case of the Screaming Beauty

The Case of the Hidden Flame

The Case of the Fallen Hero

The Case of the Broken Doll

The Case of the Missing Letter

The Case of the Pretty Lady

The Case of the Forsaken Child

The Case of Sampson's Leap

The Case of the Uncommon Witness

The Case of the Body in the Block

COLLECTIONS

Books 1-4

The Case of the Screaming Beauty

The Case of the Hidden Flame

The Case of the Fallen Hero

The Case of the Broken Doll

Books 5-7

The Case of the Missing Letter

The Case of the Pretty Lady
The Case of the Forsaken Child

ALSO BY ALISON GOLDEN

FEATURING REVEREND ANNABELLE DIXON

Chaos in Cambridge (Prequel)

Death at the Café

Murder at the Mansion

Body in the Woods

Grave in the Garage

Horror in the Highlands

Killer at the Cult

Fireworks in France

Witches at the Wedding

FEATURING ROXY REINHARDT

Mardi Gras Madness

New Orleans Nightmare

Louisiana Lies

Cajun Catastrophe

As A. J. Golden

FEATURING DIANA HUNTER

Hunted (Prequel)

Snatched

Stolen

Chopped

Exposed

Broken

ABOUT THE AUTHOR

Alison Golden is the *USA Today* bestselling author of the Inspector David Graham mysteries, a traditional British detective series, and two cozy mystery series featuring main characters Reverend Annabelle Dixon and Roxy Reinhardt. As A. J. Golden, she writes the Diana Hunter thriller series.

Alison was raised in Bedfordshire, England. Her aim is to write stories that are designed to entertain, amuse, and calm. Her approach is to combine creative ideas with excellent writing and edit, edit, edit. Alison's mission is simple: To write excellent books that have readers clamouring for more.

Alison is based in the San Francisco Bay Area with her husband and twin sons. She splits her time between London and San Francisco.

For up-to-date promotions and release dates of upcoming books, sign up for the latest news here: https://www.alisongolden.com/graham.

For more information:
www.alisongolden.com
alison@alisongolden.com

facebook.com/alisongolden.books

THANK YOU

Thank you for taking the time to read *The Case of Body in the Block*. If you enjoyed it, please consider telling your friends or posting a short review. Word of mouth is an author's best friend and very much appreciated.

Thank you,

Made in the USA
Coppell, TX
22 October 2024